GOLDEN AGE

GOLDEN AGE

A NOVEL

WANG XIAOBO

TRANSLATED BY YAN YAN

ASTRA HOUSE ⋀ NEW YORK

This is a work of fiction. Names, characters, places, and incidents are products of the
author's imagination or are used fictitiously. Any resemblance to actual events, locales,
or persons, living or dead, is entirely coincidental.

Astra House
A Division of Astra Publishing House
astrahouse.com

Printed in the United States of America

Library of Congress Cataloging-in-Publication Data

Names: Wang, Xiaobo, 1952–1997, author. | Yan, Yan (Translator), translator.
Title: Golden age : a novel / Wang Xiaobo ; translated by Yan Yan.
Other titles: Huang jin shi dai. English
Description: First edition. | New York : Astra House, [2022] | Summary: "Wang Er, whose
long affair with Chen Qinyang has attracted the attention of local authorities, is shamed
and forced to write a confession of his crimes. Instead, he takes it upon himself to write a
modernist literary tract. Later, as a lecturer at a chaotic, newly built university, Wang Er
navigates the bureaucratic maze of 1980's China, boldly writing about the Cultural
Revolution's impact on his life and those around him. Finally, alone and humbled, Wang Er
must come to terms with the banality of his own existence."—Provided by publisher.
Identifiers: LCCN 2021059054 (print) | LCCN 2021059055 (ebook) |
ISBN 9781662601217 (hardcover) | ISBN 9781662601224 (epub)
Subjects: LCSH: Wang, Xiaobo, 1952–1997.—Translations into English. |
China—History—20th century—Fiction. | LCGFT: Novels.
Classification: LCC PL2919.H8218 H83413 2022 (print) | LCC PL2919.H8218 (ebook) |
DDC 895.13/52—dc23/eng/20220114
LC record available at https://lccn.loc.gov/2021059054
LC ebook record available at https://lccn.loc.gov/2021059055

FIRST EDITION

10 9 8 7 6 5 4 3 2 1

Design by Richard Oriolo
The text is set in CenturySchoolbookStd.
The titles are set in BureauGrotesque-ThreeSeven.

CONTENTS

GOLDEN AGE

INTRODUCTION

by Michael Berry

WANG XIAOBO IS SOMETHING OF an anomaly amid the landscape of the contemporary Chinese literary world. Born in 1952, Wang was basically a member of the same generation of those superstar writers that earned great acclaim in the immediate aftermath of the Cultural Revolution—writers like Jia Pingwa (born in 1952), Wang Anyi (born in 1954), and Mo Yan (born in 1955). However, unlike Jia Pingwa, Wang Anyi, Mo Yan, and other writers, Wang Xiaobo was not a member of the literary elite that emerged during the late 1970s and early 1980s. Wang did not start publishing his work until a full decade after his contemporaries, and his career as professional writer would last a mere five years before he would succumb to a heart attack at the youthful age of forty-four. Although Wang Xiaobo only spent a few years as a full-time writer, he produced a stunning output of novels, novellas, short stories, and essays that have placed him firmly alongside Mo Yan, Wang Anyi, and Jia Pingwa as one of contemporary China's greatest writers. More than two decades after his death his books continue to top best-seller lists in China and speak powerfully to readers through his piercing social critique, sarcastic tone, sharp humor, and wild literary imagination.

Wang Xiaobo's youth in some ways mirrored the early years of the People's Republic of China (PRC), which was established just three years before his birth, in 1949. Much of Wang's youth was therefore swept up in the many political movements of early PRC history and his education stunted during the Cultural Revolution. Wang's early life experiences were rich and varied: he spent time as an "educated youth" in Yunnan and as a laborer in Shandong. During the early days of the Reform Era he worked in an instrument factory before earning a degree in trade economics from Renmin University of China in 1982. After staying on for two years after his graduation as an instructor at Renmin University, Wang's life took a dramatic turn in the mid-1980s when he traveled to the United States to pursue graduate studies. This change was also marked by a shift in his field of study, majoring in East Asian studies at the University of Pittsburgh. It was there in Pittsburgh from 1984 to 1988 that Wang would become close with the legendary sinologist Professor Cho-yun Hsu, whose work would also have a profound impact on the future writer. This experience—growing up amid the "red fever" of Mao's China, working in factories, enrolling in college during the early Reform Era, and moving to America during the height of China's "culture fever" of the 1980s—collectively contributed to an incredibly powerful and unique literary vision.

Upon his return to China in 1988, Wang took up several teaching posts, where he proved to be something of a polymath—although his degrees were in trade economics and East Asian studies, he taught courses in sociology and accounting. But, of course, his "other calling" was literature and, as a writer, Wang Xiaobo was a true innovator publishing nonfiction academic works, fiction, a screenplay, and a series of popular prose essays. He was one of the first PRC writers to win major critical acclaim in Taiwan in the early 1990s (he was a two-time winner of the prestigious Unitas

Literary Award for outstanding novella). His published works spanned numerous genres and forms. In nonfiction, he coauthored the sociological study *Their World* (*Tamen de shijie*) with his wife, sociologist Li Yinhe. *Their World* was the first serious academic study of homosexuality in contemporary China and a landmark book for its breaking of social taboos and contribution to the fight against the stigmatization of the queer community in China. Wang's research on the Chinese gay community also led to his role as screenwriter on Zhang Yuan's film, *East Palace, West Palace* (*Dong gong, xi gong*), a film often cited as the first example of "queer cinema" in the PRC. (Wang also became the first Chinese screenwriter to win an international award for his screenplay). But outside of his fiction, Wang made the biggest impact through his short essays, which were collected in several volumes including *My Spiritual Garden* (*Wo de jingshen jiayuan*), *The Silent Majority* (*Chenmo de daduoshu*), and the new English-language collection *The Pleasure of Thinking: A Collection of Essays by Wang Xiaobo*. Wang's sharp and witty observances on history and society have earned him a special place in the hearts of Chinese readers over the course of the past twenty years and have been consistent best sellers.

But standing apart from Wang's varied body of published work is his fiction. Spanning the Tang dynasty to the Cultural Revolution and into a brave new science-fiction future, Wang Xiaobo's fiction revealed a fresh perspective and stunningly original voice that hypnotized readers when it first became widely available in the mid-1990s. His trilogy—*Golden Age* (*Huangjin shidai*), *Silver Age* (*Baiyin shidai*), and *Bronze Age* (*Qingtong shidai*)—presented a wild absurdist world filled with black humor and Kafkaesque logic, punctuated with moments of penetrating insight and sublime beauty. The crown jewel of that trilogy is the novella *Golden Age,* a dark and humorous look at the Cultural Revolution. The novella also had a very interesting publication history. Certain story elements were loosely inspired by Wang Xiaobo's experiences as a sent-down youth in Yunnan, where the story is also set, and he began writing a draft as early as 1982. However, *Golden Age* would not be published until a full decade later, with its first edition appearing in Taiwan in 1991. A Hong Kong edition appeared the following year in 1992. But owing to the scandalous content, PRC publishers did not publish the book until 1994 when veteran editor of Huaxia Publishing Zhao Jieping took a chance on the controversial novella. Upon publication the novella was subject to severe criticism, but gradually began to build up a loyal readership, eventually earning a major cult following, and going on to be regarded as one of the most important Chinese literary works of the 1990s.

Over the past forty years, narratives about China's Cultural Revolution have gone through a series of evolutions—from the bare-it-all, tormented exposé stories of the "Scar Literature" movement to the more philosophical "Reflection Literature," and from the "Search-for-Roots" movement, which attempted to excavate the Chinese cultural tradition in an attempt to make sense of the "ten years of eternal chaos" that had befallen the nation, to the "avant-garde" movement, which repositioned the Cultural Revolution in a twisted world of violence and allegory. Wang Xiaobo's *Golden Age* came on the tail of this series of literary movements at a time when all narrative possibilities about the Cultural Revolution had seemingly been exhausted. But *Golden Age,* which told of the adventures of educated youth Wang Er, seemed to open up a truly new and innovative space from which to reflect upon this historical period. Here on Wang Xiaobo's absurdist canvas, "political re-education" is transformed into a "sexual re-education," struggle sessions where political victims are beaten and humiliated in public are re-imagined as S & M sessions, and political self-confessions is morphed into erotic confessions to titillate government officials. Wang Xiaobo's outrageous narrative can be seen as something of a deconstruction of Cultural Revolution literary narratives, arriving on the tail end of the aforementioned series of literary movements fixated on the Cultural Revolution and just on the cusp of when a new series of commercialized, melodramatic, and watered-down narratives of the period came to dominate. In this sense, *Golden Age* marks not only a crucial point in the evolution of Cultural Revolution narratives, but also the last breath of a "golden age" of literary innovation and experimentation, which would soon buckle under the dual pressures of censorship and "the market."

MICHAEL BERRY is professor of contemporary Chinese cultural studies and director of the Center for Chinese Studies at UCLA. He is the author of five books on Chinese cinema, including *Speaking in Images: Interviews with Contemporary Chinese Filmmakers* (2005) and *A History of Pain: Trauma in Modern Chinese Literature and Film* (2008). He has served as a film consultant and a juror for film festivals, including the Golden Horse (Taiwan) and the Fresh Wave (Hong Kong). He is also the translator of several novels, including *Wild Kids* (2000), *Nanjing 1937: A Love Story* (2002), *To Live* (2003), *The Song of Everlasting Sorrow* (2008) and most recently *Remains of Life* (2017).

GOLDEN AGE

1

WAS TWENTY-ONE YEARS OLD, STATIONED at a commune in Yunnan. Chen Qingyang was twenty-six, working as a doctor in the same place. I was in Team 14 at the bottom of the hill. She was in Team 15 up at the top. One day, she came down from the mountain to ask me whether she was a loose woman, a so-called old shoe. I didn't know her at the time, I had only heard of her. What she wanted to talk about was this: even though everyone called her an old shoe, she didn't think it was true. Her theory was that loose women steal men, and she had never stolen anything, let alone anyone's man. Even with her husband having spent the past year behind bars, she had never taken a lover. And even before that, she had never done it. Therefore, she just couldn't understand why everyone called her an old shoe. Comforting her would have been easy. I could have done it just through logic. If Chen Qingyang was an old shoe, then she must have had affairs, and those men, at least one of them, must still be around to testify. So far, no such person could be found; therefore, calling Chen Qingyang an old shoe was unfounded. But still, what I said to her was, Chen Qingyang you are definitely an old shoe, there is no doubt about it.

The whole thing with Chen Qingyang asking me to prove that she wasn't an old shoe started when I went to her for a shot. The story went as follows: during the busy planting season, our captain didn't hand me a plow, but asked me to plant rice seedlings instead, so that most of the time my back was bent downward. As anyone who knows me also knows I have an old injury to my lower back, and I stand over 1.9 meters tall. After a month of transplanting, I was in so much pain that I needed a cortisone shot just to go to sleep. Our infirmary only had a bunch of old busted needles with barbed tips that ripped the flesh straight out. They left my lower back looking like it had been shot with a shotgun, leaving lingering shrapnel wounds. It was then that I remembered that Team 15's Chen Qingyang was a graduate of the Beijing Medical University. I figured she could probably tell a needle from a fishhook, so I went to her to get treated. It wasn't more than thirty minutes after I returned from the doctor's visit that she came barging into my hut, asking me to prove that she wasn't an old shoe.

CHEN QINGYANG SAID, it wasn't that she had anything against loose women. As far as she could tell, they tended to be kind, helpful people who hated to let anyone down. She had some admiration for them. But the point wasn't if they were worthy women or not, it was just that she was not one of them. It was just like how cats weren't dogs. If a cat had found itself being called a dog, it also would have felt uncomfortable. With everyone calling her an old shoe, even she herself was beginning to question what she was.

Chen Qingyang appeared in my hut wearing a white doctor's medical gown with bare arms and legs. It was the way she had looked earlier in the infirmary with the exception of a handkerchief tied around her long hair and a pair of flip-flops on her feet. The sight of her led me to wonder: was she wearing anything under that white gown, or was she not? The fact that she didn't care what she wore was proof of Chen Qingyang's beauty. She had the sort of confidence that had been nurtured from a young age. I told her she really was an old shoe and began to explain: the term *loose old shoe* is a stereotype. If everyone calls you an old shoe, then that is what you are. It doesn't have to obey logic. If everyone says you are having an affair, then you must be having an affair. You can't reason with it. As for why everyone wants to call you an old shoe, I think the reason was this: everyone believes that the kind of married woman who doesn't have affairs should have leathery faces and saggy breasts. Your face isn't leathery and your breasts don't sag; therefore, you must be what they say. If you don't want to be an old shoe, then you should weather your face and let your breasts sag. Only then will people stop calling you an old shoe. Of course, that would be quite a sacrifice. If you aren't inclined to make such a sacrifice, then you should just have an affair. That way, even you will agree that you are an old shoe. They don't need to figure out if you really had affairs before calling you an old shoe. You are the only one responsible for making sure that no one can call you names. When Chen Qingyang heard these words, her face turned red and her eyes bulged out. She looked like she wanted to slap me in the face. This woman was notorious for her generous slaps, many had felt the heat of her palm on their cheeks. But she sighed and said, "Fine, whatever, but what is or isn't leathery or saggy is none of your business." She added that if I pondered these things too much, I would probably get slapped.

That was twenty years ago. I can still picture Chen Qingyang and me exchanging words about old shoes. My face was tawny and my parched lips were specked with shreds of paper and tobacco. My hair was like the mess of a bird's nest. I wore a tattered army coat with more than a few taped-up patches. With one leg over the other, slouching on my wooden plank bed, I looked like a hooligan.

You can only imagine how Chen Qingyang must have felt listening to a guy talk about saggy breasts, how her palm must have itched. It made her neurotic that it was always healthy, strong men coming to see her at the infirmary. They weren't sick. They weren't interested in seeing a doctor. They just wanted to see her. I was the only exception. My lower back looked like I had two farm rakes built in it. Never mind the pain, the cavities alone warranted a visit to the doctor. Those cavities somehow gave her hope that I could prove she was not a slut. Having one person believe it was qualitatively different from having no one believe it at all. But I let her down.

My thinking went like this: if I had wanted to prove that she wasn't an old shoe, and that my will to do so would have been proof enough of her innocence, then life would have been too easy. In truth, I couldn't prove anything aside from some mundane facts that needed no further proof. In the spring, the captain accused me of shooting out his dog's left eye, forcing it to constantly tilt its head like a ballerina. After that, the captain began giving me a hard time. If I had wanted to prove my innocence, I could have asserted the following:

1. The captain didn't own a dog;
2. Said dog was born without a left eye;
3. I had no hands, so I couldn't have fired a gun.

Of the three assertions, none was true. The captain did, in fact, own a brown dog. Said brown dog's left eye was, in fact, blinded after birth. And not only was I capable of pulling a trigger, I was quite a good shot. Not long before the incident, I had borrowed an air gun from Luo Xiaosi. Using a bowl of mung beans as ammunition, I exterminated a kilogram of rats in the empty silo. Of course, I wasn't the only sharpshooter in our team. Luo wasn't bad either. The air gun belonged to him and when he shot the dog blind, I was standing next to him, watching. I wasn't one to tattle. Luo and I were pretty close. Besides, if the captain had had the balls to confront Luo Xiaosi, he wouldn't have had to pick on me. So I kept quiet, and quiet meant guilty. That was how I ended up transplanting rice seedlings in the spring keeled over like a broken utility pole. After the fall harvest, I was ordered to herd oxen again. It meant no warm meal for me all day. Of course I didn't just give in. One day, at the top of a hill, when I just happened to have Luo's air gun with me, the captain's brown dog crossed my path. I took the opportunity to put a bullet in its right eye. The dog was blind in both eyes now and couldn't have found its way home for the captain to find out—heaven knows where it ran off to.

I REMEMBER IN those days, other than herding oxen and lying in bed, I didn't do much of anything. It was like the world had nothing to do with me. But once more, Chen Qingyang came down the hill to look for me. Apparently, there was a rumor that Chen Qingyang and I were having an affair. She wanted me to prove our innocence. I said, to prove our innocence, we must prove one of the following:

1. Chen Qingyang is a virgin;
2. I was born without a penis.

Both of these propositions were hard to prove; therefore, we couldn't prove our innocence. In fact, I was leaning more toward proving that we weren't innocent. When Chen Qingyang heard these words, she first turned white with anger, then red, then without a word she stood up and left.

Chen Qingyang later said, that from the start, I was an asshole. The first time she asked me to prove her innocence, I rolled my eyes and spewed a bunch of nonsense. The second time she asked me to prove our innocence, I ended up offering her a serious proposal for sexual intercourse. She decided then that she was going to slap me sooner or later. Had I known what she was up to, perhaps the following events would not have happened.

2

ON MY TWENTY-FIRST BIRTHDAY, I was herding oxen down by the river. In the afternoon, I took a nap on the grass. When I woke up, the banana leaf I had covered myself with before dozing off was nowhere to be found (the leaf might have been eaten by an ox). The dry season's subtropical sun had seared my bare skin crimson red. It was painful and itchy as hell. My little monk was pointing straight up to the sky in an unprecedented size. Such was the state of the world on my birthday. I woke up to the sun's blinding light and a sky terrifyingly blue. A layer of fine dust, like baby powder, had settled over me. Of all the boners I was to have in life, none was ever to match that one in mightiness. Maybe it was because I was in the middle of nowhere, in solitude.

I got up to look for the herd and found them crouching far off by the river's fork, chewing on grass. In that quiet moment, a white breeze hewed across the field. By the riverbank, a couple of local bulls charged at one another with bloodshot eyes, frothing at the mouth. These bulls had tight ball sacks and strong long shafts. Our oxen didn't do this sort of thing. If any of the bulls were to challenge them, they would have cowered. To avoid mating-related injuries, which would have affected spring plowing, we castrated them all.

I was there during all the castrations. For ordinary bulls, a simple slice of the scrotum sufficed. But for more temperamental animals, the crushing technique was used, which meant first pulling out the bull's testicles then mashing them to a pulp with a wooden club. Henceforth, the crushed ox knew nothing besides eating and working. It didn't even need to be tied up for slaughter. The captain who wielded the wooden club had no doubt that the crushing technique could work just as well on men. Whenever he yelled at us, he would say: all you bunch of bull testicles need is a good crushing! According to his logic, this bright red, foot-long thing pointing perpendicular to me was the very incarnation of evil.

Of course, I saw things differently. In my opinion, the thing was of utmost importance, the essence of my being. Clouds drifted lazily across the darkening sky. That day, I turned twenty-one. In the golden age of my life, I was full of dreams. I wanted to love, to eat, and to instantly transform into one of those clouds, part alight, part darkened. It was only later that I understood—life is but a slow, drawn-out process of getting your balls crushed. Day by day, you get older. Day by day, your dreams fade. In the end you are no different from a crushed ox. But I hadn't foreseen any of it on my twenty-first birthday. I thought I'd be vigorous forever and that nothing could ever crush me.

I HAD INVITED Chen Qingyang over to eat fish that evening, so I should have gotten hold of some fish in the afternoon. But it wasn't until five o'clock that I thought to check on the fish trap I had diverted

from the creek. As I was getting to a bend in the river, two Jingpo*
kids came fighting down the trail. They hurled clots of dirt everywhere, hitting me in their crossfire. They wouldn't stop until I
grabbed one of them by his ear and shouted:

"Where are the fucking fish!"

The slightly older one said, "It's all fucking Le Nong's fault! He
sat on the dam and broke it!"

Le Nong shrieked, "Wang Er! You didn't build the fucking dam
strong enough!"

I replied, "Lies! I sodded the dam myself. Who says it wasn't
strong enough?"

I took a closer look. Whether it was because Le Nong sat on it
or because I hadn't built it strong enough, the dam had collapsed
and the water that was diverted from the creek flowed back out,
along with all the fish. A whole day's work was wasted. Of course,
I couldn't say it was my fault, so I blamed Le Nong. Le Du, the other
kid, took my side, making Le Nong furious. He jumped up high in
the air and screamed, "Wang Er! Le Du! Shit! You guys are ganging up on me like brothers-in-law! I'm gonna go tell dad and he's
gonna shotgun you both!"

The little rascal tried to scamper up the riverbank, but before
he could get away, I grabbed him by the ankle and pulled him
back down.

"Just walk away and leave us to herd your oxen? In your ma's
dreams!"

The little punk tried to bite me but I pinned him down to the
ground. His mouth foamed as he cursed in a mixture of Mandarin, Jingpo, and Dai.† I returned the verbal assault in back-alley

---

*The Jingpo are an ethnic minority in northwest Burma and the adjacent
parts of China.
†The Dai are an ethnic minority native to China's Yunnan province. Their
language is related to the Thai and Laotian languages.

Beijingese. Suddenly, he stopped cursing as he lowered his eyes down my torso with a look of admiration. I looked down. My little monk had perked up again.

Le Nong couldn't help but admire, "Wow! Is that for Le Du's sister?"

I immediately tossed him aside and went to put on some pants.

WHEN I LIT the gas lamp in the water pump room at night, Chen Qingyang would appear and begin to talk about how pointless her life was, and how she really was innocent on every count. I told her the fact that she felt so immaculate was in itself the greatest sin. The way I saw it, every person was by nature horny and lazy. By going out of your way to protect your body like a precious jade, you've already committed the sin of phoniness, a sin worse than lust or sloth. She seemed to listen, but she never agreed to any of it.

That night, I lit the gas lamp and waited for Chen Qingyang for a long time. It wasn't until after nine that she appeared at my door shouting, "Wang Er, asshole! Come out!"

I went outside and found her dressed in white, looking extra elegant, but with a tense look on her face. She said: you invited me over for fish and a heart-to-heart, where's the fish? I could only answer that the fish was still in the river. All right, she said, so we are left with the heart-to-heart, we can talk right here. I insisted on talking inside. She agreed, entered my room, and sat down with a flustered look.

On my twenty-first birthday, I had wished to seduce Chen Qingyang because she was my friend, her breasts were big, her waist was thin, and her butt was round. Not only that. Her neck was also gracefully long and her face very pretty. I wanted to have sex with her, and was hoping she might agree. If she had wanted to borrow my body to explore anatomy, I would have let her; so I hoped it would have been fine for me to explore her body as well. The only problem was that she was a woman and women tend to be a bit picky. I needed to inspire her, so I began to explain the meaning of *epic friendship.*

In my view, epic friendship was the way great warriors wandering rivers and lakes would honor each other. For the heroes in *The Water Margin,* murder and arson were commonplace; but the moment Ji Shiyu's name was pronounced, they immediately bowed in respect. I, too, wanted to be a reckless hero who believed in nothing, but who would never violate the bonds of friendship. As long as you were my friend, no matter how much evil you had done, even if the whole world had wanted you gone, I would still be there by your side. That night, I offered my epic friendship to Chen Qingyang. She was so moved she not only accepted my friendship, but wanted to repay me with an even more epic friendship. She would never abandon me even if I were a wicked scumbag. Her words set my worries at ease so I went on to conclude my point: I'm already twenty-one years old, but I still haven't experienced the thing between a man and a woman, it really bothers me. Upon hearing me out, she froze, perhaps in surprise. She didn't react to anything I said. I put my hand on her shoulder and felt her muscles tense. She could have turned around and slapped me any time, it would have been proof that women knew nothing about friendship. But she didn't. Abruptly, she scoffed, and smiled. She said: how silly of me! I fell for your trick so easily!

I asked, what trick, what are you talking about?

Nothing, she replied. I pushed her to answer what I had just asked her. "Screw you," she blushed. She was acting a little coy, so I took the initiative and touched her. She shoved me away a few times and then said, not here, let's go up the mountain. So I followed her up the mountain.

CHEN QINGYANG LATER said she still couldn't figure out if my epic friendship was real or something I made up just to seduce her. But she also admitted that my words were like a spell that beguiled her; they made her feel like even if she were to lose everything, she would have no regrets. Indeed, my epic friendship was neither real nor fake. Just like everything else in this world, if you believed it to be real, it would continue to be real; if you suspected it to be fake, then it might be fake. My words weren't entirely a lie. I would always stand by them, even if they undoubtedly meant doom. It was this very attitude that led no one to trust me. Even though I thought of friendship as life's great endeavor, I somehow still only ever made a couple of friends, including Chen Qingyang. When we went up the mountain that night, we stopped halfway because she wanted to go back home for a minute. She told me to wait at the summit. I suspected that she might hang me out to dry, but I stayed quiet and made my way to the summit for a smoke. Soon after, she arrived.

Chen Qingyang said, the first time I went to get a shot from her, she was at her desk snoozing. People in Yunnan had a lot of time to snooze. As a result, everyone was always just waking up. When I approached, my shadow darkened the room. Most of the light coming into her mud-walled hut came in through the door-way. She woke, looked up, and asked me what I needed. I said my lower back hurt. She told me to lie down. I dove face-first onto the bamboo cot, nearly breaking it. My back was in too much pain for me to bend over. Had that not been the case, I wouldn't have needed to see her in the first place.

Chen Qingyang told me that even as a young man, I had wrinkly beggar lips and black bags under my eyes. I was tall, dressed in rags, and didn't like to say much. After I got my shot, I left. I might have said thank you, or maybe not. By the time she realized I could help her prove she wasn't an old shoe, I had already gone. She ran out after me but saw that I was taking the shortcut to Team 14. I swooshed down along the undulating hill, as fleet-footed as if I were wearing wings. It was morning during the dry season. Wind swept up from the valley, muting her voice as she called out to me. I never looked back. Like that, I just walked away.

Chen Qingyang said, she wanted to chase after me but knew she would never catch up. Besides, she wasn't sure if I could prove her innocence yet. She returned to the infirmary. Later on, she changed her mind and decided to look for me because everyone who called her an old shoe was an enemy. It was possible that I wasn't yet an enemy. She didn't want to miss this opportunity and allow me to become just another enemy.

THAT NIGHT, I smoked on the summit of the mountain. Despite the darkness, I could see far. The moon was bright and the air was crisp. I could hear dogs barking in the distance. I saw Chen Qingyang as soon as she got out of Team 15. Even during the day, you couldn't always see that far. But it felt different, perhaps because there was nobody around.

I couldn't be entirely sure there was nobody around because everything was just a silvery gray. If someone had walked around carrying a torch, it would have indicated to the world that someone was there. Without a torch, you might as well have been wearing an invisibility cloak, only those who knew you were there would feel you, and no one else would see a thing. As I watched Chen Qingyang move closer, my heart thumped. Instinctively, I knew what I had to do—before doing the thing, we should play.

Chen Qingyang's reaction to me was as cold as ice. Her lips were frozen. She was unresponsive to my caresses. When I clumsily tried to undo her buttons, she pushed me away and began undressing piece by piece. She stacked her clothes neatly by her side and lay stiffly on the grass.

Chen Qingyang's nude body was so beautiful. I quickly took off my clothes and went to her. Once again, she pushed me away. She handed me something as she asked, "Do you know how to use this or do you need me to teach you?"

It was a condom. In my eager state, the sharp tone of her voice barely registered. After slipping on the condom, I quickly crawled to her side. I tried to find my bearings, but it clearly wasn't working. Frostily, she sneered, "Hey! Do you even know what you're doing?"

I said, of course I know, but could I trouble you to scoot over a bit? I want to study your body under the light. I heard a crash loud like a thunderclap in my ear. She had smacked me hard. I stood up, grabbed my clothes and bolted.

3

I **DIDN'T MANAGE TO GET AWAY** that night. Chen Qingyang grabbed me and made me stay in the name of epic friendship. She admitted it had been wrong to hit me and that she had not been fair. But she added that my epic friendship was fake, and that I had tricked her out there just to study her anatomy. I replied, if I'm a fake then why did you believe me? I did want to see and touch her body, but only with her consent. If she wasn't interested, she could have made it clear without hitting me. She laughed and said she couldn't stand looking at my thing. The sight of that stupid-looking shameless thing made her angry.

The two of us kept arguing, entirely naked. My little monk remained upright, covered in plastic, shimmering in the moonlight. She noticed that I was upset and tried to be conciliatory: anyway, your thing is hideous, don't you admit?

The thing hovered like an enraged cobra, it was indeed rather unsightly. If you don't want to see it, then forget it, I said. I wanted to put on my pants but she said, come on don't be like that. So I lit a cigarette. When I finished my smoke, she hugged me. Then two of us did it on the grass.

Until my twenty-first birthday, I was a virgin. That night, I seduced Chen Qingyang to go up the mountain with me. The night began with a bright moon. After it descended, the sky was full of stars, as many as morning dewdrops on a meadow. It was a windless night; the mountain was quiet. Chen Qingyang and I had sex; I was no longer a virgin. But it didn't really make me happy because all along she didn't make a sound. She rested her head on her arms and stared at me contemplatively. From start to finish, it was a solo show; not that I held on for very long, I came right away. The whole thing left me angry and disappointed.

Chen Qingyang said, she couldn't believe it actually happened: I actually revealed before her that hideous male genitalia without any sense of shame. That thing itself was shameless too, sliding in between her legs. That men would use girls only because they have an opening in their bodies did not make sense at all. She had a husband who would do it to her every day. She never said a thing, only waited for him to one day feel ashamed enough to explain why he was doing it. But he never gave an explanation, even later when he was in jail. I didn't like what she was implying so I asked: if you're not up for it, why do you agree? She said, I don't want to appear stingy, to which I replied that she was stingy by nature. She said, let's not fight over it. She told me to come back another night to try again, maybe she would like it better then. I didn't say anything. In the morning, after the fog lifted, she and I parted ways and I went down the mountain to herd.

THAT NIGHT, INSTEAD OF going to look for her, I ended up in the hospital. The story went like this: in the morning, instead of waiting for me to arrive, a bunch of guys took it upon themselves to open the ox pen. They all wanted the stronger oxen for plowing the field. This one local fellow named San Mener was pulling on a big white ox. I walked over and told him that the ox had been bitten by a poisonous snake so it couldn't work. He didn't seem to hear me. I reached out and grabbed the ox's rein. The guy slapped me. I reacted quickly and sent him tumbling with a shove. Soon, we were surrounded by a circle of men eager to join the fight. The intellectual youths from Beijing were on one side and the local guys were on the other. They picked up sticks and pulled out their belts; but after some bickering, they didn't fight. Instead, they wanted me and San Mener to wrestle. San Mener knew he had no chance so he took a swing at me. With a single kick, I sent him flying into a manure pit. Covered in shit, San Mener got back on his feet, grabbed a pitchfork, and came at me only to be stopped by the crowd.

So that happened in the morning. At night, when I returned from herding the oxen, the captain said that because I had assaulted the poor and lower-middle-class peasants, it was necessary to hold a struggle session against me. I warned him that if he wanted to use the opportunity to bully me, he should really think twice; I just might start a riot. The captain said he had no intention of bullying me but San Mener's mother was raising hell, he had no choice. The old hag was a widow, mean as they come. He said such were the local customs. Later, he changed his tone and the struggle session became an amelioration meeting, meaning I had to go to the village to publicly apologize. If I disagreed, he would turn me over to the widow to do with as she pleased.

The meeting was pandemonium. The villagers carped on and on about how disrespectful the intellectual youths were, stealing and assaulting and all. The intellectual youths retorted, bullshit! Who is stealing things, have you caught anyone red-handed? We are here for the national border development,* we're not some exiled marauding soldiers, we will not respond to baseless accusations. I didn't offer any apologies, I just joined the fray. But I failed to

---

*In the 1960s, Chinese intellectual youth from the cities were sent to live and work in rural areas.

notice San Mener's mother sneaking up from behind me with a heavy wooden stool. Suddenly, she struck me on my old lower back wound and I blacked out from the pain.

When I woke up, Luo Xiaosi was leading a mob, calling for the burning of the ox pen. They demanded that San Mener's mother should pay with her life. The captain led another group to intervene, while the deputy captain ordered a few men to carry me onto an ox cart to be taken to the hospital. A nurse warned that if my spine was broken, I might die from being lifted. I told them my spine seemed fine so please cart me away. But no one was sure if my spine was really fine, so no one was sure if I would die the moment I was lifted. After a long wait, the captain came to check on me. He said, hurry and dial for Chen Qingyang so she can check if his spine is broken. It wasn't long before Chen Qingyang came swooping in with fluttering hair and swollen eyes. Her first words to me were: don't be afraid. If you are paralyzed, I'll take care of you forever. After a brief examination, the diagnosis was just as I had predicted. So I got on an ox cart and went to the hospital at the headquarter.

That night, Chen Qingyang stayed with me at the hospital until the X-rays came back showing no major injuries. Before leaving, she said she would come visit me in a day or two but she never came. After a week of convalescence, I could walk again so I ran off to look for her.

When I entered Chen Qingyang's office, I was carrying a backbasket overflowing with supplies. In addition to pots and pans, bowls and ladles, there was enough food for two people to eat for a month. She saw me come in and with a slight smile she said, how are you? Where are you going with all those things?

I said I wanted to go to Qingping for the hot spring. She sat back lazily and said, sounds good, the hot spring could help with that old wound. I said I wasn't really going to the hot spring but to the mountain out back for a few days. She said there was nothing back there, why not go to the hot spring.

The hot spring in Qingping was tucked away in a gorge overlooking a mud pit surrounded by weedy slopes. On those slopes, sick people with all sorts of diseases lived year-round in tents. Had I gone there, not only wouldn't I have gotten better, but I might have contracted leprosy. On the other hand, beyond the mountain out back were valleys and ridges and bounteous woods. There, I could live in solitude in a hut that I would build; alone among the flowing water and falling petals, I could cultivate my health and be one with nature. Chen Qingyang couldn't help but laugh. She asked: where do I find this place? Maybe I can come visit you. I described to her the directions, even drawing a map complete with a legend before setting off alone into the wild.

After I went to live in the wilderness, Chen Qingyang didn't come to visit at first. In the dry season, the wind blew, rattling the trees and shaking the huts. Chen Qingyang sat in her chair listening to the rustling and thought about all the things that had happened to her, questioning every moment. It was hard for her to believe that she had somehow ended up in the middle of nowhere, where for no reason, people called her an old shoe, which really had turned her into an old shoe. The whole thing was absurd.

Chen Qingyang said, sometimes when she left her office, she would look to the mountain out back and notice all the tiny trails meandering into its depths. The directions I gave her echoed in her ears. If she had gone down one of those winding trails, she would have found me. That certainly would have happened. But the more certain something was, the more reason there was to doubt. Maybe the trail didn't go anywhere or maybe Wang Er wasn't in the mountain; maybe there was no Wang Er.

A few days later, Luo Xiaosi led a group of guys to the hospital to look for me. The hospital staff said they had never heard of a Wang Er and had no idea where this person might have gone. At the time, hepatitis was going around the hospital. Other patients, who had not been infected yet, were sent to recover at home, and the doctors went to look after them. When Luo and the gang returned to our base and realized that my things were gone, they went to the captain to ask for my whereabouts. The captain said, who's Wang Er? Never heard of him. Luo reminded him that he had organized a struggle session against me only a few days ago. An old hag hit me with a wooden stool and nearly killed me. With a reminder like that, it was even harder for the captain to remember who I was. Around that time, an intellectual-youth welfare committee was coming to survey the situation in the hinterland, to learn, for example, if the intellectual youths were being assaulted or forced into marriages. That powder keg made it even harder for the captain to remember me. Luo Xiaosi and the gang went to Team 15 to ask Chen Qingyang if she had seen me, going so far as to hint at our affair. Chen Qingyang denied all knowledge.

After Luo left, Chen Qingyang felt confused. It seemed like everyone agreed there was no Wang Er. This bothered her for the following reason: if everyone insisted that something that clearly existed didn't in fact exist, then reality might be nothing but an illusion. But if everyone could agree *that* thing didn't exist, then it must have existed. For example, Wang Er. If he didn't exist, then where did this name come from? Chen Qingyang could no longer suppress her curiosity. She dropped what she was doing and hiked up the mountain to look for me.

After the old hag knocked me out, Chen Qingyang had run down the hill to see me. She had cried along the way and said in front of everyone that if I didn't get better, she would take care of me forever. As it turned out, I was neither dead nor paralyzed, which was a good thing for me, but Chen Qingyang didn't like it. She had basically admitted in front of everyone that she was an old shoe. Had I been dead or paralyzed, everything would have been fine. But I had only stayed in the hospital for a week before running off. To her, I was nothing more than a silhouette that had whooshed down the hill, a figment of her memory. She didn't want to make love to me, nor did she want to have an affair with me, unless it was for some important reason. Therefore, when she came to look for me, she really was going down the way of an old shoe.

Chen Qingyang said that when she decided to come look for me, she wasn't wearing anything under her white medical gown. She hiked across the ridge behind Team 15, where fields of green grass grew on red soil. The morning breeze that swept down the mountain was as chilly as an alpine stream. In the afternoon, the breeze charged back up the mountain, carrying a white-hot cloud of dust with it. Chen Qingyang came to me riding on that white breeze. The breeze crawled up from beneath her gown and crept up her entire body like loving kisses. She no longer needed me. She didn't need to come find me. Back when everyone was calling her an old shoe and suspecting that I was her wild lover, she came to me every day. It seemed necessary at the time. But once it was revealed that she really was an old shoe and that I actually was her wild lover, people stopped calling her anything. No one even mentioned Wang Er in front of her (except Luo). People were so afraid of loose old shoes that they did not even dare to talk about them.

EVERYONE KNEW ABOUT the intellectual-youth welfare committee coming down from Beijing except for me. It was because I had been busy herding. I left early in the morning and returned late at night. Also, my reputation wasn't good, so no one told me anything. When I ended up in the hospital, no one came to visit. After I left the hospital, I went deep into the mountain. Before going, I only spoke to two people. One was Chen Qingyang and she didn't tell me about it. The other was the captain, who didn't bring it up either. He only told me to go to the hot spring to recover. I told him that I didn't have any supplies (such as food and cooking utensils), so I couldn't go. He said he could lend me some. I said I may not be able to return them. He said it didn't matter, so I borrowed quite a bit of homemade ham and sausages too.

Chen Qingyang didn't tell me the news because she didn't care; she wasn't an intellectual youth. The captain didn't tell me because he thought I already knew. He also thought that since I took so much food with me, I wasn't planning on coming back. That was why, when Luo Xiaosi and the gang asked him where Wang Er was, he said, Wang Er? Who's Wang Er? Never heard of him. For Luo and his gang, finding me was crucial because I was proof that the city kids were being abused. From the point of view of the leadership, my absence would have been more convenient because it allowed them to say that there had never been an intellectual youth beaten unconscious here. As for me, to be or not to be didn't matter. If no one had ever bothered to look for me, I would have planted some corn and never left the mountain. It didn't matter if I existed.

In my hut, I thought about the problem of my existence. For example, when people said Chen Qingyang and I were doing the old shoe thing—that was evidence that I existed. To use Luo's words, Wang Er and Chen Qingyang took off their pants and did it. What does he know. The furthest his imagination could go was us taking off our pants. Also, there was Chen Qingyang telling me that when I rushed down the hill wearing a yellow army coat, I looked like I had wings. I learned from her that when I walked, I never looked back. I couldn't have imagined those details; therefore, I must have existed.

And then, there was my erect little monk. That also wasn't something I just imagined. I yearned for Chen Qingyang to come find me but she never came. When she came, I wasn't expecting it.

4

AT FIRST, I THOUGHT CHEN QINGYANG would come look for me right away, but I was wrong. I waited for a long time, then I gave up. I sat in my hut, listening to the rustling of leaves until I felt empty of self and of the world. I felt the monsoon clouds rumbling above my head as my soul sought to surge above me. I was like a bamboo shoot deep in the mountain, popping off one coat of fibrous husk after another, shooting up higher with every peeling layer. During the low tides, I lay low; but when the tide was high, I rose and soared with it. Chen Qingyang stepped into the room and saw me sitting naked on my bamboo bed with a foot-long penis on my lap like a bright red, freshly skinned rabbit. When she saw me, she screamed.

Chen Qingyang's journey to find me went like this: two weeks after I went into the mountain, she came to look for me. It was two o'clock in the afternoon, but she was dressed like one of those easy women who slipped out barefoot by the cover of night; she was wearing nothing under her white gown. She trekked across sunlit fields until she arrived at a dry ravine. She walked for a long time along the forking, meandering streambed without taking a single wrong turn. She left the ravine and walked toward a sun-facing dell where she saw a newly built thatched hut. Had there not been a Wang Er to give her the directions, she couldn't possibly have found it. But when she walked in and saw Wang Er sitting there with his little monk sticking up, she screamed.

Chen Qingyang later said, she couldn't believe that any of what had happened was real. Real things happened for real reasons. She took off her clothes and sat down next to me. She stared at my little monk, it was the color of a burn scar. A gust shook the hut, letting in specks of sunlight through the thatched roof that dotted her body like tiny galaxies. I reached out to touch her nipple, she blushed, her nipple hardened. Suddenly, she woke from her reverie and her face went flush with embarrassment. She wrapped herself around me.

It was the second time Chen Qingyang and I made love. Many details of our first time had left me puzzled. It was only later that I understood: she was still resentful about being called an old shoe. Since she couldn't prove she wasn't an old shoe, she was willing to become a real one. She felt like one of those women who was caught in the act of infidelity and taken to a stage on a public square to be questioned over every salacious detail. The more her lecherous audience listened, the less they could contain themselves until someone would finally shout: tie her up! Someone would go up to the stage with a rope to tie her up. She would stand there and take in all the humiliation. She didn't mind that. She wasn't afraid of being stripped, tied to a millstone, and drowned in a pond. Or like the concubines of old times, she could have been forced to kneel, neatly dressed, with a wet piece of yellow mourning paper glued to her face until she suffocated to death. Those sorts of things didn't frighten her. She wasn't afraid of being a real old shoe. It was so much better than being wrongly accused of something. What bothered her was everything that had led her to turn herself into a real old shoe in the first place.

As Chen Qingyang and I made love, a lizard crawled in through a crack in the wall. It flitted across the middle of the floor in stops and starts. Something spooked it and it darted off toward the sunlight beyond the door. Meanwhile, Chen Qingyang's moans filled the room like gushes of water. Startled by her sounds, I stopped. She said, hurry on, you bastard, and pinched my leg. After I hurried, it felt as if waves of tremors emanated from the earth's core. She said she felt full of guilt and that karma would one day come back to bite her.

AS SHE TALKED about her karma, a red flush was fading from her breast. We were still in the middle of sex, but her tone suggested that she felt guilty only for what had happened up to that point. Suddenly, my body tightened from the top of my head to my tailbone and I ejaculated massively. That wasn't a part of her karma. I was solely responsible for that part, I suppose.

Later, Chen Qingyang told me Luo Xiaosi was looking everywhere for me. When he went to the hospital to ask for me, the doctor said I didn't exist. When he went to ask the captain about me, the captain said I didn't exist. Finally, he went to Chen Qingyang. She told him since everyone said I didn't exist, then maybe I really didn't exist, to which I had no objections. When Luo heard this, he wept.

I found the whole question strange. I shouldn't exist just because some old hag hit me. Therefore, I shouldn't not exist just because some old hag hit me. The truth of the matter was, my existence was unequivocal. I felt like I needed to make a statement. In order to prove the obvious, I ran down the mountain on the day the welfare committee arrived and revealed myself at their meeting. After the meeting, the captain said, you don't look very sick, maybe you should come back to feed the pigs. He even tried to organize people to catch me and Chen Qingyang making love. Of course, it wasn't easy to catch me, I was too fast, no one could follow me very far. But still, it was a hassle. By then, it was too late for me to realize that I didn't need to prove my existence to anyone.

Feeding pigs meant I had to yoke buckets of water every day. It was exhausting work that you couldn't be lazy about. When the pigs got hungry, they became very loud. I had to chop loads of vegetables and split many logs of firewood. Feeding the pigs used to be a three-woman job. Now it was just me. It was clear that I couldn't replace three women, especially with my lower back pain. At times like those, I wished I could prove I didn't exist.

At night, Chen Qingyang and I made love in the little thatched hut. In those days, I was entirely dedicated to lovemaking and charged every kiss and every caress with sweltering passion. There was the classic missionary style, and all the others, dog, spoon, cowgirl, we tried them all meticulously. Chen Qingyang was extremely pleased. And me too. At moments like those, I knew that I had no need to prove my existence to anyone. I also learned an important lesson: never draw attention to oneself. In Beijing, they have a saying, "Don't be afraid of thieves, be afraid of thieves who remember you." Never let yourself be remembered like that.

Not long after the committee's visit, our whole intellectual-youth battalion was disbanded. The men went to work in the sugar factory. The women went to teach in rural schools. I was the only one left still feeding pigs. Apparently, it was because I wasn't reformed enough yet. Chen Qingyang said, someone must really "remember" me. That someone was probably the army cadre in charge of the farm. The guy was a real piece of work. At the hospital where she previously worked, the army cadre had tried to touch her so she had slapped him on the face. The next day, she was transferred to

Team 15's infirmary. The water at Team 15 was bitter and there was nothing to eat. She got used to it eventually, but it was meant as a punishment. She said, he'll probably torture you half to death. I wondered what could he possibly do to me? If the son of a bitch pushed me too far, I could always skip town. This notion would later prove useful.

ONE DAY AT DAWN, I came down the mountain to feed pigs. When I passed by the washing station, I saw the army cadre brushing his teeth. He pulled his toothbrush out of his frothy mouth and said something to me. I thought it was gross so I walked away without answering. A while later, he came running into the pigsty to give me a scolding. He asked me how I dared to walk away like that. I listened and stayed silent. Even when he accused me of pretending to be a mute, I stayed silent. I walked away again.

The army cadre decided to hang out in our production team; he came and just stayed. He said, until he got Wang Er to open his mouth, he wasn't going anywhere. There were two possible reasons for his stay. One, he had come down to do an inspection, came across me pretending to be deaf and dumb, and got really angry. Or two, he wasn't there to inspect anything but got wind of Chen Qingyang and me having an affair; therefore, he came down to personally make my life hell. Either way, I refused to speak and there was nothing he could do about it.

The army cadre sat me down for a talk. He told me to prepare a confession. He added, having an affair was the kind of thing that would make the people angry. If I didn't confess, it would be the people who would come after me. He added that I was a bad element and required rehabilitation. I could have tried to argue that I was innocent; who could have proven that I had done the old-shoe thing? But I just stared at him. Like a wild boar, I stared at him. Like I was deaf, I stared at him. Like a male cat staring at a female cat, I stared until he ran out of steam and let me go.

In the end, he never got a single word out of my mouth. He doubted if I could speak at all. Everyone else said I wasn't a mute, but he had trouble believing that since he had never heard me utter a single word. Still today, when he thinks of me, he doesn't know whether I'm a mute. I feel titillated by the very thought of it.

5

EVENTUALLY, WE WERE LOCKED UP. We spent a long time writing confessions. At first, I wrote: *Chen Qingyang and I had inappropriate relations. The end.* The higher-ups said, this is too simple. They told me to rewrite it. So I wrote, *Chen Qingyang and I had inappropriate relations. I did it many times and she was happy about it.* The higher-ups said it was lacking in detail. I added details such as: *the fortieth time we had illegal intercourse, the location was my illegally constructed hut in the mountain. It was either the fifteenth or the sixteenth of the lunar month, the moon was bright. Chen Qingyang sat on a bamboo bed wearing nothing but the moonlight shining in through the door. I stood on the ground with her legs wrapped around my waist. We chatted. I said her breasts were not only round but also very perky, her belly button was not only round but also very shallow, all very nice. She said, is that right, I had no idea. Later, the moon shifted. I lit a cigarette and smoked it halfway when she snatched it and stole a drag. At some point, she squeezed my nose because there was* *a local saying that the noses of virgin boys were hard, whereas the noses of those who would die from sexual excess were soft. Sometimes, she lay lazily on the bed with her back against the bamboo wall. Sometimes, she was wrapped around me like an Australian koala on a tree, puffing hot breaths into my face. Finally, when the moon would shine through the window from the door, we would part ways.*

But the confession I wrote was no longer for the army cadre's eyes. He had left the position and returned to his home village long ago. In fact, it didn't matter who the cadre was. Making a mistake like ours meant we had to write confessions.

Later in life, I was friendly with my college's human resources director. He said the best thing about being in HR was getting to read other people's confessions. I assumed he was alluding to my confessions too. I always thought my confessions had great literary potential. After all, I wrote them in a guesthouse with nothing else to do, like a novelist.

MY ESCAPE HAPPENED at night. That afternoon, I went to the superintendent to ask for leave because I needed to buy some toothpaste in the town of Jingkan. My superintendent was in charge of directing my work but also of watching me. He was supposed to keep his eyes on me at all times, but as soon as night fell, I vanished. That morning, I had given him a bunch of loquats, really tasty ones. The loquats in the lowlands were inedible because they had ants in them. The only ant-free loquats were from the mountain. The superintendent said to me that since there was no bad blood between us, and the army cadre wasn't around, he would allow me to go buy toothpaste. But, the superintendent added, the army cadre could be back at any time. If I wasn't around when the cadre returned, he wouldn't be able to cover for me. When I left the base, I hiked to the summit behind Team 15 and used a mirror to send a signal through Chen Qingyang's window. She came out. She said she was constantly under watch and hadn't been able to get away for the past few days. Now she was having her period. She said it didn't matter, let's do it anyway, but I thought that wouldn't be right. When we parted ways, she insisted on handing me two hundred yuan. At first I refused, but ended up taking the money.

LATER, CHEN QINGYANG told me she wasn't actually being watched and she wasn't really having her period either. In fact, Team 15 didn't pay any attention to her. Those who liked to call innocent people easy old shoes didn't seem to care when the thing was real. The reason she hadn't come up the mountain right away and had me wait for so long was that she was getting bored. She couldn't get in a good mood just because of sex; she needed to be in a good mood to want to have sex. On the other hand, she felt a little bad for me so she gave me two hundred yuan. I figured, if she had two hundred yuan she couldn't spend, I should do it for her. With the money, I went to Jingkan and bought a double-barreled hunting rifle.

Because I had to write my confessions, the double-barreled hunting rifle became a topic. They suspected I was planning a murder. But if you wanted to kill someone, using a two-hundred-yuan hunting rifle was the same as using a forty-yuan revolver. The gun was for shooting waterfowl. It was unnecessarily powerful for the mountain, not to mention as heavy as a corpse. When I got to Jingkan, it was already afternoon. It wasn't a market day. The one empty dirt road was dotted with a few empty government shops. Inside, one of the shopkeepers was taking a nap while flies circled in swarms. A sign on a shelf read TPTP, behind which were tin pots and tin pitchers. I chatted for a bit with a shopkeeper from Shandong and she showed me their stockroom. It was there that I saw the made-in-Shanghai hunting rifle. I ignored the fact that it had been sitting there unsold for two years, and bought it. That evening, I took the rifle to a creek for a test and killed an egret.

That was when the army cadre returned. When he saw me with a gun in my hand, he was appalled. He grumbled about things not being right, not just anyone can have a gun in their hands. He would say something to the administration and have Wang Er's gun confiscated. I was on the verge of shooting him in the stomach. Had I done that, he probably would have died, and I probably wouldn't be alive now either.

In the afternoon, when I was returning from Jingkan, I slogged through some rice paddies and stood still for a while in the middle of the flowering panicles. I saw leeches swimming toward me like little fish and attach themselves to my feet. I wasn't wearing my shirt because I had used it to wrap a bunch of molasses baos (it was the only thing they sold at the restaurant). With the makeshift sack in my hands and the gun slung over my shoulder, I trudged, trying to ignore the leeches. When I got onto a dike, I pulled the leeches off one by one and burned them. They blistered as they melted. Suddenly, I grew weary, not at all like a twenty-one-year-old. I thought, at this rate, I'll be old soon.

After that, I ran into Le Du. He told me he had collected all the fish at the fork in the river. My portion had already been dried into fish jerky. They were with his sister. She wanted me to go see her. I knew his sister very well; she was a tan and pretty girl. I told him I wouldn't be able to go for a while. I handed him the whole pack of steamed buns and asked him to deliver a message for me to Team 15: Tell Chen Qingyang I bought a gun with the money she gave me. Le Du went to Team 15 and forwarded my message to Chen Qingyang. She was afraid that I might use it to kill the army cadre. It wasn't an unreasonable thing to imagine considering how I was on the verge of shooting him that night.

In the evening, as I was hunting egrets by the river, I ran into the army cadre. As usual, I stayed silent and he blabbered on and on. I was furious, it had already been more than two weeks that he kept harping on me. He repeated the same things over and over, that I was bad, that I needed to reform, can't risk too much leniency with me. I had heard it all before but never did it piss me off as much as it did that night. Later on, he said there was some good news that he would announce to everyone soon. He wouldn't say what it was, only that from now on, me and my "little whore" wouldn't be having so much fun. The last remark made me especially furious. I wanted to strangle him then and there, but I also wanted to hear what the good news was before I did him in. He wouldn't talk, dangling the bait until we were back at the base. Come to the meeting tonight, he said in the end, I have something to announce.

I didn't go to the meeting that night. I packed my belongings and got ready to escape to the mountain. I figured something drastic must have changed for the army cadre to take care of me and Chen Qingyang once and for all. As for what the change might have been, I had no idea, at the time anything was possible. My imagination went so far as to suppose that China had returned to feudalism, and the army cadre had become a local warlord free to castrate me, crush my balls, and take Chen Qingyang as a concubine. After I was packed and ready to walk out the door, I understood that the situation was not quite so dire. There was a chant from the public square loud enough for me to hear from my room. As it turned out, the government had reclassified our base from a *people's commune* to an *army garrison*. It meant that the army cadre could become a colonel. It also meant that he couldn't castrate me or take Chen Qingyang. I hesitated for a minute before slinging my bag over my shoulder. I used a machete to destroy everything in the room and used black charcoal to write on the wall, "X X X (the name of army cadre), fuck you!" Then, I left for the mountain.

That was how I escaped from Team 14. I also explained it all in my confession. In a nutshell, it was like this: the army cadre and I had bad blood, mostly because of two factors. One, I revealed I had been beaten unconscious in front of the welfare committee, which led him to lose face; two, jealousy, which was why he continued to bully me. When I learned that he was going to become some sort of a colonel, I couldn't stand it, so I escaped to the mountain. Even now, I consider this the reason of my escape. But others insisted that because the army cadre never became a colonel, my reason was invalid and my confession unreliable. A more credible confession would have focused on my affair with Chen Qingyang. As the saying goes, no courage like lust—we could have been capable of anything. It wasn't an unreasonable argument. Except, when I first escaped, I had not planned to look for Chen Qingyang. It was only when I got to the trail leading to the back mountain that I thought, no matter what, Chen was a friend, I should go say goodbye. Who could have known that Chen Qingyang would want to join me? She said, if she didn't join this kind of thing, then our epic friendship was only good for the dogs. Hastily, she gathered up some stuff and left with me. Had she not packed up those things, I probably would have died in the mountain. Among her supplies were malaria medicine and a bunch of large-size condoms.

After Chen Qingyang and I escaped, the farm was alarmed for a while. They thought we had run away to Burma. A story like that could only have led to trouble, so they didn't report it. Instead, they put up a few Wanted posters around the farm. We were easily recognizable, especially with my one of a kind, double-barreled hunting rifle. But no one ever found us. Half a year later, we returned on our own accord to our respective production teams. A month or so later, we were taken to the people's police station and told to write confessions. It was just one of those unlucky years. There was some political movement or other, and we were ratted out.

6

THE PEOPLE'S POLICE STATION WAS a lonely old mud building at the turn leading to the headquarter of the base. You
could see it from afar because it was painted bright white.
Built on a mound, when farmers came in on market day, they would
see it surrounded by fields of sisal. Tender green sisal spikes pierced
out of the crimson earth. At the station, I answered all their questions and said everything there was to say: we planted a plot of
corn in the mountain behind Team 15, but the soil was not good,
half the corn never sprouted. We left and searched day and
night for a new place to settle. We finally remembered that
somewhere in the mountain, there was a dilapidated watermill surrounded by abandoned but good land. Inside the watermill lived
Old Man Liu, who had escaped from the leper colony. No one ever
went there, although Chen Qingyang remembered that as she was
a doctor, she had been to check on him once. We decided to move to
the clearing behind Old Man Liu's watermill. Chen Qingyang
cared for his disease while I worked his land. One day, I went to

Qingping for market day and ran into an old classmate. He said the army cadre had been transferred and no one even remembered us. So we went back down. That was the whole story.

I spent a lot of time in the people's police station. At first, everything was cordial. They said, the problem is clear, go ahead and prepare your confession. But later, things got more serious. They suspected that we had not only crossed the national border, but also had contact with enemy forces. Perhaps we had returned with a covert mission. They called Chen Qingyang in and subjected her to interrogation as well. As they interrogated her, I stared out the window. So many white clouds.

They told me to explain the border crossing. The truth of the matter was, I wasn't completely innocent. I did cross the border at some point. I had dressed up like a man of the Dai minority and went over to the other side to shop. I bought some matches and some salt. But there was no need to tell them this. I didn't say anything that was not necessary.

I led a group of policemen to investigate the place where we had lived. The thatched hut I had built behind Team 15 was starting to leak. The cornfield had attracted flocks of birds. Behind the hut was a pile of used condoms—ironclad proof of our time there. The locals didn't like condoms. They said the blockage of Yin and Yang energies would lead to frail health. Actually, the condoms there were better than any other kind I would later try. They were made of one hundred percent natural rubber.

After that, I stopped taking the police anywhere. I swore I didn't go outside the country. They didn't believe me. I showed them everything but they still didn't believe me. I no longer did what I didn't need to do. I kept quiet. Chen Qingyang also kept quiet. The interrogators started with a lot of noise, but eventually they got tired and kept quiet as well. The street was full of Dai and Jingpo farmers passing by with their fresh fruits and vegetables. The ranks of interrogators dwindled to only one man. He wanted to go shopping too, but it would have been against regulation to leave us alone there. He went to the doorway and shouted at middle-aged women passing by, telling them to stop. No one wanted to stop, most sped up. We laughed.

The comrade finally got ahold of a woman. Chen Qingyang stood up, straightened her hair, buttoned her shirt, and put her hands behind her back. The woman proceeded to tie her up, starting with her hands, then looping the rope around her neck and arms. The woman apologized: I'm no good at tying people up. The comrade said, good enough, before tying me up himself. He had us sit on two chairs back-to-back. He tied the rope around our waists before locking the door on his way out to shop. Sometime later, he came back to get some things from the office. He asked: do you need to go to the bathroom? It's still early, I'll come release you later. He walked out.

WHEN HE FINALLY released us, Chen Qingyang stretched her fingers, straightened her hair, and patted off a layer of dust from her clothes. The two of us went back to the guesthouse. Every day, we went to the people's police station. Every market day, we were tied up. On top of that, sometimes we had to join a group of people for a criticism, or struggle session. They threatened that if we didn't cooperate, they would use even harsher rehabilitation techniques—such was the story of our interrogation.

Eventually, they backed off on the whole treason thing. They began to treat Chen Qingyang with civility. They asked her to go to the hospital to take a look at the chief of staff's prostatitis. There was a group of old veterans who arrived at the farm and many of them had prostatitis. After some asking around, they learned that Chen Qingyang was the only person who knew what a prostate was. Comrades from the people's police told us to confess to our illicit relationship. I quipped, how do you know we have a relationship? Did you see it? They said, then confess to speculation and profiteering. I replied, how do you know I speculated and profiteered? They said, then confess to aiding and abetting the enemy. Either way, you have to confess to something. What, specifically, is up to you. No one gets released without a confession. We decided to confess to the relationship problem. She said, no need to be afraid of confessing to things we actually did.

Like an author, I began to pen my confession. I began with the night I escaped into the mountain. After several drafts, I eventually came up with the metaphor comparing Chen Qingyang to a koala. She agreed she was euphoric that day. It was her chance to prove her epic friendship so she wrapped her legs around my waist, grabbed onto my shoulders, and climbed me as if I was a big tree and she was a koala.

WHEN I SAW Chen Qingyang again, it was in the 1990s. She said she was divorced with a daughter, living in Shanghai, traveling to Beijing for work. When she arrived, she remembered that Wang Er was in Beijing as well. She thought maybe we might see each other again. As things would have it, she did run into me at the Longtan Lake Temple Fair. I was still the old way, wrinkly beggar lips, black bags under my eyes, wearing an out-of-style coat, squatting, eating unsophisticated street food. The only difference was the yellow nitric acid stains on my hands.

Chen Qingyang had changed quite a bit. She wore a thin woolen coat, a floral woolen skirt, a pair of high-heeled boots, and a set of gold-rimmed glasses. She looked like a publicist from some big multinational corporation. Had she not called me out by name, I would never have recognized her. Everyone, it seemed, had an essence, which could sparkle when it found its rightful place. I essentially belonged to the lot which includes rogues and ruffians. Being a professor in the city, what I wore was unbefitting.

Chen Qingyang said her daughter was already in her second year of university. She had recently learned of our story and wanted to meet me. The reason for all this was: her hospital wanted to give her a promotion but found some stuff in her permanent records. After mulling over her files, the higher-ups decided that the infraction was a relic of the Cultural Revolution and should be expunged. They sent someone to Yunnan, spending 10,000 RMB in travel expenses, to bring back the original files. The files were going to be returned to me because I had written them. She took them to her place first, where her daughter stumbled upon them and said, so that's how you guys made me!

Truthfully, I am in no way related to her daughter. I had long since left Yunnan when she was conceived, that was what Chen Qingyang said as well. But her daughter speculated something like, I could have put my sperm in a test tube and sent it to Yunnan for Chen Qingyang to artificially inseminate herself with. Or to use her original words: who knows what you assholes are capable of.

On the first evening of our escape, Chen Qingyang had been superexcited. When I had fallen asleep, it had still been light outside. Fog had oozed in through the wall cracks. She had wanted to do it again, but without the cumbersome thing. She had wanted to make a nest of offspring for me. She had complained that in a few years, her breasts would sag down low. She had pinched her nipples and pulled them down to demonstrate. I hadn't liked the way it looked so I said, let's think of something else. Let's not let them sag. So I had put on the cumbersome thing. After that, she had lost interest.

When I saw Chen Qingyang again, I asked, how are they, saggy? She said, indeed, they are a saggy mess. Was I interested in seeing just how saggy? I saw them but they weren't saggy at all. She said, they'll get there eventually, there is no way out of it.

THE HIGHER-UPS ENDED UP really enjoying my confessions. One of the big bosses, if it wasn't the chief of staff it must have been the political commissar, came to greet us. He told us he liked our attitudes. The leadership believed we did not commit treason. From now on we would only have to explain our sexual crimes. If the explanation was good, maybe they would let us get married. But we didn't want to get married. So they said, if the confession went well, they would let me return to the city. Chen Qingyang could be transferred to a top-tier hospital. I sat in the guesthouse and wrote for more than a month. Aside from a few outings, I had no distractions. I made carbon copies. The original was my confession and the copy was hers. We turned in identical confessions.

Later, some comrades from the people's police came to talk to me about a major criticism session that would be taking place soon. Everyone who had been investigated by the people's police needed to attend, including financial speculators, corrupt officials, and other types of bad people. We technically belonged to this category, but the leadership had spoken: we were young with good attitudes and well-written confessions, so we could be exempt. But someone had complained: if everyone who had been investigated had to go, why not us? The people's police were in a bind. They decided to work on us and encourage us to attend. They explained, a little bit of criticism here and there sharpens one's moral compass. It could reduce mistakes in the future. With all the benefits of being criticized, why not participate? On the day of the rally, thousands gathered from the headquarters and surrounding production teams. We stood on a stage along with many others. After listening to endless criticisms, it was finally the case of Chen and Wang. As it turns out, our problems were our lascivious thoughts and corrupt habits, choosing to escape to the wilderness rather than face ideological reform. But in the end, moved by the Party's wise exhortations, we decided to abandon the way of the shadow and embrace light. Listening to our final judgment, we were moved. We raised our fists along with the crowd and shouted: Overthrow Wang Er! Overthrow Chen Qingyang! After the criticism session, we were no longer considered problems. Yet, I still had to write my confession because the boss wanted to read more.

On the mountain behind Team 15, Chen Qingyang had somehow gotten it into her head that she wanted to breed a nest of offspring for me. I wasn't interested. Later, I thought it might not be such a bad idea and tried to talk to her about it, but then she wasn't interested. She always thought I just wanted to do her. She said, if you want to do it just do it, no big deal. But doing it just for my own sake would have been selfish, so we hardly did it at all. Besides, working the land was hard work and left me with very little energy. The only thing I had to confess about was touching her breasts while we were napping in the fields.

When we cleared more fields during the dry season, the wind was hot. It left dry sweat on your skin and a muscle ache underneath. When the day was at its hottest, we could only go nap under a tree. We used pieces of bamboo as pillows and palm husk raincoats as our bed. I wondered, why did no one ever ask me to confess about the palm husk raincoats? They were protective equipment for workers, extremely precious. I took two of them when I went into the mountain, one was mine and the other I grabbed from outside some person's house. I didn't bring either one back. I left Yunnan without anyone ever asking me about the raincoats.

I rested my head on the ground while Chen Qingyang covered her face with her cone hat. She undid a few buttons on her shirt and fell asleep quickly. I reached into her shirt and felt something round and wonderful. I undid a few more buttons to reveal her rosy skin. The sun had managed to pierce through the thin fabric that she wore while she worked. As for me, I worked topless so I was as dark as a demon.

I remembered Chen Qingyang's breasts were firm, especially when she slept. But the rest of her was soft and delicate. After twenty years, not much had changed, only her nipples had gotten bigger and darker. She said it was all her daughter's fault. When she first came out like a pink little piglet that couldn't open its eyes, she clamped her lips around her mother's nipple and sucked. She sucked and sucked until her mother became an old lady, and she became the beautiful young woman her mother used to be.

Age had made Chen Qingyang more sensitive. When we reminisced about our old feelings at the restaurant, anything explicitly carnal would make her panic slightly. It hadn't been like that before. At the time, I had been hesitant to write about her breasts in the confessions. She had insisted to just write it like it is. I had retorted that she would be exposed. She had said, so what if they know about my boobs, I don't care! She had even added that they had grown like that naturally, it wasn't as if she had done something weird. What other people wanted to think was none of her business.

Turns out, after all these years, Chen Qingyang had been my ex-wife all along. After our confession, they told us to get married. I didn't think it was necessary but the leaders said, if we didn't get married, it would set a bad example for others. We had to get married so we registered in the morning and got divorced in the afternoon. I didn't think it counted. Amid the confusion, no one remembered to take the marriage certificate back. Chen Qingyang held on to a copy. Using that useless piece of paper from twenty years ago, we were able to book a hotel room together. Had it not been for that piece of paper, we wouldn't have been allowed to stay in the same room. It wasn't like that twenty years ago. Twenty years ago, they had us living in the same room as we wrote our confessions. There wasn't such a piece of paper back then.

I wrote about our time in the mountain. The leadership asked the people's police to tell me to go easy on the digressions when confessing my next crime. Their feedback made me as angry as a mule: motherfucker, how is this a crime? Chen Qingyang tried to cheer me up by saying: in this world, there are countless people doing it every day, how many of them can consider themselves criminals? I said, they were all criminals, only the leadership couldn't investigate them all. She said, all the more reason to write about it. I began to write: that night, we left the back mountain for the scene of the crime.

7

WHEN I LATER SAW CHEN QINGYANG again and we had booked the hotel room, we went into the room together and I reached out to help with her coat. She said, Wang Er has become a gentleman. It showed that I had changed a lot. In the past, not only had I looked mean, I had also acted it.

At the hotel, Chen Qingyang and I were partners in crime once more. The room was warm with tea-tinted windows. I sat on the sofa. She sat on the bed. We chatted a bit as we eased into a cheekier mood. I said, weren't you going to show me how saggy? Let me see. She stood up and took off her coat, revealing a floral shirt underneath. She sat down and said, not yet, an attendant will come to deliver hot water in a minute. They have keys and come in without knocking. I asked, what happens if they walk in on something? She said, she hadn't experienced it herself but apparently they slam the door and mutter: fucking assholes!

Once, before Chen Qingyang and had I escaped to the mountain, I was blanching pig feed at the farm. I had to stoke the fire, chop up all the pig veggies (such as sweet potato vines, water hyacinth, etc.), and add bran and water to the pot. As I juggled the various tasks, the army cadre stood next to me and carped on and on about all the things that were wrong with me. He told me to tell my little whore Chen Qingyang that she was no good either. I exploded with anger. With the long metal ladle in my hand, I smashed a gourd that was hanging from a wooden beam in which we used to save pumpkin seeds. The gourd cracked in half. The army cadre ran for his life. Had he barked one more insult, I would have chopped his head off. I had remained so silent that now I just had to be mean.

Later, at the people's police station, I didn't talk much either, even when they were tying me up. That was why my hands were always getting bruised. Chen Qingyang talked a lot. She said, auntie, you're hurting me; or, auntie, can you pad my wrists with my handkerchief, I have a handkerchief tied to my hair. She always tried to cooperate and as a result, suffered less. We were different in so many ways.

Chen Qingyang said I wasn't enough of a gentleman back then. When they untied us at the people's police station, the rope left streaks of dirt on her shirt. This was because when the rope wasn't used to tie us up, it sat in the kitchen shed collecting ash and grease. With stiff fingers, she patted away the ash on her front side but couldn't reach her back. By the time she looked up to ask me for help, I was already gone. She tried to follow, but I was already far off in the distance. I walked quickly and never looked back. Moments like those reminded her of how much she didn't love or even like me.

According to the leadership, nothing we did in the mountain, except the koala thing, was considered a crime. The nap in the field episode, for example, was no more than a digression. I didn't write any more about it, but there was more to tell. The air was hot, Chen Qingyang was sound asleep with her hands under her head like a pillow. I pulled her shirt all the way open so that it looked like she was sunbathing topless. The sky was so blue and so bright that even the shadows had a blue tint. Suddenly, I felt an urge. I leaned in over her pinkish body. I can hardly remember what I did at the time. When I mentioned it, I assumed Chen Qingyang had no memory of it either but she said, "I totally remember! I was awake by then. Didn't you kiss me on my belly button? How dangerous, I almost fell in love with you."

Chen Qingyang said, when she woke up, she saw my messy hair hovering over her stomach, followed by a light touch on her skin. She wasn't trying to be coy, but she pretended to be asleep to see what I would do next. I didn't do anything. I looked around and walked away.

I WROTE IN my confessions, that at night we left the back mountain toward the scene of the crime. With a back-basket full of knick-knacks, we were planning to settle down in the mountains farther south. The land was fertile there. Even the roadside weeds were as tall as a person, unlike the land behind Team 15 where the weeds only grew six inches tall. The moon was bright that night as we walked swiftly over a stretch of paved road. By the time the morning fog materialized, we had already walked twenty kilometers, well on our way to the southern range. To be precise, we were in the meadows south of the Zhangfeng Outpost, beyond which was the rainforest. We settled under a big ficus tree and gathered some manure to start a fire. We laid a plastic tarp down next to the fire and piled our soggy clothes near it. We huddled into a ball under three layers of blankets and quickly fell asleep. We woke up an hour later from the cold. All three blankets were soaked and the manure fire had gone out. Condensation on the tree leaves poured down like rain with droplets the size of mung beans. It was January, the coldest time of the dry season. The shady side of mountains is always this humid.

Chen Qingyang said, when she woke, she could hear a rattling by her ear. My teeth were rattling like crazy. Even worse, I had a fever. Whenever I got sick, it was hard to recover without getting an injection. She stood up and said, this won't do, at this rate, we'll both get sick. Hurry, let's do the thing. I refused and said: just wait it out. The sun will be up soon. Later, I added: can't you see what shape I'm in? This was how we were before our crime.

The crime scene went like this: Chen Qingyang rode on top of me, bouncing up and down against a backdrop of foggy white nothingness. It wasn't cold anymore. We were surrounded by the sound of cowbells. The local Dai people let their water buffaloes graze freely. At sunrise, they came trotting out on their own. The buffaloes wore wooden cowbells that thudded as they moved. An enormous creature suddenly appeared next to us. Dewdrops hung on the steely hairs by its ears. The white water buffalo tilted its head and watched us through one eye.

White water buffalo horns can be used to make beautiful knife handles. But they are brittle, easy to crack. I had a knife with a buffalo horn handle that fortunately had no cracks. The blade was made of high-quality material as well, but the people's police had confiscated it. After our troubles ended, I tried to get it back but they said it was gone. And my hunting rifle, they wouldn't give that back either. Old Guo from the people's police had begged to buy the gun from me, but he was only willing to pay fifty yuan. In the end, I didn't get the knife or the gun back.

CHEN QINGYANG AND I talked for a long time before committing our crime at the hotel. Eventually, she took off her shirt, leaving on only her skirt and her boots. I sat down next to her and ran my fingers through her hair. There was quite a bit of white.

Chen Qingyang had gotten a perm. She said that when she was young her hair used to be so fine that she hadn't wanted to damage it. Now it didn't matter. She had become the vice president of her hospital. She was too busy to wash her hair every day. Better yet, the perm hid the wrinkles around her eyes and neck. She said, my daughter recommended plastic surgery. But she didn't have the time for it.

Then she said I could look, and she began to take off her bra. I tried to help but I wasn't of any use. I reached for her back while the clasp was in the front. She said, it seemed like I had been a good boy so she turned around. I examined her closely and offered some feedback. For some reason, she blushed and said, all right, you've seen it, what more do you want? She put her bra back on. I said, hold your horses. She said, what, did I still want to study her anatomy? I said, of course, in time, but let's talk first. Her face turned red in anger. She said: Wang Er, you will never learn, you will always be an asshole.

All those years ago when I was at the people's police station, Luo Xiaosi came to visit me. He climbed up to a window and saw me bound up like a zongzi.* He thought I was in big trouble, like bullet-to-the-head kind of big. He offered a pack of cigarettes through the window and said: bro, a little something from the guys, and proceeded to sob. Luo Xiaosi was full of emotions, he cried easily. I told him to light one and bring it in through the window. He nearly dislocated his shoulder trying to place the cigarette in my mouth. He asked if I had any unfinished business that needed to be taken care of. I said I didn't. I told him not to bring a big group of people here and he nodded. After he left, a bunch of kids climbed up to the window to peek at us. They saw me dangling a cigarette in my mouth, blinking one eye after the other trying to avoid the smoke. I must have looked like a freak. Their leader blurted out: hooligan! I said, your mom and dad are hooligans, how else did they end up with you!? The kids started to throw mud at me. After we were untied, I tracked down the kid's father and said: today I was tied up like a hog at the people's police station. Your precious offspring took the opportunity to fling mud at me. The man instantly grabbed his son and beat him. I watched until he was finished before leaving.

---

*Zongzi is a rice cake wrapped in banana leaves.

When Chen Qingyang heard the story, her only comment was: Wang Er, what an asshole you are.

I wasn't entirely incorrigible in the end. Later in my life I went on to have a home and a family, and I learned to be good. After finishing a cigarette, I pulled her toward me and caressed her breasts in that familiar way we had. When I moved on to her skirt, she said: in time, let's talk some more, give me a drag. I lit a new cigarette and puffed on it before handing it to her.

Chen Qingyang said, when she was bouncing up and down on me on Mount Zhangfeng, she scoured the wilderness around her only to see the gloomy gray mist. All of a sudden, she had felt incredibly alone. Even though a part of my body was inside her, she had still felt alone, and extremely lonely. As I was finally getting warmed up, I said: let's switch, check out my moves, before flipping over on top of her. She said, that time, you really were the biggest asshole.

When Chen Qingyang said that I had been at the apogee of being an asshole, she was referring to the fact that I had noticed how pretty her feet were. That was why I said, my friend Chen, I think I'm going to have a foot fetish. I lifted up her legs and kissed the bottoms of her feet. Chen Qingyang lay on her back with her arms outspread grasping for grass. She tossed her head. Her hair covered her face. Hidden under it, she moaned.

I wrote in my confession: *I put her legs down and cleared the hair from her face. Chen Qingyang wanted to hit me. With tears in her eyes and bright red cheeks, she restrained herself. She relaxed a little and said, asshole, what are you trying to do to me. I said, what. She smiled and said, nothing, keep going. Once again, I lifted her legs. She lay there silent and motionless, arms outspread, biting her lower lip. Whenever I looked at her, she would smile. I can remember how pale her face was and how black her hair was. That was us.*

Chen Qingyang said, as she lay there in the freezing rain, she had felt as if icy droplets were seeping into her every pore. She felt a sadness well up from deep inside, an unending sadness that was suddenly interrupted by a surge of bliss. The cold mist and rain soaked her body. She had felt like dying. She couldn't hold it in anymore, she needed to scream. But she had looked at me and swallowed her scream. There wasn't a man in this world who could have made her scream in front of him. She kept that distance with everyone.

Chen Qingyang later told me, every time we made love, she felt torn. Deep down, she wanted to scream and hold me and kiss me but she wasn't letting herself. She didn't want to love anybody, no one; even so, when I kissed the sole of her foot, a spicy sting had managed to seep into her heart.

When Chen Qingyang and I made love on Mount Zhangfeng, an old water buffalo stood near us. When it mooed and ran off, we were alone. A long time passed before the sky slowly began to glow. The fog dissipated, leaving Chen Qingyang's body covered in glimmering dewdrops. I loosened my arms around her and stood up. I could see that the outpost wasn't very far so I said, let's go. That's when we left that place and never returned.

8

WROTE IN MY CONFESSION, *Chen Qingyang and I committed innumerable crimes in the clearing behind Old Man Liu's because his fallow, fertile land was almost effortless to clear.* We settled in comfortably and as the saying goes, a warm body and a full belly lead to wanton desires. We were the only ones living in that part of the mountain. Old Man Liu was bedridden, nearing his death. The mountain was perpetually wet with rain and fog. Chen Qingyang wore my belt around her waist with my knife hanging at her side. Other than those and her knee-high rain boots, she wore nothing.

Chen Qingyang later said, I was the only friend she ever made in life. It all started in that little pump station shed by the river where we talked about epic friendship. In life, one had to pursue at least a few meaningful things. This was to be one of them. She didn't pursue any more friendships after me. Doing the same thing again would have been pointless.

I had had a feeling that was to be the case. That was why when I proposed it, I had said: sister, how about we commit some epic friendship? Confucian scholars talk about "committed matrimony," but we have no matrimony to speak of. So why don't we commit epic friendship instead. She said, okay, how do we commit? Commitment from the front or commitment from the rear? I said, from the rear. We were at the end of a cornfield. Since it was to be from the rear, we laid down two raincoats like blankets and she crouched on all fours on top of them. She said: make it quick, Old Man Liu needs his shot soon. Later when I handed in my confession, the leadership asked me to clarify:

1. What is "committed matrimony"?
2. What does "commit" epic friendship mean?
3. What is commitment from the front and what is commitment from the rear?

Once I clarified everything, the leadership told me to use fewer euphemism and to get to the point.

We committed epic friendship in the mountain, breathing wet steamy breaths. It wasn't even all that cold but the air was wet enough to wring out with your hands. Next to us were earthworms crawling in and out of the fertile soil. Later, we harvested unripe corn and ground it up with a mortar and pestle. This was the Jingpo people's traditional method. The cornmeal we produced wasn't too bad. Left in cold water, it kept for a long time. . . .

Chen Qingyang crouched in the cold rain. Her breasts felt like frozen apples. Her skin was taut like polished marble. I pulled my little monk out of her and shot my cum into the ground. She stood by and watched in horror. I said to her: it'll make the soil more fertile. She said: I know, and added: will little Wang Ers grow out of the earth? Did a doctor really just ask that?

After the rain season ended, we dressed up like Dai people and went to the street market in Qingping. What happened there I already wrote about. I ran into an old classmate who recognized me the moment he saw me, despite my disguise. It was hard for someone of my height to blend in. He said to me: bro, where have you been? I said: I don't speak Chinese! Even though I tried to put on an accent, it still sounded like a Beijinger. I outed myself in a single breath.

Returning to the farm was her idea. Personally, I had no such intention. She had joined me in the name of epic friendship, so of course, I had to accompany her down there. Frankly, we could have run away at any time but she wasn't interested. She said life now was very particular.

Chen Qingyang later admitted that her time in the mountain had also been particular. Walking through the drizzling rain under those cold, fog-shrouded peaks, with her knife on her belt and rain boots on her feet, that really was something. But doing the same thing over and over again wasn't as interesting. So she decided to go back to the world and endure all of its ravages.

At the hotel, Chen Qingyang and I reminisced about our epic friendship for a long time. We remembered being on our way down the mountain when we reached a fork in the road. It was a four-way intersection, pointing not quite east, south, north, or west. One road went out of the country, to an unknown foreign land. One road went to China's heartland. One road went to the farm and the other was the road we had come from. The road we had come from also went to the village of Husa. In the village lived the Achang blacksmiths, who had been blacksmiths for generations. Even though I wasn't of their lineage, I could still have been a black-smith. I knew many of them and they respected my talent. The Achang girls were beautiful. They wore all sorts of copper and sil-ver trinkets. Chen Qingyang was so mesmerized by their fashion that she wanted to become an Achang too. The monsoon season had passed. Blobs of sunlight flickered across the nimbus clouds ascending from all directions. We had many choices, many direc-tions to choose from. We stood at the intersection for a long time. Later, when I stood at the bus stop waiting for the bus back to Beijing, I also had two choices. I could wait for the bus or I could go back to the farm. Whenever I found myself walking down one path, I also found myself thinking about the other. I always had mixed feelings.

Chen Qingyang once said, I possessed average talent, dexterous hands, and a very muddled character. Let us consider these generalizations. In regard to my mediocrity, I didn't quite agree. As for my muddled character, there was plenty of evidence, so it was hard to deny. As for my dexterous hands, that was probably something she gleaned from personal experience. My hands were indeed very nimble and not just for caressing women. With my small palms and long fingers, I was capable of the most detailed craftsmanship. The Achang blacksmiths were better smiths than me, but when it came to engraving flowery designs on the blade, I was the champion. That was why some twenty individual blacksmiths asked us to move in with them. They could have made the blades and I could have engraved the designs. It could have been a partnership. Had I gone down that road, I probably would've forgotten how to speak Mandarin by now.

Had I moved in with the Achang, I might have lived in a dark metal shop engraving designs for Husa knives. Behind the house might have been a muddy backyard with a nest of offspring comprising four different genetic combinations:

1. Chen Qingyang and mine
2. An Achang brother and an Achang sister's
3. Me and an Achang sister's
4. Chen Qingyang and an Achang brother's

Chen Qingyang might have just returned from the summit with a bundle of firewood on her back. She might have lifted up her petticoat to reveal a firm and muscular boob. She might have picked up one of the toddlers, whether it was black or white, red or green, and offered her breast to it. Had we stayed in the mountain, that's probably what would have happened.

Chen Qingyang said something like that couldn't have happened, because it just didn't. What happened was we returned to the farm, wrote our confessions, and got denounced. Even though we could have run away at any time, we didn't. That's what happened.

WHEN CHEN QINGYANG said I possessed average talent, she clearly wasn't referring to my literary prowess. Everyone loved to read my confessions. When I first started to write, I was resistant to say the least. But the more I wrote, the more I got into it. It was because I was writing about things that actually happened to me. Things that actually happened are uniquely beautiful.

I tried hard to fit everything into my confessions, but I didn't write about the following: Chen Qingyang and I were in the mountain behind Team 15. After doing our business in the thatched hut, we went to play in the stream. The water flowing down the slopes had eroded the red soil and revealed a blue clay surface underneath. We climbed onto the blue clay to sunbathe. As my body warmed, my little monk began to perk up again. But since it had just relieved itself, it wasn't desperate like a pervert. I lay on my side. With her head resting on my arm, I slid in from behind her. Years later at the hotel, that was how we commemorated our epic friendship.

Chen Qingyang and I had lain on our sides on the blue clay. Night was approaching. The wind was chilly. We lay together peacefully, occasionally stirring. They say dolphins have sex for procreation as well as recreation. That would mean dolphins have epic friendships too. When Chen Qingyang and I had lain together, we were like two dolphins.

We spooned on the blue clay with our eyes closed like two dolphins swimming in the ocean. The sky dimmed as the sun grew redder and redder on its way down. A ring of clouds rose along the horizon, white and gloomy like a sea of belly-up fish with dead bulging eyes. Wind coursed silently into the valley. There was tragedy in the air. Chen Qingyang shed many tears. She said it was because the world was melancholy.

I kept a copy of the confessions I had written that year. Once I showed them to a friend who worked on Anglo-American literature. He said they were good and reminded him of underground novels of the Victorian era. As for the deleted parts, he said, they were good cuts. Too many details distracted from the story's flow. My friend sure was knowledgeable. I wrote the confessions when I was pretty young, not having been very well-read (even now I'm not very well-read). I had no idea what a Victorian era underground novel was. My concern was to avoid leading others astray. Quite a few people wanted to read my confessions. If as a result of reading them, they were driven to commit the old shoe, it wouldn't have been the end of the world. But if they tried to use them like guide books, that wouldn't have been very good.

IN MY CONFESSIONS, I omitted the following story for the reason mentioned above. We made mistakes. We should have been executed, but the leadership saved us and allowed us to write confessions. O benevolence! That was why I only wrote about how misbehaved we were.

When we were living behind Old Man Liu's place, Chen Qingyang made herself a tube skirt so that she could look like a Dai when we went to the Qingping market. But after putting on the skirt, it was so tight she could barely walk. On the way to Qingping, we came to a river. The water was as cold as ice and as verdant as pickled mustard greens. The river came up about waist-high, flowing rapidly. I picked her up, slung her over my shoulder, and waded across the river. Her waist was just about the same width as one of my shoulders. I remember her face turning red. I said, I can carry you all the way to Qingping and back faster than you can waddle. She said, screw you.

A tube skirt is basically a cloth cylinder with a twelve-inch circumference opening at the bottom. People who know how to wear them can do all sorts of things in them, like pee on the street without squatting down. Chen Qingyang said, that was one trick she would never be able to learn. At Qingping's street market, we watched and learned. She learned that if she was going to dress up as a woman from an ethnic group, she should have dressed up as an Achang. The journey home was all uphill. She was soon exhausted. Every time there was a creek or a ditch to cross, she would find a large stump and daintily maneuver on top of it so that I could pick her up.

On our way back, I carried her over many slippery slopes. It was the beginning of the dry season. Rows of clouds arrayed the sky under a radiant sun, but it still drizzled on the mountain. The eroding red soil made the muck planks even slipperier. Walking on a muck plank was like learning to ice-skate for the first time. With her waist in my right arm, the gun in my left hand, and a basket on my back, I trudged uphill with great difficulty. Suddenly, I began to slip. We were headed for a cliff. Luckily, I was able to plant the gun firmly into the ground and catch myself. I tensed every muscle to my human limit and barely held on for dear life. That dumbbell had to add fuel to the fire by squirming around, trying to get down. We almost died.

The first thing I did when I could catch my breath was to move the gun to my right hand and to use my left hand to spank her twice on the butt. Through that thin layer of fabric, her skin felt extra smooth. Her butt was so round. Damn, it felt good! After the spanking, she became much more docile. She did what she was told and didn't make a sound.

Of course, spanking Chen Qingyang hadn't been a good thing. But I imagine most old shoes and wild lovers didn't even ever have that sort of a connection. The incident was a digression so I didn't include it.

9

WHEN CHEN QINGYANG AND I made love on Mount Zhang-feng, she was so pale I could see the veins beneath her temples. Our time in the mountain gave her a deep tan. When we returned to the farm, she became as white as ivory again. After that, we entered the "joint military and civilian development era." On Sundays, the logistics team would send out a big tractor load of us deplorable types to a brick kiln to produce bricks. When the bricks were finished, we were taken to a production team at the border to rendezvous with a propaganda team. Our tractor was filled with counterrevolutionaries, thieves, smugglers, old shoes, and the like, rounding out examples of both class enemies and enemies within the working class. When we were finished with our tasks, we were taken to a stage to be publicly criticized. Such efforts were supposed to reinforce border defense. Trips like these came with government catering food for everyone involved. Armed soldiers stood over us as we squatted down and ate. Once when Chen Qingyang and I had finished our food, we found ourselves leaning leisurely against the tractor. A group of old ladies stopped by and appraised Chen Qingyang from head to toe. Their conclusion was that her skin was magnificently white, so it was no wonder she was an old shoe.

I once tracked down Old Guo from the people's police to ask him why we were sent on these trips. He said it was to let the scoundrels on the other side of the border know how rough it was over here, so that they wouldn't bother to come and make trouble. At first, they weren't going to send us. Unfortunately, they couldn't round up enough heads for the rally. We were no good anyway, so what if they sent us? I said, sure, so what, but why did you have to tell them to pull on Chen Qingyang's hair? If you push me too far, I can go right back to the mountain. He said he wasn't aware of the hair pulling and that he would look into it. I wanted to go back to the mountain anyway, but Chen Qingyang said, forget about it, a little hair pulling, no big deal.

When we went on these trips, Chen Qingyang always wore one of my old student uniforms. The jacket was huge on her. The sleeves went to her fingers and the collar could cover her face. For some reason, she decided to keep the jacket. Apparently, the jacket is still around and she wears it when she cleans her windows and floors. These criticism sessions were part of her routine now. As soon as she heard our names called, she took a pair of freshly cleaned old shoes out of her backpack. The shoes were tied together with a rope so that she could wear them around her neck on stage.

At the hotel, Chen Qingyang said that once, she took a shower at home and wore my student jacket as a bathrobe. She performed a reenactment of how she was criticized publicly back in the day, she performed it for her daughter. She stood, hunched over, arms bound behind her. At times, she would look up like a samba dancer so everyone could see her face. Her daughter asked: what about daddy? Chen Qingyang said: your daddy went on a plane ride. The child giggled at the thought of daddy looking like an airplane.

When I heard this story, it felt like a thorn got stuck in my back. First of all, I hadn't gone on any "plane ride." When I was being denounced, two young guys from Sichuan escorted me. They were very polite, always apologizing first: brother Wang, please forgive us. Only after that did they shove me onto the stage. Escorting her on the other hand were two floozies from the propaganda team who were twisting her elbows and pulling her hair. To imply that I was treated worse than her was unfair to the two Sichuanese lads. Second, I wasn't her daddy. When our struggle sessions concluded, entertainment usually began. We were kicked off stage and herded onto the tractor for an overnight trip back to the farm. Every time we went on a trip, Chen Qingyang's libido went into overdrive.

In our days back at the farm, the criticism sessions happened periodically. Sometimes, the colonel would invite us to his home to talk about our mistakes. He said that he had made this sort of mistake as well, and proceeded to talk to Chen Qingyang about his prostate. I would usually take my leave at such a moment, unless he asked me to fix his watch. Sometimes they were mean to us, sending us on two trips a week. The political commissar said, people like Wang Er and Chen Qingyang need to be denounced or else everyone will run away to the mountains. What would happen to the farm then? To be fair, he had a point. But more importantly, he didn't have prostatitis. So Chen Qingyang always kept the pair of old shoes in her backpack just in case. Eventually, the trips ended. One day, when the commissar went out for a conference, the colonel had a chat with the army administration. Just like that, they released me back to the mainland.

THE WHOLE PUBLIC criticism session fiasco came about like this: harassing old shoes was a form of entertainment, a local tradition. At the peak of the farm season, when everyone was exhausted, the captain would say, tonight's entertainment will be harassing old shoes. As for how exactly they did the harassing, I have no firsthand knowledge. When they went to harass old shoes, they first kicked out all the unmarried guys. Anyway, those women were usually not my type.

When veteran Party cadres took over the farm, they banned the harassment of old shoes. The reason was that it was against Party doctrine. But during the "joint military and civilian development era," harassing old shoes was allowed again. The regiment gave the order for us to report to the propaganda team in preparation for a criticism session. I was on the verge of running away to the mountain again but Chen Qingyang refused to join me. She said, she must have been the prettiest girl to ever have been harassed in the whole history of this local tradition. When she was being criticized, she was surrounded by a huge crowd staring at her. It gave her some kind of pride.

When the regiment told us to join the propaganda team's struggle sessions, they added the following: our actions represented conflict within the working class, that is to say, heavy policy action wasn't absolutely necessary; but if the crowd became agitated and demanded harsh punishment, we would have to play it by ear, policy-wise. The crowd went berserk the moment they saw us. The captain of the propaganda team was one of the colonel's men. We knew him personally. He came to the guesthouse to ask for a favor: would it be possible to ask Dr. Chen to suffer some indignity next time? Chen Qingyang said it was not a problem. Chen Qingyang came up with the idea of wearing a pair of old shoes around her neck, but that wasn't enough to satisfy the mob. The captain had to come back again and ask Chen Qingyang to suffer a little more indignity next time. Eventually, he simply said, we're all adults here, I shouldn't need to say anymore. Best of luck to the both of you.

We began every one of those sessions by waiting behind the banana trees. Then, we waited backstage. When it was close to our turn, Chen Qingyang stood up and redid her hair clips, holding each in her mouth as she went through them meticulously. Then she rolled up her collar, rolled down her sleeves, and placed her hands behind her back, ready to be bound up.

Chen Qingyang said, when they tied her up with bamboo fiber or hemp ropes, her wrists swelled up. That was why she brought her own cotton clothesline from home. They would complain, women sure are hard to tie up, all round without a corner to catch the rope on. A pair of large hands pulled her wrists together while another pair of hands wrapped the rope tightly around her wrists and then around her whole torso like a pretzel.

One person shoved her onto the stage while another pulled on her hair so that she couldn't look away. All she could do was turn slightly to a side so that she could stare at the gas lamp's pale green light. When she saw the hundreds of unknown faces out of the corner of her eyes, she smiled and thought, what a strange and unfamiliar world! What's going on here? She had no idea.

What Chen Qingyang understood was that she was an old shoe. She wore the rope tied in a pretzel knot like a body suit that accentuated her every curve. She could see the men with their pants bulging at the groin. She knew it was because of her, but why that had to be the case was beyond her.

According to Chen Qingyang, during struggle sessions, they had to pull on her hair to make her look in different directions so she braided herself some pigtails. That way, it was easier for each of her two escorts to hold one wrist and one braid. Like that, she was paraded before the crowd. Everything went straight to her heart, but she didn't understand any of it. In a way, she was pleasant. She did what she was told to and the rest was none of her business. This was how she played the character of an old shoe on stage.

When our struggle sessions ended, the entertainment began. Of course, we were never allowed to watch. We were shoved onto the tractor and dragged back to the farm. The tractor driver was in such a rush to get home to sleep that he turned on the engine far in advance. I didn't even get a chance to untie Chen Qingyang before getting ushered on. I carried her onto the tractor but the ride was so dark and bumpy that I couldn't get the rope off. Back at the farm, I carried her to the guesthouse so that I could slowly untie her under a light. Under the light, I could see her blushing. She said: can we commit epic friendship now? I can't wait another minute!

Chen Qingyang said, she felt like a gift being unwrapped. Lust and passion overwhelmed her and all her worries left her. She no longer worried about why she was an old shoe or what exactly old shoes were; as well as many other mysteries like: why did we end up here, what are we doing, etc. In that moment, she had given herself over to me entirely.

Every time we came back from a trip, Chen Qingyang wanted epic friendship. It always happened on the desk, the same desk I used to write my confessions. The desk was the perfect height; she sat on it like a koala, moaning with such pleasure she sometimes could not hold her screams. The light was off so I usually couldn't see her face. The window in the back of the room was always open. On the other side of it was a steep drop. Yet somehow, there were always heads popping in and out of view like jackdaws on a tree branch. I always had some mountain pears on my desk, the ones that were so hard only pigs could eat them. She used to grab one and chuck it over my shoulder. Her aim was mostly spot on, and the victim would roll down the hill. It made me so nervous that my load came out cold. Frankly, I was worried that someone might get killed. I should have included this in the confessions, but I was afraid that confessing to a crime I committed while under investigation might have gotten me in even deeper trouble.

10

WHEN WE COMMEMORATED OUR EPIC FRIENDSHIP at the hotel, we talked about many things. We talked about the possibilities back then, my confessions, and my little monk. The thing was thrilled to get mentioned and squirmed eagerly. In retrospect, it seemed like they had tried to crush our balls but our balls stood firm. I was as hard as ever. In the name of epic friendship, I could run three laps around the block naked. I never cared about shame. No matter what, that had been my golden age, even if everyone thought I was a pervert. I met all sorts of interesting people like the horse-herding vagabonds, the Jingpo people, and more. Just mention Wang Er, the watch repairman, and everyone would know. I sat by the fire and drank that twenty-cent liquor with them, lots of it. I was cherished up there.

The pigs in the pigsty also liked me because when I fed them, they got three times as much bran. The superintendent argued with me but I said, the pigs need to eat right. I possessed an abundance of epic friendship that I wanted to share with the whole world, but no one wanted it. So it all got dumped onto Chen Qingyang.

When Chen Qingyang and I recommitted epic friendship at the hotel, it was rather entertaining. At one point, I slipped out and there were traces of blood on my little monk. She said, she was getting old and it was getting thin in there, could I be a little gentler. She added, having lived in the south for so long, the northern climate now made her skin crack. Also the quality of hand creams on the market had fallen so much that they did nothing for her skin. As she spoke, she took out a tincture of glycerol and rubbed it on my little monk. I moved to her front so that we could converse more easily. I lay like a fallen tree between her open legs.

On Chen Qingyang's face were shallow wrinkles that flickered under the light like golden threads. I kissed her lips; she didn't resist. Her lips were supple and parted. She had never let me kiss her lips before, always redirecting me to her chin and neck, saying that it was more stimulating. We continued to reminisce.

Chen Qingyang said that it had been her golden age as well. She had been called an old shoe, but really, she was innocent. Even today, she was innocent. Her words made me laugh, but she said, what we were doing couldn't possibly be considered a crime, at the time nor today. We had an epic friendship, we ran away together, we were denounced together, and after finding each other again after twenty years, of course she was going to let me touch her. Even if it was a crime, it wasn't wrong. The important thing was, she didn't acknowledge it as a crime.

And then, her moaning sped up, her face turned crimson. She wrapped her legs around me as all her muscles tensed. Her moans were muffled behind clenched jaws. She remained in that state for a long time before relaxing her body. It had been good, she said.

It had been good, and it certainly hadn't been a crime. She wore a blissful, Socratic innocence. Even though she was in her forties, she still lived in an enchanted world. She didn't know why people had sent her to the middle of nowhere in Yunnan. She didn't know why they then brought her back. She didn't know why they had to call her an old shoe or why they had to shove her onto a stage. She didn't know why they stopped calling her an old shoe or why they exonerated her in the end. All these mysteries had explanations, but she couldn't understand any of them. She was ignorant and therefore innocent. All the law books say things like that.

CHEN QINGYANG SAID, a person lives in this world to be ravaged, unto death. Once you understood that, everything else is just water under the bridge. To understand how she arrived at such a perspective, one has to go back to the time I returned from the hospital and stopped by her place on the way to the mountain. I asked her to come see me, but she wasn't sure if she would. When she finally made up her mind and trekked on that hot windy afternoon to reach my hut, her heart was filled momentarily with beautiful dreams. But when she entered the hut, she was greeted with my little monk standing there like some grotesque instrument of torture. In that moment, she screamed and gave up all hope.

Chen Qingyang said, one winter day more than twenty years ago, she walked into her courtyard. At that time of the year, she was from head to toe in clothes so thick that she could hardly cross the doorstep. A speck of sand got into her eye. How intense the pain! Icy wind clawed at her face as tears flowed. It was unbearable, she bawled. She cried and cried on her small bed, trying to wake up from it all. It was an instinct she kept for the rest of her life. To scream uninhibited, drifting from one dream state to the next, was almost too much to ask for.

Chen Qingyang said, when she came to look for me, the woods were swarming with golden flies. The wind seemed to blow from every direction, passing through the fabric of her clothes, slithering up her body. The place where I was staying was basically wilderness. The blazing sun sliced through the thatched roof like wafers of mica. Under her thin white gown, she was naked and full of anticipation. After all, it was her golden age as well, even if people were calling her an old shoe.

Chen Qingyang said, when she came to look for me in the mountain, she hiked over many treeless hills. The wind came in from under her clothes and caressed her most sensitive areas. She felt an urge that was as ephemeral as the wind that swelled over the ridges. She thought of our epic friendship, how I rushed down the hill so fleet-footed. She remembered how messy my hair was when we discussed the problem of old shoes together, how my eyes locked onto hers. She felt she needed me, that we could fuse into one hermaphroditic whole. It reminded her of climbing over the doorstep when she was a little girl, feeling the wind outside. How blue was the sky, and bright the light, not to mention the doves in flight. The cooing of doves left an indelible impression on her. She wanted to connect. She yearned to be one with the world outside and melt into heaven and earth. If she were the only person left in the world, that would have been much too sad.

Chen Qingyang said, when she walked into my little hut, she had already thought of everything, everything except for my little monk. It was hideous, unfit for any dream state. In that moment, Chen Qingyang wanted to bawl but couldn't. It was as if some big hand had gripped her throat. That's what we call reality. Reality, you can't wake up from. In that instant, she understood what the world was all about. She made up her mind and approached me happily, ready to be ravaged.

Chen Qingyang added that the moment reminded her of crying in pain at the doorstep. That time, she cried and cried but still couldn't cry herself awake. The pain had no intention of subsiding. She kept crying. She refused to give up. She never gave up on trying to cry herself awake until twenty years later, when she was confronted by my little monk. It wasn't the first time she had confronted a little monk. But in the past, she hadn't thought there would be more of them out there.

Chen Qingyang said, when she saw the hideous thing, she thought about epic friendship. She had a female roommate in college who was ugly as a ghoul (or rather, she looked like one) but wanted to sleep in the same bed as her. Not only that, but in the middle of the night, she would kiss her lips and rub her breasts. Frankly, Chen was not interested. But to be polite, she put up with it. Later once again, she was faced with a ghoul. What this ghoul wanted was more or less the same as the first one. So let it be satisfied, even just for the sake of friendship. Happily, she approached and buried the monstrous thing deep inside.

Chen Qingyang said, she believed she was innocent even when we went deep into the mountain where we committed epic friendship nearly every day. She said that it still didn't mean she was bad because she didn't understand why me and my little monk were doing it. She was doing it because of epic friendship. Epic friendship was a kind of oath. Abiding by an oath couldn't have been wrong. She swore to help me in every way she could. But deep in the mountains, by soaking her twice I had entirely polluted her innocence.

11

SPENT A LONG TIME WRITING my confessions but the leadership always retorted they were not detailed enough, so I had to continue. I came to believe that I would spend the rest of my life confessing. One day, Chen Qingyang wrote a confession and handed it to the people's police without letting me look at it. I was never asked to write another word. Not only that, but our public criticism sessions ended. Not only that, but Chen Qingyang began to grow distant. After some time of feeling not much of anything, I returned to Beijing by myself. I couldn't figure out for the life of me what she had written.

When I departed from Yunnan, I had lost everything: my gun, my knife, my tools. The only thing I had more of were the files in my bulging envelope of shame. For the rest of my life, wherever I would go, people would know that I was a pervert. The only upside was that I got to return to the city before other people. But it wasn't much of an upside since I still had to serve in the countryside around the capital.

When I first went to Yunnan, I brought a set of tools with me including vices and clamps, and a full watch repair kit. When I was living by Old Man Liu's, I used them to fix people's watches. In the wilderness, there were occasionally horse-herding vagabonds that passed through. Some of them wanted me to appraise smuggled watches. Whatever I said they were worth, that was what they were worth. Of course, my service wasn't free. I had plenty of work to do in the mountain. Had I not come down from there, I'd have tens of thousands of yuan by now.

As for the double-barreled hunting rifle, it was quite a treasure. The locals were used to seeing carbines and muskets, but they had never seen a thing like that. The barrel was so thick and there were two of them. It was easy for me to scare people with it. Without it, we would have been robbed constantly. Me, and especially Old Man Liu, they would not have robbed. But they probably would have taken Chen Qingyang. As for my knife, it was always attached to a leather belt. The leather belt was usually around Chen Qingyang's waist. She wore it even when she slept and fucked because she thought it made her look badass. To think of it, it should really be considered her knife. But as I mentioned, the people's police station took the gun and the knife. I left my tools up in the mountain by Old Man Liu's before returning to the farm. Had things taken a turn for the worse, I could have gone back. But when I left for Beijing, I was in such a rush that I didn't get a chance to retrieve them. So, I became destitute.

In the hotel, I said to Chen Qingyang that I could not figure out for the life of me what she had written in that final confession. She said that she couldn't tell me yet, not until we parted ways. The next day she would be returning to Shanghai. She asked me to go with her to the train station.

Chen Qingyang and I were different in every way. After sunrise, she took a cold shower (the hot water wasn't running), and began to dress. From her coat down to her panties, she was a sweetly scented lady. I, on the other hand, looked like a hillbilly hooligan from head to toe. No wonder they exonerated her but not me. That is to say, her broken hymen had healed while I never grew the damn thing in the first place. Furthermore, I was guilty of abetting a crime. We had made many mistakes together but since she didn't admit they were crimes, it was all on me.

We paid the bill in the hotel lobby and exited to the street. It occurred to me, the confession she had turned in must have been obscene. The people who read those things had hearts of stone. How dirty had it been if even they couldn't stand reading it? Chen Qingyang said there was nothing special in it, only her one true crime.

The one true crime she referred to was what had happened on the road to Qingping. She was hanging across my shoulder with her tube skirt wrapped tightly around her legs and her hair dangling down to my waist. White clouds drifted across the sky. We were the only two people around. I had just spanked her twice, so hard that the blistering pain was only fading slowly. After spanking her, I had cleared my head and focused on the hike.

Chen Qingyang said, in that moment, her body had gone limp from exhaustion. As she hung on my shoulder, she felt at one with the vines, the trees, and all living things. She had not wanted to care about anything else, ever again. In that moment she forgot everything. In that moment, she had fallen in love with me and had known there was no going back.

At the train station, Chen Qingyang said, when she turned in the confession, the colonel read it right away. His face turned as red as your little monk. After that, everyone who read the confession turned as red as little monks. The people's police station tracked her down to ask her to rewrite it. She said, but it's the truth, not one word can be changed. They had no choice but to include it in our files.

Chen Qingyang went on saying, admitting what she admitted was like admitting everything. At the people's police station, they showed her other people's confessions, hoping she would realize that no one had ever written one like hers. But she insisted on her version. She said, the reason she saved this confession for the end was because it was worse than anything else she had ever done. In the past, she had confessed to opening and closing her legs. But the real reason she did those things was because she enjoyed it. Doing something and enjoying it were different. The first crime deserved a criticism session. The second deserved quartering and death by a thousand cuts. No one had the right to quarter us, so they had to let us go. . . .

After finally telling me this story, her train departed. I never saw her again.

AT THIRTY, A MAN

1

WANG ER WAS BORN IN the city of Beijing. I am Wang Er. One summer morning as I biked past my old school on my way to work, I gazed at its austere gate and the soaring chimney beyond the blacktop. Memories flooded my mind, but how any of them could have really happened was beyond me.

It seemed not so long ago that I was still a middle school student, backpack battling my classmates outside that gate. My backpack landed on somebody with a thud, sending him flying back a meter or more. As it turned out, in addition to books, there was a brick in my backpack. That pissed everybody off. They howled as they chased after me. I dashed across the blacktop, fleeing for the gray chimney. When the principal came out of his office for a stroll, he saw me high up on the chimney ladder, my young chest open to the eastern wind, screaming: "fuck your ma! Anyone who comes up here will get stomped!" I could remember it like it was yesterday.

In the blink of an eye, I had grown to over 1.9 meters, weighing over 80 kilograms. It was hard to imagine how a bunch of seventh-grade boys could have driven such a hulk up a chimney.

I got off my bike absentmindedly and parked it by the side of the road. The quietness of the empty campus sent a chill through my heart. How many times had I walked onto this silent campus, past these silent halls, into that familiar classroom to be greeted by several dozen faces turning to me simultaneously? I was always late. Written on the blackboard was a table of good and bad students. My name always had a place in the bad column. After class, the class captain, the class cadre, and two lieutenant class captains all raced to speak with me so that they could report back to the teacher and the teacher's assistant. It wasn't every day that you could find a wallet to return or an old man to help across the street. I, on the other hand, was a constant source of good deeds. Every time someone had a talk with me, a good deed was done: "I helped the bad student Wang Er!" But in the end, I grew up all right. I avoided killing any teachers or principals. I refrained from burning down any schools. I never even peed in a classroom. All that was thanks to the invaluable support of my peers.

No one twenty years ago would have believed it, not the principal, not the teachers, not the students, not even me, that Wang Er would ever get to school forty minutes early. But it happened. Wang Er had become a college lecturer who arrived in class ahead of time to prepare the biology lab. In theory, this should have been the lab assistant's job, but I didn't trust him.

Even harder to believe was the fact that it was now my turn to worry about other people. Xu You and I had been friends for thirty years. My memory of our great conspiracy to poison our kindergarten teacher was as fresh as if it had happened yesterday. I could vividly remember my bullying streak, how I beat up every kid in turn. I could remember how hard the teacher pulled on my ear as if trying to reshape them into the giant ears of the legendary

Liu Bei.* And never could I forget that afternoon, after nap time, when the teacher took us all to go poo. We formed a zigzagging row as we squatted over the winding gutter into which we defecated. The teacher observed from behind a glass door. She was supposed to wipe our butts when we finished, but she was lost in her crochet work. We squatted until our guts were ready to fall out, yet she never noticed. It smelled awful. I stood up and got some toilet paper to wipe my own butt. After pulling up my pants, I began to wipe the butts of all the other kids. My little buddies got in a line so that I could wipe their butts in turn. It would have been hard to describe how pleased I was with myself—a pioneer, the first to explore the butts of so many fine ladies-to-be, oops! Then out of nowhere, the teacher grabbed my ear and began to humiliate me in front of everybody.

I was bloated with anger. During my trip home on Sunday, I took a bottle of potassium permanganate used to wash pears with me back to school. Mother said it was poisonous, so I figured I could use it to poison the teacher. My pal Xu saw me with the red bottle of chemicals. After learning of my plan and its use, he expressed total support. He said he knew of another poison we could add, which was lime powder. Xu had a habit of putting everything in his mouth. Once, when he ate lime powder, his uncle squeezed his throat shut. His uncle said lime could burn through his stomach. After that, we began to add even more ingredients like toe mud, pee, slime from a toad's back, etc., until we ended up with a colorful concoction. But before we had a chance to put the mixture into the teacher's lunch box, we were exposed. That became the infamous Wang Er kindergarten poisoning scandal. This series of events revealed another hard-to-believe truth. Had it not been for my desire to poison the teacher, I couldn't possibly have put that much effort into a chemistry experiment.

---

*Liu Bei was a warlord in the late Eastern Han dynasty who founded the state of Shu-Han in the Three Kingdoms period and became its first ruler.

The things that happened, happened, whether I believed them or not. It was an early July morning in the year of '83. I had basically become a good person, a good teacher, a good citizen, and a good husband. The fact of the matter was, society really was a grand melting pot, capable of transforming any kind of person, even a Wang Er. Look at me now, not only a lecturer of microbiology at the agricultural department of a university, but also the director of a biology lab. Not only did I have to keep myself in line, I also had to manage others (for example, "remedial student Xu You") who I had to vouch for by patting the college president on the shoulder and making a show of confidence. That day I sprinted to the lab the moment I parked my bike in the garage. When I pushed open the door, I saw that things were just as I had feared—a bowl of leftover noodles on the lab table and a half-dozen beer bottles sprawled across the floor, pointing every which way. Last time the president came to the lab to inspect, he saw a piece of sausage on a lab table. He asked me, "What's this?" I said it was a sample for an experiment. He roared, "What experiment? Shit-making experiment!" That really shook me up. I cleaned up the room, but there was still a weird lingering smell, like a dead cat or a dead dog, or some sort of fermentation. After a thorough search, I still couldn't find the source of the smell. I went into the office and dragged Xu out of bed. He could barely keep his eyes open. He mumbled, "Wang Er, what do you want? I just found a wife in my dream . . ."

"Shush! It's already 7:40. Wake up! Tell me, what is that smell in the lab?"

"Don't interrupt me. It was my one-of-a-kind, best dream ever. I was about to . . ."

I grabbed him by his earlobe, "Answer me, what is that smell in the lab?"

"What the hell is your problem? Probably some dead rat. I put out rat poison."

"Not that kind of smell! More like your kind of smell!"

"How would I know?" He sat up. That jackass slept naked. "Hey, where are my shoes? Wang Er, don't mess with me!"

"Go to hell! I'm not your shoe keeper!"

"Oh man! Wang Er, I remember now. I put my sneakers in the oven and forgot to take them out!"

I rushed to the oven and opened the door—my God! I nearly suffocated. I quickly turned on the ventilator and put on a gas mask. After donning a pair of rubber gloves, I wrapped his stinky sneakers in some newspaper and tossed them into the bathroom. Xu had done nothing to prepare the lab for our morning work. The students would be pouring in in fifteen minutes and the lab tables were all empty. I rummaged through closets and drawers, breaking a sweat as I pulled out one instrument after another. I glanced over at Xu. The guy was wearing his lab coat, standing calmly in front of a microscope, staring at a sample. It was infuriating. I shouted, "Xu! I need tape. Go get some from medical supplies."

"All right. I'll do it in a minute."

"We have no time! The fire has reached the peacock's tail! Hurry!"

"Hold on. I still have to change."

"But you're already perfectly dressed."

He shimmied out of his lab coat. Heaven, why have thou not smitten him yet! That jackass was still naked under his lab coat. He attempted a few ballet moves, swinging through various styles like a pendulum as he pirouetted his way into the office. Moments later, he twirled back out and went on his merry way to the medical supply office. By the time I had finished setting everything up, he still hadn't returned. No matter. It wasn't as if he could have fallen down a hole and died. I wiped the sweat from my face, dusted off my clothes, and regained my composure. The students wouldn't be arriving for a few more minutes, so I decided to check out the sample Xu was staring at.

Inside the microscope was a field of white. It was full of micro-organisms, long and thin like wriggling pins. What were they?

What could Xu get his hands on that could be so unusual? All that time spent studying microbiology had better be paying off. The things looked familiar but I just couldn't quite put my finger on it.

Suddenly, Xu pulled on my collar and said, "Wang Er, my science man. Can you tell me what you're looking at?"

"You have the tapes? One for every lab table."

"Don't try to muddle through. What is it? Say it!"

I straightened up, strained to put away my director face and offered him a sinister Wang Er grin.

"You think you can stump me? I can look it up in a book and find an answer for you in no time, whereas you don't even know how to do the Gram's stain."

"True, you're a great scholar I admit. Didn't you publish two papers this year? But putting all that aside, can you tell me what's under the microscope?"

"To tell you the truth, I don't know. I can't remember. It slipped my mind, which is normal."

"That's the right attitude. Well, let me tell you. It's my . . ."

My heart lurched. Through the looking glass—well I'll be damned, his spermatozoa writhed like rat-tailed maggots. "Clean it up! Now!"

"Why so serious? Don't act like I don't know you!"

"Quiet. If the students come and see this stuff, we're finished!"

"Finished how? Doubt it. Let them see some human sperm. It'll broaden their horizon."

"They'll ask, 'Where did it come from? It's middle of the day and it's not like we're in a clinic or something.' What do we say?"

"Say they are yours of course. It was your contribution to scientific progress, at least as admirable as donating blood. The school should subsidize your caloric intake. For a married, impoverished comrade like you to sacrifice so much is really selfless beyond words."

I was on the verge of saying something mean when the first students began to trickle in. A couple of girls came over and said, "Good morning, Professor Wang. What are you up to?"

"Morning. Everyone gather around your lab tables and make sure nothing is missing. If you're short anything, ask Mr. Xu."

"Professor, what's on that slide? We want to see!"

I hovered over the microscope but this was an unruly lot. One of them used her face to push mine aside, pouring her long hair down my neck. It felt highly inappropriate!

I was ousted. The girls huddled around the microscope and chirped, "They're alive!" "They're crawling!" "Professor, what are they?"

"Uh, it's my work, it's none of your business. Return to your seats."

"We want to know! We have to know!"

I shouted, "Class captain! Class cadre! Where are you guys? Whoever doesn't return to their seats will get a zero for the class!"

"Professor, what's wrong?" "Why are you acting like an old man?" "Wise teacher, pray tell!"

"It's impolite to talk to you girls about this. You want to know? Fine, let me tell you. This is imported porcine spermatozoa, from Holland. I need to analyze the sperm count."

The class made my head hurt. Seventy percent of the time was spent answering questions related to breeding. The girls were obsessed. They wanted to know everything from artificial insemination to the concept of synthetic sows, nothing that I knew anything about, all things that tried my patience. Near the end of class, the president of the college came in and rolled his eyes venomously at me. He told me to go see him after class.

When I went to see the president, I paced around for a while in front of his office before going in. To be candid, every run-in I have with an authority figure like the college president triggers a twisted, inborn sort of servility within me that could easily be mistaken for ill will. When I entered, the president was watering his flowers. He turned and put on a smile, "Young Wang, what do you think of my flowers?"

"At your orders, Mr. President. This is of the family *rosaceae,* genus *rosa,* species unknown. Because it doesn't grow anywhere but in donkey sheds, people call it 'donkey tail flower.'"

"Are you calling me donkey tail? That mouth of yours is hopeless. Sit down, how's your work going?"

"To your orders, sir, everything is going splendidly. With regard to the previous lab incident, I already had a talk with their class supervisor. I told him to instill some discipline, and if worst comes to worst, to call the police. As for Xu You making food in the lab, I have already given him a stern warning; next time he disobeys, I will put laxatives in his bowl pot. There is a rat infestation in the lab, but I have already come up with a solution. I will buy a couple of cats."

"Total garbage. Only the cat idea isn't too far off the mark. But have you considered? I'm here right next door to you. If I am having a meeting at night and your cats cause a commotion, what will I do?"

"I have a plan. I can castrate them so they wouldn't make a fuss. I can castrate animals as big as an elephant or as small as a yellow croaker with proficiency."

"Ha. I didn't summon you here to talk about laboratory discipline. I'm moving out anyway, you can make as much noise as you like—out of sight, out of mind. Let's talk about you. How old are you this year?"

"Thirty adding two."

"Thirty years old. You're an adult now. It's time to stop acting like a child. Sunday, bring your significant other over to my place. What was her name?"

"Zhang Xiaoxia, nickname Erniuzi. I report that she is a tough woman who has repeatedly violated my civil rights. If you could enlighten her with some education, that would be duly appreciated."

"All right, we've talked enough crap. I'm going to tell you something and you have to stay calm. Your application to a sabbatical abroad has been reviewed by the party committee; they didn't agree."

"What's it got to do with them? Why didn't they agree? What's wrong with them?"

"Now, now. It is a fact that we are a new campus and badly in need of teachers on the ground. Besides, you're out of control. Everyone said that letting someone like you go to a foreign country would only end up soiling the school's reputation. My fellow comrades had their preconceptions about you. I tried my best to convince them otherwise. You should really use this as an incentive to improve your ways. . . ."

Without appearing cold or bitter, the president gave me a thorough dressing down. I didn't pay much attention. For the past two years, I had been working on a project with Professor Lü from the mining school. To be honest, I did about 90 percent of the work. I lectured at my school during the day and went over to his lab to do experiments at night. It wasn't just hard work, but I was also at constant risk of exploding into minced meat. We worked on explosives. I put my life on the line but for what? It was only because Professor Lü had a position for a sabbatical abroad. As soon as our experiment succeeded, he was supposed to move me to his department and send me off to a foreign country to see just how pretty foreign girls are. It was supposed to be a straightforward deal. Our project had won the first place at the national technology competition. Professor Lü had gotten his fortune and fame, but he couldn't do me this one little favor. I suddenly heard the president shout, "Hey, are you there?"

"At your orders, Mr. President, I'm listening very carefully. What were you saying?"

"I asked you for your opinion!"

Of course I had an opinion! But I wasn't about to say it to him. "None! I'm going to look for old Lü and give him what he deserves."

"Don't bother, Professor Lü is already gone. He said it would have been a shame to waste your spot, so he took it. To be perfectly honest, he tried his best. One night he called me seven times. I couldn't sleep. I come from the mining school. You were a student of the mining school. Let's not make this any uglier than it has to be. The important thing is: did you report your situation to your superiors ahead of time? Next time something like this happens, I hope you will give me the opportunity to openly speak up for you. First, you need to get Xu You under control. Then, get yourself straightened out a bit. Everyone says, after listening to your lectures, the students all get a little crazy."

"At your orders, Mr. President, it's not my fault. The current class of students were all conceived during the three-year famine. The people who made them were starving so they understandably took some shortcuts during production. I have read studies that say that the reason why Jewish kids are so smart and obedient is because Jews never cut corners on these sorts of things. Evidently, even small missteps can lead to catastrophe. . . ."

"Shut up, how can you even call yourself a teacher? I feel embarrassed for you. Go home and think about it. This is the end of this meeting."

I stormed out of the president's office looking to take some anger out on Xu. The moment I entered the lab, I saw him eating on a lab table. I screamed, "Eating in the laboratory again! You pig. . . ." When I paused at the end of my breath, he simply covered his ears. The president pounded on our shared wall. I stepped in front of Xu. He was eating a toona leaves and tofu salad, a giant bowl of it. I continued to admonish, "Are you trying to blow my gig? That stuff's gassy, do you know what it's going to do in your stomach? Every time I'm lecturing the class, you are in the back tooting your horn. No wonder they say my students get crazy!"

"That's enough Wang Er, quit pulling my leg. Give it a try, see if my tofu salad is as good as your wife's."

"Eat inside the office. Xu You, you are nothing but trouble!"

"Heh, don't give me that man, I know what's up. You didn't get the sabbatical. Wang Er, life is full of ups and downs, don't take it too personally. You won't get to go abroad this time but you'll get another chance. What chance have I got? I don't even know where I'm gonna find a wife."

It felt like getting ice water poured on me. Maybe he didn't mean it like that. Maybe I was overthinking it. In our thirty years of friendship, it was always me coming up with the ideas and him executing. From elementary school to high school, we did our fair share of petty crimes, but we never got into any serious trouble. Regrettably, during the Cultural Revolution, we decided to sneak into an empty lab and play with explosives. The disaster left Xu's face more scarred than if he had gotten smallpox ten times over. It was my wrongdoing.

There were still shards of test-tube glass lodged in his cheeks that could cut his hands whenever he washed his face. It was all my fault for having waved a blasting cap over a lab table. No one wanted to marry a lump of spikes so he couldn't find a wife. We had never openly discussed the cause of the accident but we knew the score. I said to him, "Do you really have to be so spiteful?"

"Wang Er, how am I being spiteful?"

"I was the one who scarred you! Remember?"

"Wang Er, you're out of your damn mind. You condescending pooch! Just because the president farted all over you doesn't give you the right to take it out on me. I will leave you alone to think hard about this!"

He stormed off.

After the fight with Xu, I felt anguished. It was my first fight with him. I must have really been off. It was said that when some people's plans for a sabbatical abroad went south, or if they didn't make the full professorship, they would hysterically beat and yell at their wives and kids, and turn their homes into a war zone. Was I just another scumbag like them? It would have been news to me.

Forlorn, I paced around the lab. It felt like one of those Tibetan torture techniques where they wrap you up in a wet cowhide. Then, they would dry you under the sun until the hide shrank and hardened, squeezing you until your eyeballs popped. Life was like that also. Day by day, you get older. Day by day, the cowhide gets a little tighter. This cowhide is the great regulator of life: go to work, get off work, eat, shit, fuck; each is a rung that squeezed tighter at a regular interval. Inside the cowhide there would still be a few tiny little hopes: sabbatical abroad, associate professor. But as soon as that hope oozes out, in comes hysteria. What a load of crap. What a crock of shit!

I found myself sitting on a tall laboratory stool, holding my chin, staring past the test-tube stands at the blackboard. There were a few lumps of coal drawn on the blackboard. What was I doing drawing lumps of coal? Eventually, I remembered. I was drawing yeast balls. Sickening thoughts surfaced in my mind. For example, if I was going abroad using the mining school's program, why would my school block me? Also, how was it any of their business what kind of a person I was? But why should I spend time thinking about any of this shit? It wasn't any of my business in the first place.

I stared at the test tubes arching along their stands. Their ethereal forms put me into a trance. The smell coming from the incubator reminded me of the swamps of the Southern Kingdom;* it was the smell of life, a blend of birth and decay mixed with the scent of water. The southern sun radiated white and bright at the apex of the sky. The meadows were lush with flora. Opalescent oil slicks seeped out from the roots and floated on the surface of the water. A dream, like a story, must be savored.

Once, there was a group of people who were banished from the imperial capital to the southern wilds. One day, one of the Neo-Confucian scholars went to look for a place to wash up. On his way to look for a river, he fell into a putrid bog. He quickly lifted up his robe, revealing the black muck on his lily-white legs. The blazing sun and the pungent herbaceous muck made him dizzy. He was alone in the wilderness. Suddenly, his member became erect for no reason, so much so that it terrified him. He loosened his clothes only to see his member brighter than a cooked prawn, not to mention hot to the touch. But it had no reason to be, he wasn't even

---

*A time of turmoil and war (420–589).

thinking about women. Around him, the earth steamed with a primal desire that had long predated men and women. Suddenly, a laughter shattered the scholar's daze. A pair of a man and woman passed by on the back of a mighty water buffalo. Naked, they held on to one another as they smirked at the scholar's chagrin.

Someone was talking to me. I looked up and saw this guy, no more than a boy, wearing a red school pin. He might have been a new faculty member, I didn't recognize him. He was saying something about clogged pipes on the first floor. He asked me to look into it. I was flummoxed, "Go look for the director. What do you want me for?"

"Mister, the director has already left. Please take a look, you're not doing anything anyway."

"Is that so! I'm not doing anything, but you are, is that what you're saying?"

"That's not what I mean. I'm a teacher. You're the boiler room guy."

"What boiler room guy? Hey, so what if the pipe's clogged. What's it to you?"

"School sanitation is everyone's responsibility. Can't you boiler room people take some responsibility?"

"Fuck off. You're a boiler room guy! Get the hell out of here!"

After I had gotten rid of the guy, I realized why he might have thought I was a boiler room janitor. It was because I was often in the boiler room. That and my demeanor, I did not much look like a teacher. Maybe that was the reason why I wasn't allowed to go abroad. No matter. I was a plumber by training; I wasn't going to forget my roots. If it hadn't been for the fact that he said I wasn't doing anything, maybe I would have gone to check out the pipe with him. But how can you say to a blue-collar worker, "You're not doing anything anyway"?

The sun was shining in through the west-facing windows. It was time to get off work but I didn't want to go home yet. I had pent up frustration and needed someone to talk to. Xu came in and asked me if I would be eating dinner on campus. Xu was a real pal. I wanted to pour my heart out to him but he wouldn't have understood. He wouldn't have had the patience for it.

I was reminded of a fable by Jean de La Fontaine. There were two friends who lived in the same city. One of them went out in the middle of the night to look for the other. The other friend jumped out of bed and put on an armor suit. With a sword in his right hand and a bag of money in his left, he asked his friend to come in. He said, "Friend, you must have some urgent reason to visit me in the middle of the night. If you owe someone money, here is a bag of coins. If you have been dishonored, I have a sword to avenge you right now. If you are sleepless and bored, here are beautiful slave women to entertain you."

Xu was that kind of a friend, but I had no use for him at that time. The weight on my heart could only be unburdened by a woman, but who could that woman be?

2

RODE MY BIKE OUT THE school gate, but I didn't want to go home. I wanted to wander the streets for a bit. If my wife had found me sulking at home, she would have made a fuss, which would have only made things worse. Melancholy was in my nature.

Many years ago, when I was stationed at a commune on the outskirts of Beijing, I often took long walks home. This time it was autumn. The road seemed to go on forever. My heart felt knotted and gnarled. I didn't know where I was headed or what would happen when I got there. The road was lined with cottonwood trees. A gust of wind untethered countless leaves that fell like a golden rain. At times the wind wailed and at times the wind whimpered. It scooped up the fallen leaves from the gutters and poured them over the dirt road like a golden flood. I walked alone, no one in front of or behind me. I started to relax. I felt as if I were leaping headfirst into the blue sky; the leaves falling around me were like the golden gates of heaven. My heart stirred with poetry. In that instant, I shed all of my worries and returned to being myself.

The sky was as blue as if it were ink dyed. In the murky dusk, there was another figure walking down the dirt road. That someone was walking quickly, kicking up dust with every step—such familiar steps! I caught up and tapped her on the shoulder. When she saw me, she rejoiced, "No way! Is that you? Get the fuck out of here! It is you!" It was my girlfriend from the commune, Little Bicycle Bell.

As we strolled into the wind on our way home, I read her a part of a poem I had just composed. It went:

> *Walking in silence, walking the sky,*
> *but the penis hangs downward.*

Even though nothing on her body hung downward, she could still relate, she said. Little Bell was a rare friend. She could always empathize.

I should have been biking back home to Jinsong, but somehow, I ended up past Shian Men, near where Little Bell was living. I couldn't tell you why I decided to go that way; I definitely had no intention of looking for her. But then, I had run into her.

She stood on the side of the road wearing a pale-yellow blouse and a red skirt. Her lips trembled on the verge of tears. Apparently, she had already recognized me from afar. I leaped off my bike to greet her, "Bell, how are you?"

She said, "Wang Er, you motherfucking . . ." before breaking into tears. I had a bad feeling—maybe we shouldn't have seen each other.

Little Bell asked me to have dinner with her. Seated inside the newly opened Moon-Taker Pavilion, I took one glance at the menu and nearly cursed out loud. How could a restaurant without any reputation charge such exorbitant prices? Had they no sense of decency? This wasn't a meal I could afford. But I also wasn't shameless enough to ask her to treat me. Back in the day, I could have just said: Bell, I got twenty yuan, what have you got? But no more. I was someone else's husband and she was someone else's wife. So I spoke hesitantly, careful to avoid eye contact. When Bell saw me like that, she first pouted sadly, but quickly it turned into anger.

"Wang Er, if you're in a hurry to go home, then get out! If we're still friends enough to eat a meal together, then stay. But don't act like a dog ran off with your head."

"What's the matter, I was just thinking. Nowadays when you go out, you really have to think about how much money each person has before you order. We wouldn't want to get stuck with a bill that will leave us embarrassed, would we?"

"Thank you for stating the obvious! If I didn't have money, I would have mentioned it already! Wang Er, you really break my heart. That Erniuzi must have you on a tight leash!"

"You don't mean that. I wouldn't say that about you."

Bell blushed. She said, "It's exactly what I mean. All right, let's talk about something else. How have you been? Are you still writing?"

I said I didn't have the time. I was busy making bombs. She pursed her lips as she listened. In the middle of our conversation, a waitress came to take our order. Bell ordered way too much food just to prove her point. I didn't like to leave food on the table, so maybe she was trying to gorge me to death.

Ten years ago, I often drank with Little Bell. I felt sick after consuming alcohol, but it was always my idea to go drinking. Bell's constitution allowed her to drink liquor like it was iced water. Like a sieve, she was fine no matter how much she poured. That summer in Shahe town, we drank a kind of plum wine, which tasted quite palatable at first, but later left you feeling like your brain was getting squeezed out of your orifices. The restaurant we were in only served one kind of bar food, pig brain. Bell said just the thought of it made her sick, but I ordered a plate anyway. I tasted it; it was gamy like blood. She didn't even want to look at it. She shoved it to a corner of the table and began to look for something to talk about.

We were used to just shooting the shit. That day, we talked about history and philosophy. Supposedly, the rise and fall of the Roman Empire was determined by Cleopatra's nose. By extrapolation, all great events can trace their causes to something minuscule. In fact, as early as billions of years ago, or maybe even before the beginning of the universe, some tiny coincidence determined that there would be a Bell and a Wang Er who would have a drink together in that very moment, when they would order a plate of pig brain for Bell to refuse to eat. You could call it the law of probability or you could call it fate. Bell said she would rather die than believe that. To prove that she wasn't bluffing, she forced herself to take a bite of the pig brain. The moment the flesh touched her tongue, she wanted to spit it out. I told her to spit it out, but she forced it down her throat anyway. Like a frog, it found its way into her gut one hop at a time. Little Bell sure had chutzpah!

Bell took everything seriously, while I was always half-kidding. Being with her often left me feeling guilty. I grabbed a bottle of beer and chugged it. My face turned red instantly.

Bell said, "Wang Er, I'm feeling unusually cheerful today. Please pace yourself and don't end up a puddle of mud. Do you remember that time in Shahe town, what a fool you had made of yourself?"

I had no memory of my drunken folly, only what happened afterward when she carried me home. It was hard to imagine her carrying me, but it also seemed like if she really wanted to, she could carry just about anything. I made my way over to the counter and ordered a bottle of brandy. When Bell asked me what I had in mind, I said I didn't want to go home that night. I wanted to sit in a park all night with her, so the booze would come in handy later on. Little Bell rejoiced, "Wang Er, you can always think of ways to cheer me up. Let's skip the park and go to my house; it's close by."

"Is that wise? I'd probably end up in a fight with your husband."

"I divorced him ages ago."

"How come?"

"No reason!"

I said that divorces aren't easy, especially going through the court system. She said, ain't that the truth? The newspaper where she worked sent an editor to persuade her to not go through with the divorce. "Phonies! A bunch of phonies!"

"What did you say to him?"

"I said, there are some people in this world who are qualified to fuck my pussy and there are some people in this world who are not. The gentleman fainted on the spot and no one came to meddle after that."

"You're just trying to sound scandalous. You didn't actually say that."

"I did too! When have I ever lied to you? Not like you, blushing after every honest word. I still have your treatise! I learn something new every time I read it!"

At the mention of the treatise, my heart sank like I had just stepped off a ten-thousand-story building. I had forgotten that in addition to essays on explosives and microbiology, I had once written a philosophical treatise. How could I have forgotten? I had this uncanny suspicion that I had blocked it out for a reason.

In the last winter of my days as an intellectual youth, everyone else had returned to the city. I was the only one left in the men's dormitory. I told Bell to move in with me. We lived like husband and wife. I brought a bunch of books back from the city. The sight of all those exquisite tomes on the bed-stove lit fireworks in my heart!

That year, one of the China Bookstores in the city opened an internal services department that carried old foreign books. I had a reference letter from my mother and some money from my father and got myself into their stockroom. They had everything one could dream of. Many of the books had handwritten notes next to name stamps on their title pages. Many of the writers had passed, others were lost to history. Standing before those majestic shelves, I felt like a tomb raider. I remember there were thousands of books with the stamp Zhimo Collection—once upon a time, there were many thinkers like Xu Zhimo, attempting to erect a lone city out of literature in the middle of a desert. The city had collapsed and the people were gone; one couldn't help but weep for the fallen!

In my intellectual-youth phase, I read a winterful of books while lying on the bed-stove. When my head began to hurt, I would stare at the frost crystals forming on the windowpane. Bell would huddle up to me and say: Wang Er, please explain! She was constantly scouring the dictionary, so she could only get through a few pages a day.

I grew up on my family's hand-me-down colonial education. My English wasn't too bad, enough for me to appreciate the pleasures of text. But after blurting out some half-cocked reply to quiet her, I buried my head back into the tome I was reading. After dark, I lay like a dog on the bed-stove with my hair glistening yellow under the kerosene lamp. When my scalp tightened and my lids grew heavy, I said, "Bell, we should sleep." But I kept on reading, barely noticing Bell shuffling and organizing our space, even removing the clothes from my body. When she finally blew out the light, I found myself naked, snuggled under the bedcover.

In the dark, I began to describe the story I was just reading. The combination of excitement and exhaustion left my body weak and limp. While taking the necessary measures, Bell managed to occasionally mumble, "And then what happens?"

When we started to do it, she was quiet. But as soon as we finished, she began to repeat, "And then what happens?"

How inappropriate! I said, "Hey, are you trying to be rude?"

"Sorry, sorry. But really, what happens?"

"I don't know yet. I would have to turn on the light to read it!"

"Don't do that! You're weak right now, I can tell. Get yourself a good night's rest."

One night, when I was having trouble falling asleep, I thought about Descartes's famous proposition: "I think, therefore I am." It didn't surprise me that Descartes could think himself into being, what I didn't understand was why I wasn't Descartes. What was I missing? Full of angst, I got up and smoked two cigarettes before firing up the kerosene lamp again. Looking down from the intellectual height of Descartes and his peers, our way of thinking must seem muddled, perhaps even deranged.

Bell woke and asked what I was doing. I said I wanted to undertake a Cartesian thought experiment, so I proceeded with a series of logical inductions. She cheered, "Go, Wang Er! Induce it! Induce it!" That was how I ended up with the treatise.

I had no desire to think about what I had written, so I said to Bell, "Bell, we sure had a swell time! A whole winter devoted to books. Could we ever have that again?"

She put down her liqueur glass and said, "Reading books wasn't half as fun as reading your treatise."

That treatise again! It was like a perfectly heated hot tub that I didn't want to jump into. I couldn't help but recall how the treatise began: if Descartes were Wang Er, Descartes would not have thought. If Don Quixote were Wang Er, Don Quixote would not have battled windmills. Even if Wang Er were already standing on the Island of Rhodes, Wang Er would still not have been able to jump. Because Wang Er did not exist. And not only Wang Er, but most of the people in the world did not exist either. That was the root of the problem.

After penning that bizarre thesis, I set out to provide evidence. Suppose that Wang Er did exist, then he couldn't possibly not exist. But the world inhabited by Wang Er didn't provide such clarity. Therein lay the difficulty. Take for example, the following syllogisms:

Every human must die. The emperor is a human, long live the emperor.

And:

All humans must die, the emperor is a human, the emperor will die.

Wang Er was okay with either; now do you see how hopeless he was? Clearly, there exist two systems in this world. One comes from the need to survive and one comes from the essence of being itself. Therefore, every question has two right answers. That is the basis of phoniness, so my treatise was titled "On Phoniness."

I was too young when I wrote the thing. The arguments were erratic at best. But there was one thing I was clear on: I didn't pass judgment on phoniness itself. Not only that, I thought phoniness was a monumental cultural achievement. Little Bell protested. She wanted me to delete that part, but I declared with the confidence of youth: a word, a thousand ounces of gold cannot buy. In retrospect, I think I had gone a little overboard.

These memories led me to imbibe one drink after another. It was getting dark, there were only a few patrons left at the restaurant. One of the waitresses stood outside the kitchen and watched us with her hands on her hips, like Lady Sun Erniang* staring at minced meat-to-be. Instantly, I was pulled into the kitchen by her gaze and chained onto meat hooks. The butcher said, "This calf is all tendons and no meat. What little meat there is is stiff and malodorous. When you grind him up, add in some pepper."

Cannibal Lady Sun said, "Might as well keep him alive as my plaything. Little calf, what do you think?"

There was a thin mustache above her upper lip and a pair of hot-water balloons swinging from her chest. I said, "Give me

---

*A fierce woman warrior character in the Chinese classic *The Water Margin*.

death." She kicked me and hissed, "Ungrateful little calf, please stay put. I'll be back in a minute for the bloodletting," and left. The butchery was quiet. Suddenly, a Chausie cat, white as snow, leaped like a dream before me.

Bell said, "Wang Er! Are you drunk? What the fuck?"

I wasn't drunk, far from it. I sat up straight and thought about my treatise. It was true, I had written: phoniness wasn't the end but the means. Proceed from there, and everything would improve.

Phoniness could be compared to an on-off switch in the brain. At every decision, you must make a distinction: pragmatism or logic, and proceed to turn the switch. If your switch turned to pragmatism, then shout: long live the emperor! If your switch turned to logic, then determine the major premise, minor premise, and end up with a rock-solid conclusion. But phoniness could also be a burden, the phony ones tend to be sluggish, often making blunders.

One could also take a more sophisticated approach and think dialectically about pragmatism and logic. The synthesis of pragmatism and logic could lead to such a phenomenon: one could profess with complete sincerity, *long live the emperor* and *the emperor must die*, and believe that there was no contradiction between the two. For some reason, that path to success never interested me. I always believed that everything would eventually revert back to its true nature.

In my view, life already held infinite beauty, more than enough to outweigh any amount of fame or fortune. I didn't want to lie to anyone, except when circumstances forced me to. As a result, I was never in line for any perks. But if I had surrendered my existence, what good would perks have been?

At the time I also wrote, from now on I must do everything with sincerity. I must think like Descartes and fight windmills like Don Quixote. Whether I was writing poetry or making love, I needed to do it with the utmost authenticity. I was already there on the Island of Rhodes, all I needed to do was jump—doing so would have been for nothing else, but for the sense of existence itself.

In my view, the tender sprout in the spring had no agenda. The stallion in heat, bucking against the wind, had no agenda. The grass wanted to grow and the stallion wanted to mate, and none of it was for show; it was existence itself.

I was determined to go through life with the authenticity of the stallion and of the grass. I would no longer sheepishly play a role. It was through performance that we had lost our true selves. I wrote a lot of great things, but I didn't go through with any of them it. That was the main reason why I didn't want to be reminded of that treatise.

The waitress began to sweep the floor. She wasn't really sweeping the floor so much as trying to close down. There was still half an hour before closing time. Still, we had no choice but to stand up and reluctantly show ourselves out. That long-ago winter, Bell and I were similarly reluctant to leave communal living behind.

Bell and I stayed in the dormitory for about twenty days until we had eaten all the food and burned all the firewood. As we were leaving, we heard fireworks going off in the nearby village. It was the eve of the Lunar New Year. Heavy snow was falling, blanketing the earth, stopping all traffic. There was no one else out on the street. Only the two of us were walking through silence back to the city.

On our way to Bell's home, we trekked across a dike partitioning two crop fields. I had never been there before so I didn't know the way. Going over to Bell's house this time made me feel anxious. Perhaps it was because she was still as passionate about life as she had ever been.

All those years ago, we were trudging through heavy snow. If not for the billowing of snowflakes and the crunching of fresh powder, the silence would have been complete. The chilly air cured my lingering headache. I suddenly felt a yearning as deep as never before: I wanted to love, to live, and to use my one life as if it were a hundred. It all seemed so simple: I thought, therefore I was, and there was no pretending that I wasn't. No matter what, I had to take responsibility for myself.

When we got to Bell's house, we washed up and sat down in the courtyard for another round of drinks. For some reason, even though I should have been drunk already, I felt soberer than ever. Little Bell sat in a recliner in front of me in complete silence. As I watched her, I felt moved.

The year we had trekked home through the snow, I had also been moved. The world was such a blur that it was hard to know where the sky was. The sight of her trudging through the knee-deep snow had made me want to pick her up. Her little face was red from the cold. Thick white breaths coursed out of her mouth as if pouring from a fountain. It felt like we were the only two people left in the world. I wanted to protect her and to possess her.

No one could possess Little Bicycle Bell. She belonged to herself. This woman was incredibly brave, and even crazier than I was. The first time we made love, she bled quite a bit. She wiped the blood from our legs and jumped up with a smile: Wang Er, shameless! You stuck that huge thing inside of me!

We broke up during college. Before that, we had lived together for some time. The sex wasn't exactly harmonious but we got used to it. Little Bell was asexual and needed to use lubricants, but she never refused or ever complained. I got used to her slim body lying silently under me. But in the end, we still broke up. I had a feeling it was fate.

Little Bell sat in front of me wearing a leopard print bra and a short skirt. Under the moonlight she was beautiful. I noticed that she had pierced her ears, but it did not change her much. The tips of her shoes were a scuffled mess, which meant she was still kicking up rocks. I guess that's why they say: it is harder to change a person than to move a mountain.

I knew that if Bell had said, "Wang Er, I need you," the result would have been difficult to imagine. Bell also knew that I wouldn't have withstood the temptation. But she didn't say anything. She put down her glass and picked up another cigarette. She really wanted to say it, but she wouldn't.

Bell once said she needed me as a friend. In order to never part from my shadow, she was willing to become my wife. But spending a lifetime with a friend might be rather tiresome. So my reply to her was: maybe we weren't meant to be. Maybe she would one day meet someone to whom she wasn't just willing to be married, it would feel as if they were married already. Either way, Little Bell would always be Wang Er's friend, that fact would never change. That was how we broke up.

If that night Bell had said, "Wang Er, I am your wife," all hell would have broken loose. Erniuzi would not have condoned someone divorcing her. But none of that happened. We sat until the moon leaned west and I said, "Bell, I should go home."

For a moment, her lips quivered as if she was about to cry but she caught herself and said, "Go ahead, come see me again when you have the time." I rushed home but it was already two o'clock in the morning!

3

TIPTOED OUT OF THE COURTYARD and rode my bike home. I carried it up the apartment stairs and locked it to the handrail. Quietly, I opened the door and stepped into a pitch-black room. After kicking off my shoes, I leaned onto the bed but somehow ended up on the floor. The lights turned on. My wife was sitting on the bed. She must have kicked me off it. Her face was crimson red and her hair stood on ends.

"Where did you go? I thought you had died! I called the school, the mining school, and even went to the police station. You were out drinking? Who were you with all night?"

Though I knew how to lie, I never lied to my wife. To tell only truths to some people and to tell only lies to other people, that was one of my rules. So I began to mutter, "I ran into Little Bicycle Bell, had a couple of drinks."

She screamed and did some backstroke-type moves under the bedcover. At that point, nothing I said would have mattered, so I went to wash my feet in the bathroom. When I returned, I turned off the light and lay down on one side of the bed. Suddenly, I was being chocked to the point of seeing stars. Erniuzi growled by my ear, "I'll show you who's the boss!"

That shrew was a wrestler with thick arms and a thick neck. It was common for her to challenge me, but I was never intimidated. No matter what move she tried to put on me, I could always just pick her up and throw her on the bed. She was in the 47 kg weight class and I was in the 90 kg weight class, which made a difference of over 40 kilograms. But on that bed with her hands around my neck, I was in real trouble. She was always practicing this stuff, what they called "ground game." I failed twice to flip over. The veins beneath my temples were getting ready to burst. With my last remaining breath, I bellowed and pushed only to hear a loud crack. The bed collapsed. We rolled around on the ground for a bit until we knocked over the tea table and shattered everything. I was finally able to push her aside. I got up and turned the light on only to see her crying on the floor. That was my opportunity to strike.

"It's three o'clock in the morning! Have you lost your mind? You feral zombie!"

I spoke with such fervor that she was stunned for a moment. When she came to, she said, "Asshole! Divorce!"

"I will accompany you in the morning. Right now, I have to sleep."

"I'll tell your mother!"

"Go ahead, but just so you know, you're not in the right."

"How am I not in the right?"

"The fact of the matter is: Little Bell is an old friend of mine, so I couldn't just ignore her. Having a meal and a couple of drinks with her is perfectly acceptable."

"A couple? How many is a couple?"

"Maybe half a pint. But not the clear stuff, it was brandy."

"You son of a gun, you drank that much. Where did you eat?"

"Moon-Taker Pavilion by the Jijia River. The food was awful; Little Bell paid the bill."

"Son of a gun! Showing off her money. We're going to eat there tomorrow. Or I'll castrate you. Dishes! Name every last one of them."

Was this ever going to end? It was the middle of the night and my head was pounding. "Fried pig vagina!"

Erniuzi laughed and cried. By the time we finished talking, it was four o'clock. Just as I was closing my eyes, Erniuzi told me to bring the bike inside, but it was already too late. The air had been emptied out of both tires. Although, it was nice of the culprits to put the nozzles back on. It must have been the neighbor's way to protest against our midnight fisticuffs.

I practically went all night without sleep. Erniuzi tossed and turned incessantly. Just before sunrise, as I was beginning to doze off, a pair of small hands gripped my vital region. She wanted me to prove that I was still true to her. Proving it wasn't a problem, but I no longer had a chance to sleep. In the morning, there was a faculty meeting where the president assigned responsibilities. A quarter of an hour into the meeting, I collapsed and rolled on the ground. The president screamed, "Wang Er, get up!"

"At your orders, Mister President, I have already stood up!"

"Stand there and wake up! The reason I always let you off sleeping through meetings was because you were doing experiments at night. You even got an award, so it was understandable. But you're not doing overtime anymore. What were you doing last night?"

He shouldn't have asked. But since he did, I lost it. Why was I the only one who worked overtime? A roomful of smug faces, all a bunch of frauds! Patience, just wait until I show them: "At your orders, sir, my wife beat me."

The room exploded. There was applause from the back row.

"Reporting to you, sir, I stood up for the honor of our school and defeated my wife in the end. I didn't lose face for the school!"

The brothers in the back stood up with thundering applause. The president's face turned purple as he roared, "Get out! Wait for me in my office!"

When I got to the president's office, I began to regret my outburst. I put him in a difficult spot and didn't offer him a way to save face. The president treated me like one of his own, sticking up for me in front of everyone. He had nominated me to be the director of the biology lab. Even though I was going to only have one person under me, Xu You, people had still complained. The human resources director had had my file in his hand and said: Wang Er has some troubling history. He and Xu You were implicated in an explosion incident. These guys could blow up the whole building, maybe just make him a codirector and move the fat lady from the canteen over to be the director. The president had laughed: two kids getting into trouble during the Cultural Revolution, what's so remarkable about that? The fat lady from the canteen was unscrupulous. Putting her in charge of the biology lab was just asking for trouble. The award Professor Lü and I won had come with a 2,000-yuan prize. He had taken the bulk of it and left me with 300. When the money had gotten to the school's accounting department, the head of accounting had wanted to confiscate all of it. His reasoning was that Wang Er was working for other organizations at night when he was still on the school's payroll. He yawned so much in the morning that the students seated in the front row could see his tonsils. The president had stood up for me and said Wang Er's project was a contribution to the nation and brought honor to the school. Withholding my prize would have been like scraping gold off the Buddha's face. In the end, I got most of the money, even more than Professor Lü.

I felt a bit ashamed. I didn't want to be known as the ungrateful type. But upon further reflection, my heart hardened again: fuck it, who's to say I'm his guy? I'm my own goddamn guy. On that note, the president entered the room. He sat in silence for two minutes before solemnly declaring, "Young Wang, I need to discipline you."

"At your orders, president, I should have been disciplined long ago!"

"Don't get so emotional. The whole sabbatical abroad thing left you feeling disappointed, I understand. But you didn't have to make a scene at the meeting! If I don't discipline you, people will harbor resentment."

"Yes, sir, I wasn't being emotional. I only ever tell the truth to my colleagues. Erniuzi did attack me. Look at the purple bruises on my neck . . . and that's me, if it had been somebody else, they would be dead already."

The president took a look at my neck and couldn't decide if he wanted to laugh or cry. He said, "You little son of a gun! Even a couple's quarrel should have limits!"

"President, you misunderstand. This wasn't a couple's quarrel! My wife assaulted me for real. She's on the wrestling team! Last time, she dislocated my elbow, I had to apply tiger-bone paste bandages. See, it's still on there now."

The president pondered for a moment before walking out. I thought with glee: how are you going to discipline me now? A minute later, he returned with the chairman of the labor union and the head of human resources, both of whom were my enemies. The president spoke to them in an excited pitch.

"Take a look at that, completely unacceptable! To use so much violence on someone! When our male comrades beat their wives, the organization has to intervene. So when our female comrades beat their husbands, should we just stand by and watch? Don't laugh! It's a special matter! Give the athletics department a call, tell them to discipline their athlete! The labor union and human resources have to be involved. An injury like this has negative effects on the workplace. Young Wang, why don't you take the rest of the day off. But if possible, hang in there for a little longer until the meeting's over."

Hang in there my ass. The moment I walked off campus, I slapped my butt and laughed: what a one-of-a-kind college president! I took a nap the second I got home and didn't wake up until three in the afternoon. My wife had left a note telling me to meet her at Moon-Taker Pavilion at four. She had laid out my suit on the table. I dressed up and took a look at myself in the mirror. The more I looked, the more it didn't look right. I wasn't the type to appear stylish. Once out the door, I walked close to the walls to avoid being spotted by my neighbors. When I got to New Bridge, close to the restaurant, I saw my wife right away. She was wearing a bright red satin cheongsam that looked more like a duvet cover. With rouge and lipstick, she looked like a streetwalker. I walked up to her and took her hand in my sweaty palm.

She whined, "I'm gonna die!"

"Don't be scared, keep moving, where's that bone-shattering spirit of yours? Don't look at the ground; there's no money there, even if there was, I'd be the first to see it. Chin up! Chest out!"

"I'm afraid people will see that I'm wearing makeup!"

"What are you afraid of? You're pretty good-looking. Wearing a little powder is still better than having no nose. Walk like a super-model. Swing those shoulders, sway that ass!"

The walk seemed to have given her a renewed sense of confidence. Her joints were cracking again. When my wife dressed casually, she turned quite a few heads on the street. But now, everyone seemed to be turning away from her. After sitting down in the restaurant, she began to cry.

It was an uncomfortable meal, like we were a pair of mannequins eating in a restaurant. After we got home, I pondered for a long time in silence, which seemed to have led to some sort of a breakthrough. Next morning at work, I was more of a jerk than usual.

The first thing I did when I got to school was to meet up with Xu. I had come to terms with the fact that a sabbatical abroad just wasn't in the cards for me. Our fight two days before had left us at odds. We were due for a good talk. Ever since we were little, he had been my bodyguard. I couldn't let distance grow between us. Just as we were reaching the height of camaraderie, there was a banging on the wall. That was the president's signal for me to go see him.

When I walked into the president's office, I could tell something was off. On his desk was the annual budget proposal for the biology lab. He let out a long sigh.

"Wang Er, oh, Wang Er, your conduct can be summed up in just four syllables!"

"I know, selfless comrade."

"No. Young and feckless! Take a look at your budget proposal. What do you mean by three units of two-hundred-liter refrigerators, for storing the fat lady's milk?"

"She's always putting milk in the fridge, saying it was empty and wasting electricity. I use the fridge to culture mold. She took all the cultures out and they died. Now that she got knocked up, don't you think it's time to plan ahead?"

"You can make suggestions but don't write a bunch of nonsense. Besides, why three units? Someone thought you were trying to make it a bigger deal than it is in order to subvert group unity."

"President, this will be the fat lady's second child. The first child only warms up the belly; there won't be much produce. The second pregnancy could easily lead to eight or ten kids, that is, if we were talking about sows with that many nipples. The big lady has two, but we still have to take the young ones into consideration. It's all in the proposal."

"Rubbish! This perfectly reasonable concern is now ammo in someone else's gun. Sit down. Let's be honest with each other. Are you aware that our school is going through difficult times?"

"At your orders, sir, I've seen the news. Too many new colleges have been built. Consolidation is a wise strategy on the part of the Party Central Committee. Take our school for example, there's no money for teachers or equipment. It may as well close."

"Again, with the nonsense! Our school was built out of nothing. But through hardship and grit we have trained thousands of graduates for the nation. Our success is as clear as day. We now have hundreds of faculty members and loads of equipment. How can we just close? If the school closed, where would you go?"

"I would go to the mining school. Professor Lü has tried to transfer me several times, but you've always put a stop to it. Take a good look at me. Wouldn't it be better if I was out of your hair?"

"Dream on. The school is in difficult times. Many people want to transfer. If I let you go, how I can stop the others? The committee has decided that not a single person can be let go. Whoever decides to quit will get handed a punishment that will stick with him all his life. On the other hand, we will aggressively promote young talent. Those who are capable will get to go abroad and be promoted to full professor. Take you for example. You break every rule in the book, yet we still let you be the biology lab director. How has the school let you down?"

"In so many ways. Take housing for example. My classmate who was assigned to the agriculture department got a house the moment he graduated. Me? After countless applications, I ended up with a wet and dark basement perfect for growing mushrooms. Even if I was subpar, I don't think I deserved that. Mushrooms are of kingdom *fungi,* division *basidiomycota.* Me, I'm at least mammal, primate, *homo sapiens*, of the East Asian variety, just like you. Do I look like a mushroom?"

"All right! Nobody is a mushroom here! We need to take care of our fellow humans. The housing will be there. Please don't cry poor. You live in a bigger flat than I do!"

"That's because it is from the athletics department's housing. My wife said, I got the better end of the bargain, so I have to let her have her way with me. Of course I can beat her in a fight, but I'll never win in the court of public opinion. I'm a nearly two-meters-tall man. It's only because I'm stuck in this school that I have to take abuse from my wife and I can't even get a divorce—I'd be homeless if I divorced. That or I would have to share the lab office with Xu You. Do you have any idea how bad Xu's feet smell?"

"Is that why you want to turn the school upside down? Let me be frank with you, I'm not the only person who makes decisions around here. You can mouth off all you want to me but it's no use. Even if you manage to transfer, it won't do you any good. I have already prepared your political assessment: do you want to hear what it says? 'Comrade Wang Er, despicable character. Reactionary in political thinking, lackadaisical at work, and reprehensible in everyday life.' We can stick that in your permanent files and let you carry it for the rest of your life, how does that sound? Do you want it?"

The president sneered at me, giving me goose bumps all over. I had no choice but to back down.

"President, your honorable, how can you treat me so? I really do want to learn to be good. I just wasn't born with the talent, and it doesn't come across right. It's all right, I can rewrite the budget proposal. I'll keep my eyes on Xu You. Is there anything else you need? Let's have it out in the open, no more backstabbing."

"If you really wanted to learn to be better, you could start with your mouth. Your attitude just now, is that the right attitude for a faculty member to take with the president?"

"Understood. Next time I come here, I will first say goodbye to my true self. Anything else?"

"You must hold political seminars! You're the class supervisor for Ag-3-Beta, do you understand?"

"What's Ag-3-Beta, sounds like the name of a pesticide. All right, I understand. Every Wednesday afternoon, talk to the students. What do I get if I do all of these? Do I get to go abroad?"

"In your dreams! The political committee submitted their report accusing you of reactionary speech. What was it that you said during the last faculty meeting on spiritual pollution?"

"A paper was read during the meeting that was obscene, talking about why jeans should not be worn. Criticizing spiritual pollution should be a serious matter and shouldn't be trivialized. What's this about jeans constricting airflow, squeezing girls' reproductive organs, leading to mold? Question, who's gotten any yeast infection? How did you come to see this? If the Chinese will grow mold after a few days of wearing the thing, wouldn't American cowboys have grown mushrooms by now?"

"You're thinking too narrowly. You have to look at the bigger picture. All the foreign stuff coming in must be resisted. What's so great about jeans anyway? I don't see it."

"With your three-foot waistline, wearing a pair of jeans would turn you into a big radish, of course they shouldn't be worn. But skinny people wearing them just look good—anyway, it's pointless to argue. But even suppose it did cause mold. We could improve upon it and install a battery-powered fan on it. If it turns out to be a good invention, we can export it and make a fortune. If it doesn't sell, then whoever wrote that paper can carry the losses. That's what he gets for making stuff up. That was my only input."

"And it is incorrect! I chose for that paper to be read. When there are female instructors in our college wearing the thing, we need to raise public awareness; but we're not talking about dress codes anymore, so I don't need to say any more about it. Of course, you're the expert on yeasts and molds, but don't make everything so radical, do you understand?"

"I don't fully understand. Why are you staring at me like that?"

"What do you mean? I care about you. I want to nurture you."

"Why do you want to care about me!"

"All right, allow me to say a few things to you unofficially. Right now, the school is still in a developing stage; it needs entrepreneurial talent. People have their doubts about you, but I look at you in this way: no matter how many problems you have, you know what you're doing and you're willing to do things. As long as you satisfy these two conditions, I'd take you even if you were a green-eyed demon with fangs—young people these days, how many of them are really willing to work? That's how things look from where I stand. From where you stand, how do I treat you? The ancients have a phrase, honor your benefactors! After all that work with Old Lü from the other school, what did you get out of it? He left the country without even telling you. But I was the one saying good things about you in front of the committee. How many wishes did Professor Lü grant you? Did he come through? Irresponsible. I'm just going to lay it out for you: as long as you behave, you will be prioritized for every opportunity. There are young people who are much better ass-kissers than you, but I won't consider them, because I consider you a talent. Is that clear enough for you?"

It all made sense now. I had always wondered why the president was like that! So that was the reason. It was because I was a talented individual! Knowing that he believed in me, I couldn't let him down. I decided to not transfer to the mining school.

That afternoon, I took the students out for a field trip. They were waiting for me eagerly. I took them to the reception office to wait for a school car. While waiting, I called the breeding station that would be receiving us. One of my old classmates was the manager there.

"Breeding station? I'm looking for Manager Guo. No! I'm not bringing anything in . . . I'm not interested personally . . . we have both male and female. Guo Er, we're coming. I know it's not season yet, we just want to take a look. Who was that on the phone just now?"

"There's no supervisor here. Wang Er, come on over. It's not yet the season but we can stimulate them artificially. Our livestock have had their shots. They're trying to take over the place! I designed a synthetic sow using the latest electronics; the boars can't get enough of the thing!"

"We don't need to see too much of the synthetic stuff. Our class is introductory, we don't need to get into advanced topics."

"We got the natural kind as well. I have a little jack donkey from Yunnan about the size of a dog. Its dick is even longer than a Guanzhong's jack.* Nobody has ever seen it and not laughed. Hurry on over!"

"Not so loud, I have a bunch of students here. They can hear everything you're barking."

---

*Guanzhong is a Chinese breed of workhorse.

"Hey, who are you trying to play? Can't fool me. Let's talk shop when you get here!"

"Man, you are getting sleazier by the day! Students, cover your ears. All right, that'll do. See you in half an hour."

After putting down the phone, I felt ambivalent. Maybe I shouldn't be taking the students to a breeding station. Maybe it would make me look deviant. We waited for a long time but no car came. Just as I was about to send someone to check, the dean of the agriculture department, Mr. Liu, arrived. His lips were puckered like he was sucking on a nipple.

"I'm sorry, Mr. Wang, I'm sorry fellow students, our car-riding plan has been canceled. Please everyone return to your classroom. The field trip can wait until next week."

"Dean Liu, as an agricultural scientist, you shouldn't joke around like that! At this time of the year, breeding requires artificial stimulation. If we keep doing last-minute changes, what are they going to tell the jackasses! But since you're already here, there's nothing I can say. Let me give the breeding station a call."

When Guo Er heard that we were rescheduling for next week, he screamed, "No way, mister, you are not welcome next week. You think this breeding station is for your personal use?" He slammed the phone down. I said to Mr. Liu, "Just listen to what they're saying about me! My personal breeding station. What does that make me? Students, we will not be going on a field trip today. Next week, we'll have an exam."

The students began to clamor. Some of them threatened to strike. All this commotion blocking the school's front gate was too much for any authority to handle. I said, "Fine, let's go! We'll walk there. The weak and the wounded are exempt; we'll have to walk over six kilometers after we get off the bus. We'll snap some overhead slides to share with those who stay back."

That didn't work either. One of the students was on a sports team. He had injured his leg and had come to class on a pair of crutches just to visit the breeding station. The other students offered to carry him there. What a joke. I turned to Mr. Liu and said, "So, what if we had a small car? At least we could carry the wounded."

"Mr. Wang, it's not that I don't want to send a car. Our department isn't as obtuse as some others. To keep first-year agriculture students from visiting a breeding station, that would have to be some sort of a joke! But if the administration says there's no car, there's nothing anyone can do. Those buffoons, didn't even think to warn us ahead of time."

"Really? I don't believe it. Let me try." I picked up the phone and called the driver's office, "Who's this? Young Ma? Send over a large sedan. I need to take my students on a field trip."

"Wang Er, are you the one who needs the car? Our director must have made a mistake. Let's see, would sitting in a truck cabin do?"

"No! Someone else can sit in the truck. I want the sedan."

"The director told us to hide the sedan so no one would see it. He wants to use it himself. Let's let him save some face, all right?"

"What about my face? Whose face do you think is more important?"

"It's Wang Er's of course. Wang Er is my big brother! The car will be there shortly."

Mr. Liu didn't leave. Apparently, he didn't think the car was going to show up. Moments later, when the car pulled in from the road, the students cheered and ran to it. Old Liu was red in the face, fists clenched, quaking in anger. I immediately offered him a save, "Mr. Liu, Young Ma is putting himself on the line for us. Someone's bound to try to put the small shoes on him. But this is for the good of our department . . ."

The old man roared, "Don't you worry. I won't let any harm come to Young Ma. I'm going to go find the president and talk to him about people hiding cars!"

The students came back from the field trip changed. They gathered in small groups, whispering secrets. I took several rolls of film. I called the class captain over and gave him instructions.

"Take these films to be made into slides and hold onto them. Remember, don't let anyone borrow them, other than Ag-3-Beta. They will only get to go to the botanical garden, so they might feel left out. But if you lend the slides to any other class, I will never take you guys on another field trip ever again."

"Teacher, our class is completely loyal to you. The Beta class bad-mouths you, but there's no one like that in our class. I won't lend these slides to anyone. I'll just say they were overexposed."

"Sounds good. What did they say about me?"

It was nothing out of the usual. They said I dressed sloppily and that when my lectures reached a fever pitch, I sounded like a country yokel. I knew all these things before he even mentioned them, but I wanted to hear it again anyway. When I returned to school, the president called me into his office. What's with all the talking? I was starting to lose my patience.

The president wanted to talk about the incident concerning the administrative director hiding the car—in fact, he knew more about the situation than I did. The administrative director had wanted to use the car to take people from a different organization on a tour of the Great Wall, only for me to have foiled his plan. The president heaped me with praises and all sorts of encouragements. But I wasn't that interested: I was only a faculty member and did not want to get involved in the affairs of the upper echelon. The plan for that afternoon was to take the students to the botanical garden. The students were full of complaints.

"Teacher, the Alpha class said they saw a donkey at the breeding station that looked like it had five legs. Its middle leg was five times longer than its other legs. They must have been exaggerating, right?"

"Don't listen to their nonsense. This is science, not playtime. But yes, that donkey was rather special."

"Teacher, you're playing favorites! We want to visit the breeding station too!"

"That's enough. The animals need to rest. Do you know what season it is? They were only able to perform after getting shots."

"Give 'em more shots! The more shots the better!"

"Shush! You can't treat them like machines. They are flesh and blood just like us. What if we gave you a shot? If you guys could bad-mouth me a little less, maybe I'll let the Alpha class show you the slides."

"Teacher, don't listen to those provocateurs! Only Erjunzi bad-mouthed you and we've held three class meetings criticizing him. Tang Xiaoli from their class said you ate during class, and many other mean things about Mr. Xu. Bad-mouthing Mr. Xu is just like bad-mouthing you. If you think they are the good class, then you've been duped!"

I had heard it too many times already. I figured: bad-mouthing me meant loving me, the more the better. When we got to the botanical garden, I left the students with an assistant researcher in charge of guided tours and slipped away to enjoy the flowers in peace. I knew it wasn't going to be some short little break when I ran into my old mentor Liu Er.

Liu Er was one hell of a character with eyes the size of a pair of balls (bull testicles) and a face as black and bumpy as the bottom of a burnt wok. He knew how to do everything, but back in '75, when I became his apprentice at the factory, he was unwilling to do anything. He grew up in an orphanage and married a country bride. He raised a couple of pigs in the countryside, which was where he poured all his heart and soul. When he told everyone that he refused to work, the factory manager and team captains all had to put their own skills to the test. Meanwhile, he hummed a little song, putting his own lyrics to the tune of the northeastern classic "Red Sorghum." I sang the accompaniment. Whenever he got to the end of a verse, he would call to me, "Oh me, oh my ma!" and I would return, "Aye." We were both off-key; anyone listening couldn't help but laugh.

I could never keep track of all the verses in Liu Er's song. The words seemed to change every time. Every version began with his childhood. He was raised by whores, which was bad luck. Then, he sang about how when he joined the factory, he had entered from the wrong door. Our factory was built in '58 by a bunch of old ladies doing street organizing. When the factory was built, he was fifteen years old so he became an apprentice. Then, the song talked about how he never got a raise in over a decade, always the same old twenty-six yuan and fifty cents. That was followed by how he couldn't find a wife. Only the crippled and infirm were willing to marry a street mechanic, finding an intact specimen just wasn't in the cards. With no other option, he looked for a country bride and ended up with a really lazy one. As they say, marry a man, have clothes to wear, and food in hand. His wife slept all day on the bed-stove (a so-called *kang*) and ate a pound of pork meat at every meal. Then, the song talked about his two, waddling rat-browed sons. Their eyes glowed whenever they saw white steamed buns. Those two ate him into oblivion. He had to find some way to make money, but every way somehow involved capitalism (at this point, someone would just cough and be pointed out as reactionary—this was in '75). His only way out was raising pigs. After that, he only sang about pigs. They were his mother, his father, his food and clothes and everything else. One of the pigs he called Father, and he sang an ode to Father describing everything from its long mane down to its trotters. His love for it knew no bounds but he needed the money, so he had to castrate it. Another pig he called Mother. She was as beautiful as can be, and pregnant with a litter of his little brothers, which meant she had to eat well. If his little brothers came out with tiny snouts, nobody would want to buy them. Thus, the next part of the song was about finding food for the pigs. If someone didn't interrupt him, the song could have gone on for a hundred years. Liu Er sang about what it was like to reap grass, what it was like to gather vegetable stumps, and a hundred more adventures like such. After those endless verses, he went on to sing about how he couldn't only feed his Father and Mother vegetables, because that would have been unfilial, so he went around gathering kitchen swill. Later that year, the agricultural college had a new initiative. Every household was given a vat to collect kitchen swill to make fertilizer for farmers. When the season got warm, a foul stench filled the air. Snow-white maggots crawled everywhere, there wasn't a soul in Beijing who didn't complain. My mentor complained too, but not about the stench. He complained that the new policy took away his father's and mother's food source. The song suddenly changed to the subject of stealing swill at midnight. As he and I (I would sometimes help him), with our criminal implements (ladle and bucket), moved stealthily toward our target, everyone listening to the song couldn't help but pinch their noses. Suddenly, my mentor disappeared. The old man was hiding under a workbench, signaling me to be quiet. If you listened closely, you could hear an old lady cursing from beyond the factory gate. Her curses were in verses that metered and rhymed, all the way to the factory gate. The old lady was in charge of collecting swill from the vats. She was cursing Liu Er. With her hands on her hips, she stood outside the gate and screeched, "Wang Er, where's your mentor? Tell him to come out!" I said my mentor had the swine flu and was resting at home. She continued to curse verse after verse, saying basically how everyone hated her lot and blamed them for all the stinky swill vats. On top of that, they were only making twenty-five yuan a month, working through the cold and rain. When the vats froze, they had to break up the ice, what a horrifying job. When it got hot and they fell behind on the collection, the vats filled up with maggots. The whole community pinched their noses and cursed at them. In short, they were up to their necks in frustration. Then came the aria, describing their state of disbelief: how in the world was there a creature like Liu Er who would actually steal swill. They would have loved nothing more than to have their swill stolen, but this Liu Er was so afraid that people would notice that he replaced the stolen swill with rocks and dirt, giving them even more work to do. It was one thing for the community to scorn them, but what Liu Er did to them was simply sadistic. Her piece ended with an upbeat hymn in which heaven was invoked to put a lightning bolt through Liu Er. The factory manager came out to invite her into the office to talk. She declined and walked away cursing. My mentor crawled out from under the bench, his dark face purple from anxiety. He pretended like nothing happened and went on to do his thing.

I often advised my mentor to stop stealing swill, why not just ask for it? Even if he had to steal the swill, why fill the vats up with rocks? He wouldn't listen, something about dignity and reputation. At the time, I couldn't understand. How can you worry about dignity when you're stealing swill? But later, I understood: swill was something that you could steal but you couldn't beg for because even pigs didn't stoop that low.

My mentor was very down to earth. In all the years that I had known him, that was the only time he had ever worried about his reputation. But when I saw him this time around, he was different. You wouldn't believe me even if I told you. He was wearing a checkered suit with a thick gold ring on his finger. The moment he saw me, he offered me a Hilton cigarette. It turned out that after he was suspended from the government factory, he became an independent contractor. He was leading a band of migrant workers in the construction of a greenhouse for the botanical garden. He was a bit surprised by my appearance and quietly asked me if I knew anyone personally from his client's side (as in from the botanical garden).

I said I knew one person but it would most likely amount to nothing. We felt embarrassed by our very exchange. It was almost worse than getting caught stealing swill. I asked about his wife and two sons, but there wasn't really much else to talk about. He looked awkward in his pristine white shirt and I assumed he felt uncomfortable in it as well.

I could only guess what my mentor thought of me. So, this little Wang Er turned out to be a teacher, scurrying around with his little pack of students! Frankly, I didn't like my role either, not one bit.

4

WHEN I GOT HOME THAT NIGHT, I was in a foul mood. After work, the president called me to a faculty meeting. Present were the deans of various departments, the academic director, and so on, it was a bit of a reach to call in a mere lab director like me. Besides, I never acknowledged the title, lab director. Everyone already knew what I was! Being at that meeting felt like having my balls clutched.

After a shower, I walked naked onto my patio. The sky was full of stars, like a storm frozen in place. It was a seductive sky. When I was together with Little Bell, we often walked out into the night under the starry sky. Back then, we had nothing, but in turn nothing prevented us from enjoying the silent night.

When we went out, she wore a backpack. Inside were a few measly items: pieces of a hemp sack, matches, cigarettes (I liked to smoke after sex), a small bottle of oil, condoms. When the inventory was complete, there was a sense of accomplishment, but the inventory was rarely complete. After one disaster involving hot chili oil, she tasted every bottle of oil I brought before rubbing it on, which was somewhat of a mood killer.

Even so, every time we prowled through the sorghum field was a moment of great happiness. Sitting on the piece of hemp sack, I undressed Little Bell and entered a whole other world. I recited a poem of mine: tight at the beginning and a mess by the end, a final verse that is as distant as the stars. When Bell heard the final verse whispered into her ears, she screamed and pushed me aside. She lay naked on the ground and by starlight, she transcribed my poem into a notebook.

I began to look for constellations. A line of poetry read: *like flour under a flour sieve, the stars shower us with their tears.* On that silent moonless night, the stars showered their tears on Little Bell's body like bioluminescent flour. I realized there was no use in writing poems for others to read. If anyone had come to enjoy the silent night, my poem would have been of no use to them. If someone else had read it out loud, it would have only interfered with the sheer joy of the silent night's own poetry. If a person couldn't sing, then all the songs of the world would be of no use; if a person could sing, then they must want to sing their own song. That is to say, poetry as a profession should be eliminated. Everyone has to be their own poet.

I stepped toward the kaleidoscope of stars. No one could tell me where I was, or what sort of a person I was. I went to sleep bewildered.

5

HAD TO GO TO SCHOOL even when there was no class because I was the biology lab director. I sat in the empty lab, slowly dozing off. I began to hate the president and his nurturing hand. If only he had been more like my father or my old teacher who saw me as irredeemable, how happy I would have been! All of a sudden, my mother called, telling me to go have lunch with her. It was something I had to do. Why else would she have had a son? So I hit the road that very instant.

Thirty-three years ago, something happened that would determine my whole life. That afternoon, after finishing a twelve-hour night shift at the Union Medical Hospital, she came home, which I still have some vague memories of. The small, room-and-a-half tiled-roof house had been built during the Ming dynasty and was situated in a small *hutong** branching out from the Forbidden

---

*A *hutong* is a small alleyway in a Chinese city.

Palace. The house next to it was taller, so our house got very little light. My mother wore an embroidered cheongsam and in her high heels, she stepped gingerly around the gutters along the hutong path. She bought a small amount of meat, not enough to feed a cat, but enough to make noodles in meat sauce. After she and my father ate said noodles in meat sauce, they did the deed.

I don't like noodles in meat sauce because I was made from noodles in meat sauce. That night, the condom they were using (vintage from the Japanese occupation, washed many times, dried and powdered) broke, and I got leaked out. After rinsing everything off, they thought they were in the clear, but in less than a month, my mother was puking until she was green in the face.

Maybe it was because of the rinsing, I ended up having recurring nightmares of a great floods; maybe it was because of the rinsing, I was early by two months, entering the world floppy and hairy like a rat drowned in a swill vat. My mother cried the moment she saw me and moaned, "Oh my ma! What have I created!"

I waited for my mother on the third floor of Dong Lai Shun, which was our usual place. I couldn't go to the hospital because my story was so well-known there. Back then, I rolled around in a makeshift incubator in the preemie ward for several months. In those difficult times, they managed to rig something out of a tinplate for me, it needed to be filled with hot water regularly. One time, someone added a whole bucket of boiling water and I nearly became lamb hot pot. Whenever I show up at the hospital, even unweaned little interns have the nerve to call me "the unboilable mouse!"

Periodically, my mother would sit me down for secret talks, it was a twenty-year-long tradition. The origin of this tradition goes back to when I was in third grade. My father and I lived in the small courtyard. My mother lived in a single-person dorm at the hospital. Father was in charge of my education. His methods were harsh, always caning me with the feather duster. My shenanigans were a part of it, but another part of it was simply that I was a mistake, so he didn't think anything good could have come from me.

After I had damaged a classroom desk, my teacher wrote a letter that she told me to take home. I ate the letter, envelope and all, like it was a hawthorn-flavored fruit roll-up. The next day, the teacher asked me for the return letter, but I said my father didn't write one. She knew I was lying and sent the class captain to deliver another letter. I led a gang of little misfits to block the entrance to the hutong, attacking anyone who dared to come within a hundred-meter radius. The teacher had no choice but to deliver the letter herself. As soon as she left the house, my father grabbed me by the ear and beat me until the feather duster broke. Just as he was grabbing for a fresh duster, mother returned. When she saw father lifting me off the ground by my ear (having suffered enough punishment, my ears were remarkably tough), she wailed and leaped to save me. She went on to give father a vicious scolding. My father tried to explain himself by saying, "This child is like an earth spirit, he'll vanish the second he touches the ground," but my mother didn't listen and rescued me.

After rescuing me, she took me to the otology wing of the hospital to get my ears checked. The doctor puzzled over my ears and determined that they weren't ears but rather the hooks of a construction crane. Mother then grabbed a cot from the postnatal ward and made a place for me in her dorm room. She left me a key and three ground rules: one, I didn't have to go to school if I did not get at least ninety points on tests. Two, if I didn't go to school, I couldn't go outside to play either because I wasn't to be seen. Three, there was money in the drawer that I could use at my own discretion, but I had to bring back receipts to show that the money had been put to proper use. If I had no objections, then that was to be our deal. If I broke the deal, she would hand me back to my father for discipline. I raised my hand and swore to heaven: if Wang Er broke any of the above three rules, he would willingly go to hell or live with dad. Mother laughed and said she had been foolish, with a big boy like me around, why had she been living alone all this time?

I moved in and turned the second floor of the women's dorm into my own little kingdom. Many of the young aunties bought me snacks and listened to me tell ghost stories from *Liao Zhai*.* During the day, I was often out visiting the zoo with a night-shift nurse. But after a winter of that, I grew bored of the world of women and needed things to fiddle around with. My mother found a few tutors for me. I studied calligraphy one day, tinkered with radios the next, and learned chess the day after. At night, my mother read her medical books while I monkeyed about. When we were tired, we chatted. I pointed out all the funny ticks each tutor had. When my mother was pleased with me, she would bury me in her bosom. It was all right in the winter across thick sweaters but in the summer, it was too intense and I had to push her away. She raised her eyebrows and chided, "Hey! A big man now are you? Don't you remember suckling on your mama? So you want to be all serious like your father. Fine, you can play by yourself, I'm going to read!"

My chess education failed because the tutor didn't like my game. The old man was a venerable elder of Beijing's chess world. He had mastered the opening, the setup, and the execution but unfortunately, he was old and lacking in blood dynamism and courage. He was no match for the brisk viciousness of my game. He said to mother, this child is undoubtedly talented but he lacks self-restraint, there is blood in his eyes. Give him a few more years and I can recommend an appropriate teacher for him. After he left, mother asked if I had been causing trouble in the old gentleman's home. He was famously restrained so why couldn't he tolerate me? I told her,

---

Liao Zhai is a collection of classical stories by Pu Songling. They are fantastical tales also implicitly criticizing societal issues. Many have been adapted to film and TV.

I noticed that he had a problem: he couldn't stand risky plays, his fingers trembled every time he found himself in a situation. So when we played, I always tried to create those risky situations. That was how I won twelve matches out of twelve. The story made mother laugh. She said I had a bellyful of demons! Whenever I talked about the things I did during the day, she would crack open a xiangfei nut and say, "Gosh, son of mine, how did I ever make you!"

I stayed at my mother's place for three years. For the first two, I was eager to share all my stories and listen to her cheer me on. But slowly I became reluctant. I was growing up. Things were changing inside of me. During that last summer, when I saw the aunties in the dormitory in their shorts and tank tops, I got goose bumps all over my back. I didn't like seeing my mother show so much skin either. Sometimes, she wouldn't wear a bra and I complained, "Ma! Put something on!" At the time, my mother had long legs and full breasts as if she were in her twenties. It became extremely uncomfortable living with her. I needed my own privacy. For middle school, I got accepted into a boarding school and moved out.

After that, she spent the next twenty years playing detective. She tried, in every way she could think of, to pry into my private life. In response, I came up with any lie I could think of. I can't even remember the last time I told her anything true.

My mother was getting old. Her once bright eyes were turning presbyopic and her rows of white teeth had been replaced with dentures. Her once full breasts shriveled and her long legs walked with a slight limp. My mother had transcended her corporeal self and transformed into a dainty old lady. I loved my mother and used that love to repay her thirty-two years of care, but I still had to lie to her.

My mother asked me why I didn't come home on Sundays. I said I was busy. She said it didn't matter how busy I was, I still had to go home because our four-bedroom apartment was allocated on the basis of having four residents. If people saw that it was only a lonely old couple living there, they would complain. What a lame reason. But saying that I was too busy was also a lame reason. The truth was, I was avoiding my father's biliousness. Confucius says: the downfall of a man is his pompousness—the great sage Confucius, how wise he was! I did my chemistry and my father did his math—the well water stayed clear of the river water—but he just had to ask me how my math was coming along. If I said I didn't do math, he would get mad and say if you don't study math, how can you ever amount to anything? If I said I knew math, it was even worse, he handed me a math quiz. After a week of work, I returned home only to do math problems? That wasn't a home, that was hell. My mother knew exactly what I was thinking, so she said, "You can avoid your dad but don't avoid me too! Besides, your father cares about you, you needn't be so petty."

"I'm not petty, ma. Dad's a sadist. He likes to watch me drenched in cold sweat when I can't figure out a problem. I can do the problems fine, but the equations he sets up make no sense. I was just too polite to point it out. If I had made up some random numbers, he wouldn't be able to solve the equations either. Then he'll know what it's like to feel that constipated, but I bet you would never let that happen to him."

"Oh you. You could have just humored him, why take him so seriously? He's been like that his whole life, even I can't change him, much less you."

"He's always trying to prove that I'm worthless. So I admit I'm worthless but that's not good enough. How can he ever be satisfied? He wants to prove that I'm not worth even one of his pubes. What is that? After thirty-some odd years, I'm still just some spermatozoon he shot out. . . ."

My mother laughed, "Rubbish! Don't you think that's an inappropriate thing to say to your mother? But seriously, when are you going to have kids? I want a grandson."

That old question. "Ma, I'll have one for sure, I'm just busy right now. I need to do more research and become a full professor.

Full professors have it good, they get a big flat right away. But lecturers? Forget it. One of my classmates was assigned to Tsinghua University. His kid's already nine years old, but the three of them are still crammed into a tiny place. People in their thirties still have strong sex drives so the kid ended up telling everyone at school that mommy and daddy were doing it again last night. That was embarrassing. So now they wait for their colleagues to all leave for lunch before locking the door and taking off their pants. You know how hard office desks are. Can't imagine it being very pleasant."

"What are you telling me all this for? Our house isn't lacking in space!"

"True, but the house is dad's, not mine. I envy the house with all its fancy fixtures and I want to get one too. As soon I as get a house like that, I'll have a son!"

"Oh please. By the time you get a house like that, I'll be dead."

"To be honest, I don't really think I'm able to be a good father. Look at how you've made me, carefree, lackadaisical. Besides, it was that time before I was born when you tried to rinse me out with cold water that led to my recurring nightmares of a great flood . . . and what if I give birth to an idiot son!"

"Don't you try to change the subject; do you know who I am? I'm a childbirth expert. So give birth to something! If it's good, I'll take it."

"I still have to design explosives and become a famous professor. When am I going to have time to raise a kid? Dad has me on a crusade. I have to make a name for myself no matter what!"

Mother put on a sly smile and said, "You think you can fool me, I know all about your work. If you really are what you say, that would be some miracle!"

My mother's words sent my heart racing: what else did she know? Ever since I started middle school, she spied on me continuously. When my father was assigned a new house, mother spent her weekends at the mining school. I had a small room there with three sets of locks on the door. My mother was somehow able to pick all of them without leaving a trace, like a consummate rogue. I knew she had such abilities, so I hid everything and killed my diary habit. I kept everything that was important at school, but that still wasn't enough to prevent her investigation.

Back then, going home on Saturday was like torture. I had to fabricate lies for my mother and butt heads with my father. Whenever mother wasn't home, father was always on the verge of kicking my ass. Eventually, I ended up with a large stature and the agility to walk on walls. He couldn't beat me anymore so he began to preach. My father had a fabled youth, from elementary school to high school, he always scored number one; and when he got into Tsinghua University, he was also number one. Had it not been for his poor health, he would have been the first state-sponsored scholar to go abroad. According to mother, my father was a marvelous machine that could solve all sorts of problems.

My father said of me, he's doing pretty good out there, living in housing that's usually reserved for senior professors. He's famous at the mining school. Not only the teachers and students but even the janitors give him two thumbs up. He said, "Your mom is always complaining that I hit you. If you can achieve just one percent of what I have, I will spare you down to your pinky!"

As father blew himself full of hot air, mother sat by with a cold smile. After the meal, when I had returned to my own room, mother came in to whisper, "Don't listen to your dad. He's a real bore; you do what you love to do. Just be a decent man and preferably a happy one too. What's with all this road to glory and fame and fortune, we're not into all that, you're my son!"

These things were all fine to talk about, but she always had to digress into unrelated matters, leaving me crimson-faced. "I was washing your undies and noticed a little problem. How are you feeling?"

Out of exasperation I screamed, "Who told you to wash my underwear? I'll wash my own underwear!"

"Come now, your mother's a doctor, every boy goes through this stage, it's totally normal. Back before the revolution, you would have been given a wife by now."

"Nope! What would I do with a wife? What the heck is a wife good for!"

On Monday morning, I went to school and my mother went to work. As I rode on my bike, she rode on her Hungarian cruiser bike next to me. It was a relic from the Austro-Hungarian Empire with the chain falling off constantly. By the time she got to the hospital, her hands were covered in black grease. She insisted on riding her bike so that she could continue to question me, but I changed the subject.

"Mom, why don't you divorce dad?"

"Why would I divorce him?"

"The sooner you leave him, the sooner I'll stop getting beaten up."

She laughed and jumped down from her bike. During the Cultural Revolution, she finally found something out about me: the story of our explosion incident got out. I was under police custody. This proved my father's hypothesis about me: he's a bastard, bound to bring down the house.

My mother continued to love me nevertheless. She said to Little Bicycle Bell, life is a lonely road, you need a good long novel to get you through. My father's novel was a bore, she regretted ever having taken it off the shelf. She was happy that Little Bell had a rather good one. But this novel of mine can only be read using carnal knowledge. Not many people knew about Bell and me. The fact that she found out about it proved her abilities. My mother adored Little Bell, she said Bell "sure is a swell girl"; but in the end, I got stuck with Erniuzi. It had something to do with me butting heads with my mother somehow.

I was confident that neither Erniuzi nor Little Bell would betray me, so I asked with confidence, "Mom, what is it that you know?"

"You really are nothing like your father. You're of my making!"

"What?"

"Your poems, I read *all* your poems, you really hit the nail on the head. You even said, life should be lived in accordance to the *dao,* but also with excitement. You still haven't figured out what the *dao* is have you? Let me tell you, the *dao* is your mother, it's the way your mother made you!"

She cracked open a xiangfei nut. For a moment, a youthful revolutionary zeal returned to her face. I felt all of my blood surging to my brain like I was going to have a stroke. Writing poems was my biggest secret, sharing it was tantamount to lovemaking: when inspiration strikes, it is like an orgasm and when the words appear on the page, it is like cum. Only girls that I was sexually involved with were allowed to read my poems. How could they have ended up in my mother's hands! I felt like a chicken without a tail, with nothing at all to cover my sphincter. The matches, cigarettes, and chopsticks sitting on the table splattered across the floor. Furiously, I roared:

"That goddamn Little Bicycle Bell! I will murder her. Mom, did she give you the manuscripts? Give them back!"

"The manuscripts are still with her; I just made copies. If you want them, pay up, three hundred-yuan printing fee!"

"Outrageous, how about half the price? Forget it, it's not like I can pry them out of your eyes. Don't ever mention my writings again; they aren't for others to see, okay? Especially not dad, if he saw them he'd kill me."

"Okay, I won't show him anything. But really, it's not like it's a big deal, why keep them from me? What else have you written? I want to read everything."

After returning from my mother's place, I made an important decision. I would never write poetry again or get involved in anything that wasn't my business. I would go on the straight and narrow path like my father and seek personal advancement. I was my mother's creation, that was indisputable, and I loved my mother, perhaps even more than my wife. But I had to prove that she and I had different aspirations.

6

THE NEXT DAY, IT WAS the biology lab's turn for sanitation duty. In the past, I never paid attention to it as long as there was a mountain of toilet paper in the stalls. This time it was different. I needed to make sure everyone was impressed. I got to school early to drag Xu out of bed and started sweeping.

There were about thirty departments of various sizes occupying our building. Each department was on rotation for sanitation duty. When it was the president's turn, he would scrub the toilets personally. The school wasn't winning hearts and minds, so he had to work hard if he ever wanted to win over any hearts and minds. If Wang Er wanted to go on the straight and narrow path, he would have to go down this way too. After scrubbing the toilets, I used some of the waste acids from the chemistry lab to make every bathroom implement glisten. Then, it occurred to me that it wasn't enough just to clean the bathroom, I also had to let everyone know who had done it. I got hold of large sheets of red paper so that

I could write a couple of slogans down. The one over the men's room door read:

"Welcome to the toilet!—Biology Lab."

Above the urinal, I posted "Step forward, please—Biology cordially invites you to."

On the back of the bathroom door, it read, "Farewell. We know you will come to miss this immaculate environment, but unfortunately it is time to work. When shall you return? Adieu from the Biology Lab."

The slogans inside the stalls were even more spectacular. In the men's room, it read, "Big marbles, small marbles, they all drop into the jade bowl" and "A heart as pure and white as virgin ice in the jade vase." In the women's bathroom, it read, "Our front gate and courtyard are overgrown with weeds, but a path has been cleared today in your honor." Above their door was a banner that read "Gazebo of Dark Fragrances." As for Wang Er's calligraphy, nice would have been an understatement. If I added up all the paper I've used studying the masters' engravings, it would have weighed dozens of kilograms. Just as the bathroom was starting to look like a calligraphy show, the president stormed into the biology lab and harped, "Did you write all that stuff in the bathroom?"

"Yes, sir. Do you think they are prizeworthy?"

"Prize my ass! The committee on higher education will be arriving for an inspection. You have ten minutes to clean everything up!"

Pasting up slogans was easy but scrubbing them off turned out to be hard. The committee on higher education arrived before I was finished and laughed their assess off. A green vein on the president's forehead went *rat-a-tat*. After the entourage left, the president called me over.

I said, "President, in any case the bathrooms have been cleaned. I should get some sort of a praise for that right?"

"What praise? You'll be reprimanded by name at the next meeting."

"What the hell, man! Take a look at how sparkling clean the bathrooms are! Forget it, I'm tired of playing the sucker. It's back to business as usual."

"Stop! Sit down. Cleaning the bathrooms was a good thing but posting up slogans was a mistake. In the future, when the administration brings you up, everyone will remember today and call you a troublemaker! It's not like you don't do enough hard work, but it all gets forgotten because of stuff like this. You need to take care of your reputation. Go home and think about it, don't just mindlessly rush into things!"

After leaving the president's office, my teeth itched with anger. He made us scrub toilets and we weren't even allowed a little sense of humor, what the hell. When the clock struck, I walked into class with a projector in hand. I wanted to salvage my reputation so I threw myself into the lecture. The topic for the day was the shapes of bacterium under the microscope. When I introduced the ball-shaped coccus bacteria, I squatted down and puffed up my cheeks. When I talked about the rod-shaped bacillus, I stretched out like a diver. When I mentioned the S-shaped campylobacter, I nearly twisted my back. At the mention of the helical-shaped helicobacter, I twisted my legs like a braid of onions. The students turned away in fear. When I explained that bacteria had hard hairs called pili that they used to move around with, I likewise walked the walk. When I got to cell division and was getting ready to tear myself in two, the bell rang. The room was littered with pencils, on which I nearly slipped. I returned to the biology lab frothing for breath. I looked in the mirror and saw a hairy crab. When I ran my hands through my hair, chalk powder fell like snow. By the time I finally had a chance to catch my breath, Dr. Zhang from the medical office came to see me. He said someone in the agriculture department called and said Mr. Wang was acting strange during class. He came to check my temperature to see if I had a fever. After doing away with Dr. Zhang, Xu You snickered at me as well, so I did away with him as well. I sat alone to clear my head.

I felt nauseous so I went for a walk around campus. Our school used to be an old church. Inside the campus were ornate flower beds and cast-iron railings. The school's tall steeple was covered in iron slate. I couldn't tell you how many of its dark hallways were lit with only one transparent roof tile or how many of the attic rooms exited right out onto the roof. Old buildings had a way of triggering my imagination. I walked alone and saw no one. This was all a story, a puzzle, that I needed to slowly mull over.

First of all, the roof wasn't made of rusty iron, but of heavy gray lead instead. Eunuchs with ashen faces in black robes scurried out of every corner. The president, with his long, hooked nose, questioned and prodded to test the purity of everyone's faith. The cast-iron rails were really Turkish torture devices that still carried the smell of blood. At the same time, some people were on the roof making love. I had seen that cat before, fur as white as moonlight, passing on the roof.

Can you tell me what the cat signifies? Or the ornamental flowers beneath the walls? A contour was starting to emerge from the deluge of images. It was time for me to search for some of those clarion phrases, pure as moonlight . . . still in my trance, a series of loud rings nearly gave me a seizure. Just like our little Wang Er, the rest of this story was buried in that sorghum field beneath the midnight sky.

I was standing right under a large electronic loudspeaker. The ringing of the class bell was like an explosion above my head. Students flooded out of the building shouting, galloping to the canteen—it was the lunch bell. I made a sudden decision: dammit, I'm going home. I didn't even want lunch!

Outside the campus, I saw people sweeping the street. It dawned on me that it was Patriotic Sanitation Day, the whole city pitched in to clean the space in front of their institutions and businesses. It was also the day when class supervisors and students were scheduled to meet. According to school regulations, I was supposed to give an ethics seminar, then take the class to go sweep the street.

This was an important test. Had I fled home, it would have destroyed any chances I had of getting on the right, straight and narrow path.

Reluctantly, I returned to school. It didn't necessarily mean that I was all that ambitious about getting on the straight and narrow path or seeking advancement. It was more that once I had made such an important resolution, I had to go through with it for at least one morning. After I filled my belly and took a nap, it was time to head to class. I first visited the substitute class supervisor, secretary of the Youth League, Young Hu. After being briefed on the situation, I continued on my way.

I taught four courses, interacted with eight classes from two departments, and Ag-3-Beta was my least favorite. The students in this class were always picking on their teachers. Old professors got by all right, but when young lecturers like us taught, nine out of ten times there was carnage. Putting me in charge of this class must have been a conspiracy. But maybe that was why I had to give this ethics seminar!

I had a migraine from the moment I entered the classroom. These were the very students who said I was having a fever in the morning. They stared at me like they were birds of prey. When the masses point their fingers, there is only death ahead. How many hairs was I going to lose after this class? I stepped onto the podium and cleared my throat.

"Students, men and women, that is to say, male and female students. As I stand here and look into everyone's eyes, it is like I am looking into the eyes of Comrade Dzerzhinsky;* I dare not look. It isn't a joke. I can tell from the way you look at me that you have two questions. First, you want to ask: doesn't Mr. Wang have a fever? Why is he here instead of being dead? Is this correct? Class captain please answer."

---

*Dzerzhinsky was a Bolshevik revolutionary and head of the secret police for the Soviet regime.

Unimpressed, the class captain said, "Someone called the infirmary saying that Mr. Wang was sick but it was not the opinion of the majority of the class. The class committee met and decided that Mr. Wang's exceptionally lively lecture was not a problem. We have already reprimanded the student who made the call."

"Very good. The teacher is very pleased to receive acknowledgment from the students regarding his hard work. The second question you must want to ask is: what is this guy doing here? The next microbiology class isn't until Thursday. Let me tell you. I am, in fact, your class supervisor. I had been busy as of late, so by instructions from above, Mr. Hu was your substitute class supervisor. From today on, I will return to my post. Today's topic is morality and ethics . . . captain, do you have a question?"

"Teacher, do you have a lesson plan?"

I swallowed the "screw you" I wanted to throw at him with some difficulty and said instead, "Of course I do. I didn't bring my notes because I can remember it all. You can be confident in your teacher's memory, please sit. Since I will be starting the ethics seminar for the first time today, I thought it would be fitting for us to learn a bit more about each other. If anyone has any questions for me, please don't hesitate to ask."

"Teacher, are you a Communist Party member?"

"Not yet, but I'm working on it, thank you for that question."

"Teacher, do you have a graduate degree?"

"No, just a bachelor's. I'm a little old to start graduate school. According to our regulation, holders of bachelor's degrees can teach basic courses, anything else? Try to be more specific."

"Teacher, why did you call us frozen pork?"

"Did I say that? I think I said entering this room was like entering a cold cellar when you all looked at me like I was a hanging corpse. All right, I can take back the cold cellar comment. What else?"

They didn't ask anything more so I put on a grave expression.

"Fellow students, my flaws are open for you to see. You are supposed to be a model class. But what is the reality? Is it all hype?

Cheating during tests, I've seen it. When things go missing in the class, you just buy more with the classroom budget before even catching the thief. There's enough blame to go around for everyone. I am your class supervisor and I hereby declare an immediate crackdown. The thieves need to be caught and the cheaters need to be disciplined. Also, you pretend to be loyal to professors from our department but you pick on teachers from other outside departments, why is that? You are not the first and only ones around here! Your attitude should not be made-to-order! In fact, tomorrow I will convene a meeting with the teachers from the other departments and draft a report for the president. I know someone must be goading you on, but I'm afraid even that person won't have the gumption to encourage a student rebellion. I know about the female teacher who went home crying after your class. What about her eyebrows? Too bourgeois? That's a rather big hat to be throwing on someone. Are you the student body or the political council? Seems like there are more than forty people trying to interfere in politics in this class; I wonder what the Party Central Committee has to say about that . . . You call yourselves students? And you bully your teachers? What's there to cry about, stop crying!"

I continued to lecture until I had unleashed all my anger, then announced that it was time for small group discussions. The class cadres gathered at the front of the room. They were the obedient ones, sweet talkers all of them.

"Teacher, where have we offended you? Why are you punishing us?"

"No offence taken, I'm only doing this for your own good."

"Teacher, we're wrong, please forgive us!"

"It's not my place to forgive, but our class spirit must be rectified!"

Speaking with such authority made me feel godlike. It wasn't until I got the bunch of kids on the verge of tears that I was finally able to relax a little.

"Of course, the teacher will always forgive the students. But why do you antagonize your teacher? Tell the truth!"

I already knew the answer. It was only because there were some people who had it out for those of us who were transferred here from other schools. The despicable part was that they gossiped with the students, spreading mean rumors about me probably related to something promiscuous. I turned to them solemnly.

"It's all bullshit. I will deal with them on my own. As long as you all behave, I won't drag you into it. In the future, report these things to me immediately; I'm the head teacher of this class. Now, enough talk, it's time to sweep the streets!"

My class marched into the street in a formation as tight as an army platoon, much better than any of the other classes. I led the way wielding a bamboo broom. Sand and stones were pushed away and dust filled the air. After a few strokes, I handed the broom to the class captain. I left him with a few words before going to the president's office to report. As soon as I entered, I could tell that he was pleased with my ethics seminar. As it turned out, he was eavesdropping the whole time. When I explained what I learned from the students, he nodded.

"I see. These people don't know what's good for them, ganging up, building factions. I will bring this up at the presidential meeting. Young Wang, you're getting the hang of this at last. But the slogans you wrote in the bathroom this morning, those were a fiasco."

"At your orders, sir, what about the insinuations on my character? As they say, there are no waves without some wind. Old Man Yao needs to be taught a lesson, he keeps making up rumors about me!"

"Old Yao is a different sort of problem altogether. He is an extremely loyal comrade, not to mention assiduous. But he's not the most capable and he can't keep his mouth shut. All the petty crimes at school get reported to him. He couldn't solve any of the mysteries so he bad-mouthed you out of frustration. Don't take it too personally. There is something I want to discuss with you: last night when he was on patrol, he took a hard fall—have you heard about this?"

"I had no idea. If I did, I would have toasted to it. People like him are nothing more than manure machines, what was he doing as the head of security? What did you want to discuss with me?"

"He's hurt pretty bad, dislocated a hip. The hospital requested for people to take turns watching him. Old Yao's wife will take the day shifts, it's up to the school to send people for the night shifts."

"If that's what the hospital says, then we should send someone. But what does this have to do with me?"

"It has everything to do with you. Old Yao's department and your department are both considered core departments. But the core young people refuse to attend to Old Yao, so maybe you could take the lead and set an example. After that, no one will be able to refuse."

I screamed, "Fuck your . . . loved one." I wanted to say, "Fuck your ma," but when I remembered it was the president I was talking to, I withheld my words. "What I meant was, I deeply respect your mother. But please explain to me why I should go to the hospital to watch him."

"That darn mouth of yours! If you talk like that to me, I don't want to imagine how you talk with other people. Listen, the higher-ups want all the schools to apply for research grants—we can't get left out of that. I am preparing to build a research center and fill it up with projects from all the departments. I'm afraid your bomb research might be the most important project. So let's lay the groundwork of it, what do you say?"

"Not sure, can I build bombs in this building?"

"Who said you would be doing experiments here? The experiments can still happen at the mining school; we just want the projects to be based here. If it's based here, then we can apply for research grants. One day, we'll build a research center and buy all sorts of equipment, but that's far off in the future. As for the choice of director for the research center, we'll leave that blank for now, but the codirector position is all yours, you're the only one who can really carry the project forward. That would move you up by several notches. In the future, whether its professorship or foreign sabbatical, you'll have top priority. You almost look like you're not interested, what's wrong with you!"

"I didn't say I wasn't interested!"

"But it's not enough just to convince me. Think about how other people see you! Take a look at yourself, I shouldn't need to say any more. There are only a few more weeks before the naming of the leadership for the research center. You need a few outstanding performances to turn your reputation around. This thing with Old Yao is the perfect opportunity. If you don't take it even after someone serves it up to you, then you're just thick!"

"If it's as you say, then I really should do it. When my father got sick and I offered to keep him company, I was told I wasn't needed. Who does this Old Yao think he is, stealing my father's thunder! And I have to wipe his ass? Yikes! When do I start?"

"Tonight there's no one watching him, you go. Tomorrow, I'll send Xu You. Once the two of you have gone, the brats won't dare to make excuses anymore."

It certainly wasn't easy trying to be good. In addition to jabbering with students, I had to wipe Old Yao's ass, and feel thankful for the opportunity that his broken leg offered me. When I returned to the biology lab, I gave my wife a call telling her that I wouldn't make it home. Without a word, she slammed the phone. When I told everything to Xu You, he stared at me in silence for a long time before blurting, "Wang Er, please stop mocking me." After I ate dinner, I made my way to the hospital.

7

HAD OLD YAO NOT MADE up all those rumors about me, he could have been a sweet old man. His face was red and plump, covered in a coat of peach fuzz, tender as the nation's flowers. White stubble of varying lengths sparsely populated his chin and jaw. This person wore a cloth hat all year round with a pair of white-rimmed glasses saddling his nose as he would creep around campus looking for thieves. There were plenty of thieves at our school but he never caught a single one. Most security departments of most organizations had a hard time actually catching criminals. They were mainly there for intimidation purposes. But Old Yao didn't intimidate anyone. In fact, he became their prime target. When he put down his guard for even a moment, his face towel would somehow end up in the public shower, where everyone used it to wipe their feet. When Old Yao got it back and washed it before using it again, he ended up with athlete's foot on his face. The one who stole his towel was his assistant Wang Gang. Wang Gang had no sense of decency. After Old Yao fell, he didn't even bother to visit. He said his mother-in-law was visiting Beijing, so he had to go see her. In fact, his mother-in-law had been in town for half a year; he was just making up an excuse.

When Old Yao couldn't catch any thieves himself, he enlisted the help of the people. Whether it was an all-campus meeting, a department meeting, or even a meeting within a specialized field, he would make himself heard. Everyone had to be on high alert and do everything to assist him in catching thieves. He was such a wastebasket of words that even after an hour, he had still not gotten to his point. So everyone tried to avoid having him at meetings. When the core departments met, we often hid in the basement and appointed people to keep watch. As soon as someone saw Old Yao approach, we would disperse immediately. He put up a dozen suggestion boxes everywhere, but no one ever submitted anything, except once in the men's room, someone wrote in an ancient style, "Yonder Old Yao by the ditches of defecation; the trash bin empties." What blasphemy against the elders!

Those were his problems, not mine. I only blame him for making up rumors about me when he couldn't catch any culprits. Whenever something went missing at the school, he always suspected one of the young janitors. It wasn't entirely ridiculous since he was working off the police station's data: 80 percent of the crimes committed in the city last year were committed by the rural youth, followed by young factory workers; our school didn't have any rural youths. He narrowed down his list of suspects, circling in on the rougher-looking young plumbers who worked in the boiler room. Every time something went missing, he blamed those guys. Do you really think they were going to remain silent about it? What happened was, a toilet was clogged and they couldn't clear it out with a bamboo rod, so the brothers dug up the ground and solved the mystery. They pulled up a ball of condoms, several dozen at least. They took the bamboo rod with the condoms, stuck to it over to the security office, and slapped it on a desk, splashing juices everywhere. They demanded the culprits be found immediately or else the next time the toilet clogged, it would be Old Yao doing the digging. So Old Yao had to solve the case of the condom ball. Who knows how he got it into his head that there was a biology lab on campus where he could get me to analyze the evidence. The moment he came through the door, he heard me joking with Xu You, saying how my condoms were probably somewhere in that ball as well. That was the trigger, Old Yao took it literally and went around bad-mouthing me to everyone. Rumors are as hard to take back as water out of a bucket. Until this day, I remain the scapegoat. Any given moment, I would have loved nothing more than to strangle him to death, and yet now I was going to the hospital to be his night guardian. I think I must have taken the wrong pill or something.

I went to the hospital reception to ask about Old Yao. They said they had no record of such a person, maybe he had already been discharged. I knew the hospital had a dubious reputation, but to have Old Yao bureaucratically eliminated in one afternoon seemed a bit extreme, even for them. I tried to get more information. They asked me when he was brought there. I said that very morning. The guy asked me if I personally knew any doctors or administrators. I said I didn't. He said in that case, the emergency ward was probably the place to look. I was advised to find someone who knew someone at the hospital or else the patient might just lie in the emergency ward indefinitely. I looked for the emergency ward but the signs took me in circles. Somewhere near the back of the hospital, I found a door with the Emergency Ward sign, which was strange because I was clearly in the morgue. As it turned out, the emergency ward was being renovated so the patients had to squeeze in with the dead. Anxiously, I paced back and forth at the entrance. My heart pounded like it was my first time talking to Little Bell.

The first time I had spoken to her, I made up all sorts of excuses to approach her, but none of them really covered up my ultimate aim of wanting to do her; back in those days, had it not been for this need, boys and girls could have lived their entire lives without ever having talked to one another. In the same way, I had no way to appear like a truly kind person in front of Old Yao without revealing my ultimate aim of upward mobility. We weren't family or even friends. In fact, I usually felt nothing but resentment toward him. So what was I doing there?

Ever since elementary school, I liked to mock the Goody Two-shoes, but now was the time to forget about all those wicked prejudices. I needed to get off my high horses because everything mean I had said about other people was now true of me as well. What if I just walked away? No! That would have been even worse.

I began putting together my story. "Old Yao, the president asked me to look after you." It sounded like something the groom said to the bride back before the revolution. He would have felt shy being in a room with an unfamiliar female so he would have said, "By the will of father and mother, and the wisdom of the match-maker . . ." Notice how innocent he appears, yet in a moment, he would fuck her. The words of a groom are the words of self-deception. My words were also self-deceiving. It wasn't as if there were armed policemen escorting me to the hospital. If I was unwilling to do this, I didn't have to!

I could have also said, "Old Yao, I heard that you were sick with no one to watch over you, I felt worried. Us young men who grew up in the 80s have a duty to start taking care of the elderly." Beautifully said. Sadly, it was too out of character for me. I could have said it in a slightly different way, "Old Yao, we work together and I'm younger than you, so it seemed only right." Why wasn't it Wang Gang there saying those words? I was overthinking it. I decided to walk in first and figure out what to say later.

Upon entering the emergency ward, I was shocked. A mercury lamp lit up the room like a skylight. Its purple-green light made everyone beneath look like feral zombies. Countless patients lay stiffly on uneven two-foot-wide beds, resting on precariously thin boards. They were such familiar beds! When I was a kid living in the hospital, I had often explored the basement. Once, I found my way into the morgue and saw those same beds.

One summer, I had seen a young woman lying on one of those beds. Yellow beads of oil oozed out of her pores like fresh pine sap. Nothing in the emergency ward now looked nearly as beautiful as she was, especially not the big lady in the middle of the room. She looked like a deflated balloon saddled across two adjoining beds. Her body was so swollen that it was becoming translucent. Her eyelids were like two tiny bags of water. A striped hospital gown covered the upper half of her body, leaving her lower half naked. She sat over a bedpan with her white bush hanging out like an oily cotton ball. The old lady hummed as she poured her kettle. Her flesh looked like it was ready to explode, but she was still connected to pipes and IV drips; the sight of it all made me weak in the knees. But thank goodness for the splashing sound coming from under her. Regardless of whether it was pee or poo, at least it let people know she was still alive. The room was filled with bodies of various shapes and sizes, but one thing they all had in common was that none of them looked like they were going to be alive for long.

The smell in the room was awful. One sniff of it would have been enough to last a lifetime. Piss, shit, decaying flesh, rotten apples, moldy oranges, I can only assume that the blend of all those odors would not please anyone. The sounds weren't as remarkable, just a few sighs and hums here and there. The worst by far was the sound of excretion. I found a young lad keeping watch by a bed near the door, so I asked him if he had seen a red-faced old man with a broken leg. He said he was in the back. I got on the tips of my toes and looked. Indeed, Old Yao and his wife were in a back corner. It must have smelled even worse back there. I wasn't in a rush to see him yet so I had a little chat with the lad. I offered him a cigarette and when he saw that it was a Double Nine, his eyes lit up.

"Where did you get these?"

"At the Yunnan Shop. Who is it that you're watching over?"

"My grandma, throat cancer, no hope. Bro, where's the Yunnan Shop?"

"Dashilan, ask around when you get there. Damn, this place is the worst, why don't you take her home?"

"Got my woman at home; she's afraid of dead people. This room is probably full of nearly dead people who don't have enough space in their homes. When they were brought to the hospital, there was nothing that could be done, so they ended up here, waiting for their last breath. We're almost done. That'll free up some space so you guys can scoot closer to the door. The air is much better here."

The grandmother suddenly opened her eyes and gestured. Her body was as red as a brick. Her mouth emitted the foul stench of cancer and oozed a dark red fluid as it opened and closed like a catfish; judging from the shapes it formed, she was asking to be taken home. The young lad lowered his head and said to her, "Grannie, hang in there, they have this thing here (he squeezed the oxygen tube connected to grandma's nose), it makes you feel better!"

The old lady's mouth twitched, as if to tell us that she had heard everything we said. She wanted to make a sound, to scold her impious grandson, but all she could do was stare angrily. She turned her vengeful gaze toward me and I fled immediately. I looked around the room and thought about all the death-fearing wives who had banished these people from their own homes. I felt the need to point fingers! Wives, oh wives!

When I got close to Old Yao, I tried to think of something to say; but Old Yao's wife was one step ahead of me.

"Are you the one the school sent for night watch? What took you so long! Old Yao broke his leg watching over your school every night, and this is how you repay him? Let me be straight with you: no good! Get him into a hospital room immediately!"

Her pressure tactic annoyed me, "Mrs. Yao, talking to me won't do you much good, why don't you ask our president?"

"I will go to him tomorrow and ask for an explanation! Does your school even have any standards? Old Yao is a Party Committee member and when he gets hurt you send him to the dog pound?"

What she said was reasonable. If I was sick or hurt, I wouldn't want to end up in this dog pound either. I supported the idea of Old Yao's wife raising hell in front of the president. I said, "Go ahead and make some noise. In this day and age, if you've got guts, you get fat; if you have got no guts, you starve. If you can stir something up, maybe the school will move Old Yao to the Peking University Hospital."

She left. Old Yao glanced at me out of one eye and closed it again. He and I had nothing to talk about. I tapped his leg and said, "Let me know when you need to pee!" before resting my eyes. Sometime later, I was struck by a terrible sound and smell. I opened my eyes and saw a person being carried out. An old man, with nothing left but skin and bones, had passed. I wanted to go out for some air but Old Yao grabbed me. In a hoarse whisper, he said, "Don't go! I'm afraid to be alone in here!"

Just my luck. As I sat down, I thought about a famous line by Li Si:* "Men are no different from mice!" This was something the venerable elderly man learned when he was the manager of a grain silo. He explained that there were two types of mice. The granary mice ate as much as they pleased. Government granaries opened their gates only once every few years. The mice in there were practically living in luxury resorts, free to party and gamble when they pleased. But then, there were the toilet mice who ate shit. Whenever a person went in to do their business, the mice had to screech and flee. Heartbreaking, but that was why he said, men are no different from mice. The successful ones are like the granary mice, the losers are like the toilet mice. What a courageous thing to say! Christians like to say that people are the sons and daughters of the Almighty. Li Si said, the same rules apply to mice and men. By comparison, it seemed like our ancestors wrote better papers, got more to the point. I always believed that people were what they

---

*Li Si was a calligrapher, philosopher, writer, and politician of the Qin dynasty.

made of themselves. Clearly, I had never considered the problem from the lofty heights of a mouse. Facing the scene before my eyes, I was forced to reconsider. Calling this place a shithole would not have been a metaphor. Had I been in my waning hours, lying on a wooden plank listening to a fat old lady pour her kettle next to me, how would I have felt? Even if I were a poet, and could reimagine the sound as raindrops trickling from the leaves (there is an impossibly beautiful guitar tune like that), I still would not have been able to outwit the bouts of torrential excretions accompanied by a fog of stench. Every breath would have felt like trying to swallow an iron ball. My head would have hurt like I was standing on the deck of a ship in a Category 8 storm. With all those sounds and smells, I'm afraid I wouldn't have even been able to gulp down my last breath. My Erniuzi (her hair would have been white) would have lain on top of me pouring buckets of tears. The sight of my pitiful state would have made her want to put me out of my misery by stabbing me with a knife, but she wouldn't have been able to do it. That wasn't the kind of future I wanted to think about, so I tried something else.

In fifty years, Wang Er is the top engineer in some university department as well as an academic consultant to half a dozen other departments. The hospital bed this Wang Er lies in is in the VIP ward of the capital's finest hospital. Like a corpse, I can't speak or even move a pinky. The sofa bed is submerged in a dark green ambient light. The pillow is gently sloped. There is fancy machinery behind a glass window. I can see my pulse beeping on the heart rate monitor.

A female nurse walks in, fully made-up, with a fine face. She is the strong kind of woman, with breasts like mountains, and muscular arms. She unties my pajama and yanks it off my body. Oh, Wang Er, what have you become! My chest is wrinkly and my belly sunken. Legs, oh my legs, are like a pair of logs rotting deep in the woods. My puff of pubes has only a few dark strands left. The thing is as soft as an overcooked noodle. I wonder how exactly a

1.9-meter person shrinks to such a size in old age. The female nurse flips me over with one finger and proceeds to massage my back and arms. My heart races but my body is as stiff as a board. My urethra feels a warm tingling and a single drop of fluid squirts out. When she finishes the massage, she notes that my body is behaving strangely. Hee-hee, that's what she gets for touching me. Wang Er isn't dead yet after all. The woman gets a wad of cotton and dries my turtlehead before gracefully flicking it into a waste basket. Wang Er, you're done for! I can't even blush, I am so old. After dressing me, she walks out. I suddenly have this feeling that I have lived long enough and am ready to die. The heart rate monitor stops beeping, an alarm sounds. White-gowned warriors charge in and stick needles in my arms, my legs, and my chest. They strap an oxygen mask over my face but it's no use! The red light on the machine turns on. A clock records the time. Several men in woolen Mao suits enter and take off their hats to pay their respects. At twelve fifty-seven and twenty-seven seconds, the great scientist, social activist, star of the Chinese scientific world, Wang Er, has fallen. The cadres exit. A bunch of nurses work together to undress me, flip me over, part my butt cheeks, and stuff a big cotton ball deep into my innards. So that's what that feels like! Then, they flip me back and spray me with perfume. It no longer matters that the perfume is cold; they are no longer worried about me catching a cold. A pretty young nurse straightens out my thing and tucks it into a jockstrap while several others begin padding my stomach with foam. They set my body upright and dress me in suit and tie. Hey! That's not how you tie a tie! Are you trying to lasso a cow? Is that how you tie your husband's tie? Of course, my screaming from the beyond has no impact on them. Then enters a middle-aged guy with a suitcase. He gives me a shave and stuffs cotton balls in my mouth. That's not pleasant. Hurry! Rigor mortis is setting in! They smother on some lipstick and glue on some fake eyebrows. A casket arrives. A bunch of people pick me up and place me inside. Western-style coffins sure are nice, comfortable, and spacious. In my breast pocket is a flower and resting on my chest is a ceremonial hat. In my hand is placed a cane so that I can beat people with it in the afterlife. At last, Wang Er has got style! Comrades, this is what we call service! Now I'm ready for that memorial service!

My head banged against the wooden bed and I woke up. I was so exhausted I wanted to shove Old Yao off his cot and sleep in it myself. I looked around and noticed that just about everyone was asleep. Even the fat lady had fallen asleep on her bedpan. In the short time that I had been dozing off, several people had disappeared from the ward. The young lad by the door who smoked a cigarette with me was gone and so was his granny. That woman must have already gone to heaven. I couldn't sit still anymore so I went out for some air.

The black sky had a purple tint to it; the stars were tiny white dots. Little Bell and I often scurried through sorghum fields on the outskirts of Beijing, so we knew more about the night sky than most. This was a solemn night sky. Its mood was as tense as a drumhead and as dense as a jungle. My hairs stood on ends.

Nights like these, one couldn't help but ponder death and eternity. Death was always at your back, an infinite darkness coming to swallow you. I felt minuscule. No matter what I did, I would still be just as minuscule. But so long as I could walk, I could outrun death. In that moment, I was a poet even though I had never published a line of poetry. For that reason, I was an even better poet. I was like those traveling poets who spoke poetry to themselves on horseback just to get through the cold night.

I had long transcended mouse-hood, so I wasn't dreaming about any granaries. If I could choose my death, I would choose something bloody and glorious. I would want to be tied to a tank and paraded around. When they would drag me to the gallows, the executioners of my choosing—beautiful young girls clad in black leather dresses— would approach me and offer me wreaths and sweet kisses. The girls would strap me carefully to the scaffold and circumambulate the platform a few times. They would use sharpening rods to sharpen the sabers hanging from their belts until the blades gleamed. Then, to the sound of a cannon shot, they would step forth and deliver to me their blade tips along with their sultry smiles. I would rise from earth to the cheer of a massive crowd.

I returned to the emergency ward and dozed off on a stool. At eight o'clock in the morning, Old Yao's wife woke me up. I was still feeling sleepy and home was too far away, so I rode my bike to the school, hoping to take a nap in the laboratory.

The wide street was confused with traffic, with everyone looking for ways to push ahead. I thought about how thirty-three years ago, when I left my father's body behind, I was also in the middle of crowded rushing traffic. That time, I charged ahead with everything I had. I took first place among my billion compatriots and grew from a microorganism into a hulk. Trying to get ahead on that wide street was like trying to grow another few hundred million times bigger, into a more macroscopic world. But did it even make sense to compare the race of life to the pursuit of fame and fortune? The truth was, my desire to go on the straight and narrow path was nothing more than the desire to die with a cotton ball stuffed up my innards.

I didn't need to be doing what I was doing. I didn't really even need that cotton ball. Even if I did, I could always stick it up there myself before my last breath and quietly die thereafter. Isn't there pleasure from just doing things for yourself: when I lay down on Xu You's stinky bed, I thought: if I really wanted to think this through, I would need a lot of time. I didn't have the time yet, but perhaps I would when I got old. In any case, I had to do it before I died.

YEARS AS
WATER FLOW

1

1952, born.

1966–1968, Cultural Revolution. High school student living at
the mining school, witness to Mr. He's suicidal plunge and
Mr. Li's blood-swollen turtlehead.

1968, played with explosives with Xu You in a basement, had
an accident, extremely unfortunate. First disciplined, then
arrested, took many beatings.

1969–1972, regained freedom. Stationed at a commune in
Yunnan. Met Chen Qingyang.

1972–1977, stationed at a commune on the outskirts of Beijing.
Entered relationship with Little Bicycle Bell. Met mentor
Mr. Liu; the Old Mr. Liu passed. Transferred back to the
city and worked as street mechanic.

1977–1981, attended college.

1981–1984, graduated, after thirty, a man. Married Erniuzi.
1985–1990, reacquainted with Line, shocked to learn she
    married Mr. Li. Earned degree overseas. Father passed.
    Got divorced. Returned to China.
1990, 40 years old.

Years as water flow, I have reached my doubtless forties. I am divorced, living with my mother. Bell visits occasionally, but sometimes after a fight she disappears for weeks. I am basically single.

I live in my father's house, but he is no longer with us. I was finally transferred to the mining school and took a teaching position in father's former department. Living across from us is my big boss, Mr. Li. Mr. Li's wife is an old classmate of mine. Back in the day, she was called Line. Line was wild during the Cultural Revolution years. She began hanging out with boys at a young age. I shouldn't really talk about her like that, but I don't think Line would find it surprising. After all, I was the boy she played with. You could even say we were old lovers.

As for Mr. Li, he wouldn't mind either because he doesn't care about such old things. Besides, we're old friends. When he returned from overseas, the first name he could think of was mine. He isn't a sociable man; other than his wife, I am the only person he talks to. I don't know what his situation was like overseas, but here in China, if he wanted to talk to someone about something, it would be either to Line or Wang Er. That really isn't very many people. In his own words, other people just aren't in his stars. I consider Mr. Li a friend as well and I never hesitate to offend a friend. Real friends don't get offended—if you get offended, you're not a real friend, that's always been my rule. You can probably guess why I have so few friends.

Even the few friends I do have aren't around anymore. Xu You got a job in the Middle East building expressways. Chen Qingyang is nowhere to be seen. Bell says I'm still in love with Line, and that it's like a toad yearning for a swan—she can be a real gourdful of vinegar sometimes. I am in love with Mr. Li's wife. Mr. Li has no idea, he thinks fate has brought us together. And that we should be friends.

According to Mr. Li, our stars crossed one winter morning twenty-three years ago. I was a seventeen-year-old high school student, as tall as I am now but much skinnier, like a bamboo pole. On my head was a dog-fur hat; over my blue uniform was a thick winter coat; on my feet were a pair of bulky leather boots; that was just the way we dressed back then. My clothes were dirty, which was also normal. The hat was given to me by a friend, who had probably gotten it by some crooked means, stolen or snatched, which would have been the way of the time. Back then, other than the few flimsy sensitive types, all the high school students did their fair share of petty crimes. Stealing a hat would have been nothing out of the ordinary. That was how I was dressed as I approached the big plaza in the mining school to check out the new big-character posters.* By '67, big-character posters weren't shocking anymore, but there was still plenty to gawk at: during his student years in Japan, a certain gentleman hired a prostitute but refused to pay; during the era known as the Three Years of Difficulties,† a certain professor who had been sent to the mines stole a steamed bun from the guesthouse and hid it in his jacket; a certain party secretary embezzled money and made himself a silver cigarette box, and etc., were among the more interesting posts. Reading big-character posters was addictive. Before long, I felt like a villain myself. If we were to have another "cultural revolution," I definitely would not read big-character posters again. But back then, I had a habit of trying to read every big-character poster on campus. The mining school was huge, with countless posters, it was impossible to read

---

*These were usually handmade, handwritten posters in Chinese characters plastered on walls and used to protest, or for propaganda or denunciations.
†Known in the West as China's Great Famine (1950–1961), millions died of starvation.

them all. Sometimes, I just read the headlines, other times I skimmed for the basic gist. Occasionally, I found something interesting and read it carefully. Even so, I had to maximize each day. I woke up early in the morning to get a head start. By the time I got to the plaza, it had already been sectioned off into pavilions, forming a maze of big-character posters. I was early, and wandered through the empty maze all by myself. It wasn't until after I had circled the plaza several times that I saw another person. This person was lying on the ground like a dead fish. It was Mr. Li.

Turning back the calendar twenty-three years, Mr. Li had just come back from Hong Kong. The winter clothes he wore must have been a temporary solution. His blue hooded coat was what Beijingers called a "cotton monkey." It was old and tiny, someone must have given it to him. Mr. Li was of a small stature but the cotton monkey was too small even for him. It was probably some child's hand-me-down. Under his cotton monkey was a pair of tweed pants, something he had brought back from overseas. Below his tweed pants was a pair of oversize cotton shoes with plastic soles, which he had gotten in Beijing. He had stubbly facial hair and a pair of spectacles that looked like the bottoms of glass bottles. That was how he looked when I saw him collapsed on the ground. He was squinting but only the whites of his eyes showed. I shuddered as I was reminded of Mr. He crashing to the pavement after he had jumped off a building only a few days prior. But upon closer inspection, this situation was different. Mr. He's brain had splattered across the pavement whereas Mr. Li's brain was still inside his skull. That was the most obvious difference. When Mr. He jumped off the building, I wasn't actually there, but I rushed there as soon as I heard about it. Even though I got there immediately, I still missed out on a lot of the action. Apparently, when Mr. He first landed, he rolled around on the ground. I didn't get to see any of that. Also, Mr. He's hands clenched a few times, but I didn't see that part either. Sadly, I had missed most of what happened prior to the moment of Mr. He's death, I only got to see his very last couple of twitches. So when I saw Mr. Li on the ground, I was thrilled, even though I couldn't be sure if he was dead.

Had I known that Mr. Li wasn't dead but had merely fainted, I definitely would have offered him a helping hand. Even though I was thin, young people before the Cultural Revolution paid attention during physical education class and had formidable strength. Mr. Li wasn't heavy; I could have carried him easily. But at the time, I thought that he was probably beyond saving. Had I been right, the thing to do would have been to preserve the scene of death until the police arrived. But since I wasn't sure if he was dead, there was also a third possibility: I could have gone to call some people over to check if he was dead or alive. That was my least favorite option. Suppose Mr. Li was dead, and I had left only to have someone else find him, how could I then claim to have been the first to have found him? No one would have believed me and it would have been worse if they did. They would have said Wang Er was afraid of a dead body and had run away. Now, in my doubtless years, I was no longer afraid of being called a coward. After decades spent in communes and factories, I had already made my reputation as the cavalier type, ruthless, fearless, reckless, especially when it came to sex, etc. Even if someone were to call Wang Er a coward once in a while, I wouldn't think much of it. But back then, it was the one thing I feared the most. That was why I decided to go with a fourth option. I decided to stand by and observe if Mr. Li was twitching harder and harder or if he was coming to a rigid stop. Had it been the latter, I would have called for help. Had it been the former, I would have picked him up and carried him. But who could have guessed that he would just open his eyes and sit up. What a disappointment! I turned and was about to leave.

From Mr. Li's perspective, the morning's events proved much less uneventful than for me. He had just returned from Hong Kong to participate in the Great Proletarian Cultural Revolution (which he later said was the biggest mistake of his life). He had just arrived at the mining school the previous night and that very morning, he was out there putting up his big-character poster. Somehow, he found himself in a heated argument with some guy and received a painful kick that left him writhing on the ground. After regaining consciousness, he was shocked. He wasn't lying in a hospital bed and there was no crowd around him. The person who kicked him was nowhere to be seen. There was only a kid, a stake and a half tall, standing by, watching him. The kid looked like he was getting ready to leave, so he quickly called me over to give him a hand. Mr. Li said he was in so much pain that he couldn't stand up without help. I shook my head and reluctantly walked over, which left him feeling insecure. When I got close enough to him, he wrapped his arm around my neck and held on tightly, afraid that I would run off. By the time we got to the hospital, my neck was purple and green. Of course I wasn't going to help him get back to the school. I left as soon as I could, which was unfortunate for Mr. Li because he didn't know his way around and wasted a lot of time trying to get back.

With regard to the situation, I feel the need to provide a few more hypotheses. I didn't know Mr. Li at the time and was unaware of his affiliation with the mining school. Had I known, my rescue would definitely have been more proactive. I was also unaware of the fact that he had been a victim of assault. I thought he was having a seizure. Had I known, my rescue would also have been more proactive. With those two caveats in mind, I admit that I was overly interested in dead people at the time, and not so much in the living. Mr. Li thought that my feelings back then were understandable. What he couldn't understand was why that kick to the groin had to be so merciless. Had it been just a little bit harder, he could have become the sort of person that I was interested in.

The story of Mr. Li getting kicked went like this: back in '67 everyone wanted to write word posters. They wanted their posters to be read and discussed by a head-bobbing crowd for the same reason that I want my books to be published now. The most infuriating thing at the time was to have your big-character poster that you spent all night writing get covered up right away by someone else's big-character poster. That was why the posters often read: SAVE FOR FIVE DAYS, or SAVE FOR TEN DAYS; but of course, no one ever saved your poster. Back then, fights and arguments over poster space were too numerous to count. Mr. Li's poster went right over a poster that a bunch of hooligans from the driver's office had just painstakingly put up. They had caught him in the act. He tried to calmly reason with the young men, but there wasn't really anything to reason about. That was why they ended up kicking him down there, but even they didn't expect for the kick to land so firmly. Everyone knew what the driver boys were like, except Mr. Li. That was why he wasn't at all prepared for the kick. After the kick came trouble. Blood drained from Mr. Li's face and his eyes rolled back into his skull. His limp body fell into his attacker's arms. The gang was afraid of ending up with death sentences, so they left him on the ground and fled. Who knew if he could have been saved? And what if they had gotten him to the hospital but he couldn't be saved?

Nowadays, everyone at the school calls Mr. Li "Blood-swollen Turtlehead" behind his back. This is true even of unmarried young women. They would say, Mr. Li was originally Japanese, surname Turtlehead, given name, Blood-swollen. That's incorrect. Mr. Li has never been to Japan in his life. The reason he ended up with the nickname was because after being kicked, he furiously copied out his hospital diagnosis and posted it up in a quest for justice. A part of his diagnosis read, "damaged scrotum, blood-swollen turtlehead." The justice he received was the nickname Blood-swollen Turtlehead. After twenty-three years, he is still the blood-swollen one.

2

MORE THAN A DECADE LATER, I was studying abroad at the school where Mr. Li had gotten his PhD. After graduating, Mr. Li taught there for two years, so there were still quite a few people who knew him. People at that school described him in the following ways: fiery temperament, stubborn to a fault, and overflowing with talent. When I heard this, I thought that maybe something was wrong with my English: Mr. Li with a fiery temperament? He was the least temperamental person I knew!

But I could attest to Mr. Li's overflowing talent, especially after his turtlehead had become blood swollen. He was prolific in writing big-character posters that discussed the problem of blood-swollen turtleheads. The first entry began like this: a certain Li was met with misfortune in the hands of underhanded scoundrels, a full hospital report was released to the public via big-character posters. But instead of receiving compassion from the gentle people of the mining school, he was met with public ridicule; as an anonymous peer, I must bring up the topic of blood-swollen turtlehead once more for all the good people to reconsider.

The context for posting such a big-character poster was this: he turned his hospital report into a drawing and posted it for all to see. The poster received harsh criticisms such as: what kind of a big-character poster is this, disgusting! Obscene! But as for the kick he received, no one seemed to give a damn. That was why Mr. Li felt the need to emphasize: this certain Li's turtlehead was not born blood swollen but had become so after being kicked.

Mr. Li wrote in his big-character poster, he wasn't looking to get even, he wasn't even looking for an apology. All he wanted to say was that blood-swollen turtleheads were not good, that they hurt. Blood-swollen turtleheads needed to be condemned so as to avoid the blood-swelling of further turtleheads in the future. His posts were regarded as being somewhat screwy. By this point, he had been back in the Mainland for some time and people began to recognize his face. The head chef in the canteen urged him: Young Li, forget about it. Look at where you were kicked, you shouldn't draw attention to that. But Mr. Li was stubborn, he raised his voice and argued: chef, it isn't like that. They kicked me *there*. It wasn't as if I pulled out my turtlehead and offered it to be kicked! If there is no consequence to kicking someone down there, then everyone will kick down there!

Even though no one agreed with Mr. Li's point of view, his big-character posters were still widely read. He wrote one entry about the problem of blood-swollen turtleheads, then another, then another. In his third entry, he explored the following question:

In our recent discussions about blood-swollen turtleheads, many have failed to understand the seriousness of the issue. Instead of taking the matter seriously, they offer only derisive laughter. Let it be known that all men have a turtlehead, this is an indisputable fact. When a turtlehead is kicked, it can become blood swollen, which is very painful, also an indisputable fact. When it comes to indisputable facts, what is there to laugh about? Being the indisputable fact that it is, how can you not take it seriously? The only effect his line of reasoning had was to give everyone a bellyache from laughing too hard. In my view, the nickname Blood-swollen Turtlehead was something Mr. Li worked hard to earn for himself.

Mr. Li kept on arguing until someone finally wrote a big-character poster in response. It was entitled: "Blood-swollen Turtlehead can take a break." Its premise was: a blood-swollen turtlehead is a small matter, not worthy of so much discussion. In the Great Proletarian Cultural Revolution, big reasons trump small reasons, and big problems trump small problems. A tiny little turtlehead, whether it is blood swollen or not, is irrelevant. It should not distract from the direction of the overall political movement. Even if there were a hundred blood-swollen turtleheads, it would still not rise to the level of importance of the central mission of "expose and criticize." When this big-character poster came out, it was met with immediate controversy. People thought that its author was the kind of person who had nothing better to do. If said person understood that "exposing and criticizing" was important, then why didn't the person write something to "expose and criticize"? Why did they instead choose to talk about a blood-swollen turtlehead? According to one critic, Mr. Li's posts were irrelevant, but then why pay attention to them? A big-character poster response to an irrelevant big-character poster was irrelevant itself. Mr. Li felt the need to offer a serious rebuttal. He noted that big reasons trumping small reasons was in itself an unreasonable statement. Big problems trumping small problems could only lead to a mixing up of priorities. Even if "exposing and criticizing" were more important, it didn't mean that people deserved to live with blood-swollen turtleheads. Focusing only on the size of the problems rather than on their consequences was wrong. He was pleased with his own arguments but he failed to recognize where the theory of big vs. small problems came from. Soon, some people arrived at his home to teach him a lesson. But because he was a leftist who had recently returned from overseas, he was only given a warning on account of his ignorance. Had that not been the case, the consequences of questioning party doctrine would have been much more painful than a blood-swollen turtlehead. Even Mr. Li appreciated the gravity of the situation and contained himself. The matter of the blood-swollen turtlehead was temporarily laid to rest.

Years as water flow, in the blink of an eye, I have reached my doubtless years. Many things have changed. Today, Driver Feng would never dare to aim his flying kick at Mr. Li's groin. But back then, he even had the guts to bully us. The campus kids took quite a bit of abuse from him. Once we had a scheme to swarm him when he was walking alone. Our plan was to shower him with ten pounds of coal briquettes before attacking with our hands and feet. We heard that he knew kung fu. We wanted to know how much kung fu he would have left after a coal storm. In order to teach Feng a lesson, we formed a "chicken-slayer" war party, I was the captain. On three separate occasions, the boys and I hid in a dark alley waiting to ambush him, all to no avail. Driver Feng was a scout in the military and was extremely alert. When he saw shadows shifting in the alley, he went around. On our fourth attempt, we used a slingshot and broke several of his windows. In the pitch-black of night, he didn't come out to chase us. After that, the driver's gang no longer beat up campus kids.

As for the matter of the blood-swollen turtlehead, we the campus kids reached our own conclusion. We concluded that Mr. Li's approach was all wrong. As far as we could see, there were two types of people in this world, people with blood-swollen turtleheads and people without blood-swollen turtleheads. It was impossible for people without blood-swollen turtleheads to understand what it was like to be someone with a blood-swollen turtlehead. The only way someone could understand was if you kicked him in the groin and made his turtlehead blood swollen as well.

In regard to Mr. Li's blood-swollen turtlehead, I have the following to add: in those days, Beijing was shrouded in a dark cloud like a mouthful of sticky condensed phlegm that never went away. Many people died at the mining school. In addition to Mr. He who jumped off a building, there were people who hung themselves, who took poison, and even ones who stabbed themselves with scissors, leaving a grotesque mess. Mr. Li's situation was at best laughable. It could hardly have been considered a big deal.

3

THE YEARS FLOW LIKE WATER; some stories pass by quickly while others linger on. In addition to the matter of Mr. Li's blood-swollen turtlehead, there was the matter of Mr. He jumping from a building. Of course, Mr. He was Mr. He; he had nothing to do with me, but his death is still etched deep inside my consciousness. I have to think it through before I can sort my own life out.

Before jumping to his death, Mr. He was being held in a lab building. According to father, Mr. He wasn't particularly old, but he had academic seniority over even my father's teachers. Before the Cultural Revolution, he wasn't officially retired but he no longer ran things. In his own words, "I've done all I set out to do in this lifetime; all that's left is to live a few more years." Father also said that even though Mr. He was an elder, he didn't seem old because his mind was still sharp. Whenever you asked him something, he would always have a complete reply. When he had said what he needed to say, he stopped and there were no extraneous words. Based on that, my father predicted that he would live even longer than the people who were in their fifties at the time. Mr. He was arrested because he had been a very high-ranking official once upon a time. So he jumped off the fifth floor.

When Mr. He was getting ready to jump from the building, Xu You happened to have been passing by. Mr. He even spoke to Xu You, which meant he didn't jump right away. Later, I questioned Xu You dozens of times, asking him what Mr. He had said and how he had said it. All that dummy could remember was Mr. He saying, "Kid, move!"

"And then?"

"And then splat, like a watermelon!"

I pressed and pressed but all I got was *kid, move* and *watermelon*. I wanted to punch Xu.

When I was young, I often thought about death. Mr. He was the first dead person I had seen. I wanted to learn what death was like from him in the same way that I would later want to learn what women were like from Chen Qingyang. Sadly, both of these specimens were poor choices. Take Mr. He for example, I never got a chance to speak to him when he was alive. That dumbass Xu was so shaken up by the event that he forgot everything. How can anyone possibly believe that someone who was about to kill himself would leave the world with the last words, "Kid, move"?

I saw everything, after it happened. When his head hit the pavement, brain matter splattered everywhere. Using his point of contact as the center, there were bits and pieces of a fresh pork lung-like substance spread throughout a five-meters' radius. In addition to the ground, there were also bits that splashed onto the first-floor walls and windows. With such a dramatic death, I refused to believe that aside from "Kid, move," he said nothing.

For a long time after Mr. He's death, dark stains remained on the ground around where he had landed. The human brain contains large amounts of oil. Mr. He was known to calculate and predict just about everything (playing chess against him gave me a taste of that), he must have known this would happen. A person who chose to have his organ of thought become one with the dust under other people's shoes must have possessed a spirit that was beyond my ken.

Even though Mr. He died without ever having his name exonerated, my respect for him remains undiminished. In fact, my love and admiration for him know no bounds. No matter what other people say about him (reactionary academicism, KMT* bureaucratic tendencies, etc.), my respect remains unwavering. In my heart, he will always be that great man who created a great spectacle around which the countless masses circled and stared.

---

*Kuomintang, Chinese nationalist opposition party in Mainland China (1927–1949).

4

EARLIER, I WROTE THAT MR. LI once said, returning to participate in the Cultural Revolution by way of Hong Kong was a mistake. That wasn't to say that he realized it was mistake after his turtlehead became blood swollen. At least he didn't say anything so counterrevolutionary to me. What he said was, he shouldn't have stopped in Hong Kong. In Hong Kong, he met a group of Trotskyites. He mingled with them and later kept in touch via mail. During one of the purges, he was exposed and criticized for this mistake.

After Mr. Li's true face of Trotskyism had been exposed, Line and I saw him get beaten up in a small auditorium. A bunch of people shaved his head and held a contest to see who could make the best bumps on his noggin. In the heat of competition, they snickered that Mr. Li was literally becoming a "blood-swollen turtlehead." That was when Line fell in love with him. Twenty-three years ago, Line was only a yellow-haired girl-child; even her eyelashes were still yellow. She was as thin as a wafer with a waist small enough to hold in one hand. Her two itty-bitty breasts were like flower buds that only appeared seasonally. Decades later, she basically still looks like that, except with a patina of weariness. She was the ballsiest woman I had ever met. Even so, I never imagined that she would actually marry Blood-swollen Turtlehead.

It would be appropriate now to describe the scene of Mr. Li's beating. The small auditorium could fit about four to five hundred people. It was filled with benches made from wooden planks nailed together. There were a few dozen of us onlookers who were lying on the benches, watching Mr. Li and the contestants on stage. Someone turned on a spotlight to set the mood. Once shaven, Mr. Li's skull revealed its awkward shape: it was pointy at the top and under his occipital bone in the back of his head, there was a deep long ridge. Heads like these were difficult to shave even for professional barbers. No one present was an experienced barber so they could only try their best, leaving patches of greasy black stubs here and there. Once, in the countryside, a bunch of intellectual youths and I had slaughtered a pig and ended up with similar results. By the time Line and I showed up, there were already a couple of bumps on his head, some green, some purple, and some that had popped, oozing blood. Even so, the contest continued because they weren't competing to see who could make the biggest bump, but rather who could make the roundest. Some of the bumps were shaped like branches while others were more like amoebas. The best bumps were close to oval in shape, which meant they were still far from perfection. Mr. Li stretched out his neck, furrowed his brows and wore an expression halfway between crying and laughing. He closed his eyes like an old monk entering a trance. Several people tried their hands, but he showed no reaction. It wasn't until Driver Feng, the one who had given him the blood-swollen turtlehead, showed up that he finally opened his eyes. Driver Feng curled up his right index finger and began to hammer away at Mr. Li's bald head. *Pop, pop, pop*, bright and round bumps rose to the popping sound. Mr. Li couldn't help but be impressed: that's some kung fu!

Line later told me: that time we saw Mr. Li getting beaten on stage, the helpless expression on his face was just adorable! I wasn't all that surprised. The way Mr. Li looked wasn't unlike E.T. If people thought E.T. was adorable, then it should come as no surprise that some people would find Blood-swollen Turtlehead adorable as well. Line said she felt something digging into her heart that nearly drove her mad. She wanted to leap onto the stage, hold him in her arms and smooth out all his bumps with her delicate fingers. That didn't surprise me either, she was always acting crazy. The only thing that came as a surprise was the fact that she actually married Blood-swollen Turtlehead.

I once loved Mr. Li too. A man who could get bopped on the head and still keep a poker face was a hero in my book. And before that incident, in spite of all the criticisms, he fought passionately to raise awareness about the plight of his turtlehead. Even though his reasoning was a bit abstruse, it didn't take away from the fact that he was a fighter. So when he was locked up in a little dark room, I walked over roofs and walls to deliver steamed buns to him. Line said, we need to support Mr. Li. I didn't disagree. She wrote him a bunch of notes, all of which I delivered. She wrote: *Blood-swollen Turtlehead, hang in there! I love you!* I figured, brother, you sure had it rough, nothing wrong with letting my woman show you a little love. Who would have known that what began as child's play would turn into reality, that Line would actually become Mrs. Turtlehead!

5

THAT YEAR, AFTER MR. HE JUMPED off the building, he twitched a few times and stopped moving. Not long after, the police arrived to conduct an autopsy. They first stripped Mr. He of all his clothes. I stood at the front of the crowd and rooted myself to the ground as if my shoes were cleats. That was how I got to see the whole autopsy process. By the time they finished examining the body, Mr. He had gone hard so they couldn't put his clothes back on. The comrades from the police station wrapped Mr. He's pants around his butt, covered him with his jacket and carried him onto a car to be hauled off. They didn't find anything interesting from the autopsy aside from a purple mark on his butt cheek. A young police officer muttered: dead man! At the time I thought he was being banal. The "man" was clearly "dead," do you not see his brain matter everywhere? But quickly, I realized that the policeman might have been speaking in jargon. When I got home and flipped through an encyclopedia, I found it was indeed the case. The young police officer had no evidence to suggest foul play, but in front of the crowd who all noticed the black and purple blotch on the butt cheek, he felt the need to say something. In the end, the cause of death was of course, suicide. Indeed, a blow to the butt was neither life-threatening nor even likely to cause injury; it is a rather humane form of violence. Later, when Old Mr. Liu, who had been locked up together with Mr. He, was freed, people asked him who it was that hit Mr. He. Old Mr. Liu wasn't clear on the details because remembering might have gotten someone somewhere another beating. The only person he singled out was Feng the driver. He didn't even say that Feng was violent, only that he wore a pair of black gloves, wielded a rubber tube, and touched his victims as he abused them, which made everyone a bit squeamish.

Later, the victim's family wanted to sue Driver Feng, but by then Old Mr. Liu had already died of a stroke and was no longer available to testify. That's the ins and outs of Mr. He's death. My only conclusion is that there is no need to be too hard on Driver Feng. No matter what, he wasn't some evil villain. Feng was a Red Guard for a while and did some nasty stuff, but not even that much. Back when there were Nazis, they committed genocide on the Jews. In comparison, Driver Feng, who was only kicking his victims on the butt, was pretty gentle. He wasn't the problem. And most of the people in the He family weren't the problem either. Mr. He's mother was seventy years old with tiny bound feet. She wanted to take Feng to court because she lacked imagination. Mr. He's older brother was over fifty years old, so you can't blame him for lacking imagination too. But the young prince of the He clan, called He Qi, was about the same age as me. Once upon a time, he had quite a reputation on campus, a real champ. What the hell had happened to him?

6

WHEN WE WERE SENT DOWN to the countryside, Line didn't go with me to the commune in Yunnan. Instead, she went with her parents to labor at a cadre school, because that was where Mr. Li went. Of course, their situations were entirely different. Line was a child, a dependent, she did what she liked and it was mostly a breeze. Mr. Li, on the other hand, was a Trotskyite, he was forced to do everything. After a while, they stopped calling him Trotskyite, but the factory workers who ran the cadre school couldn't stand Blood-swollen Turtlehead, so they made him suffer in many ways. In the parlance of the village folks back then, there were the "four back-breakers": digging wells, making bricks, harvesting wheat, and fucking pussies.

With the exception of the last activity, Mr. Li did them all. He also carried piss and shit, leveled fields, made roof tiles, did woodwork and more; dredged the river in the early spring and watched over things turning green in midsummer. Sometimes, he was the night watchman. If anything got stolen, the old village farmers gave him hell. It was a good thing he grew up eating beef, which gave him a robust constitution. Plus, he was rather on the young side, not even thirty years old; had that not been the case, Line would have been way out of his league.

When people in our department talk about Mr. Li, they always mention how impressed they were with his performance at the cadre school. They thought that for an intellectual who grew up overseas to take on so much responsibility was really quite extraordinary. He never complained about the forced labor or the criticisms that he took. After everything was over, he had nothing bad to say about the nation or the Party. He was a good comrade and had the potential to be brought into the Party. But Mr. Li said, as he was still carrying the ugly name of Blood-swollen Turtlehead with him wherever he went, and as he didn't want to sully the Party's good name, it should perhaps wait.

Line said, Mr. Li's behavior was fascinating. He did everything he was told and always had that same silly grin on his face that he had when he was getting bopped on the head. She thought Blood-swollen Turtlehead, the big E.T., was a real hoot. Had there not been so many eyes and ears at the cadre school, she would have done it with him long ago.

Later, Mr. Li said to me personally: my brother, we went to the same school, worked in the same field, are colleagues in the same department, and back in the day, you brought me steamed buns— what an extraordinary bond. What I mean is, I would like to speak honestly with you. During my time at the cadre school, I got hung up the way young people sometimes do, and thought that I had fallen under some sort of a curse. For someone who studies the scientific method like me to harbor such a notion is hard to believe, I know. But considering everything I have seen in the Mainland, the blood-swollen thing, the Trotskyite thing, the headful of bumps thing, superstition no longer seems so far-fetched. And strangest of all: every day after work, there is always a note on my bed. So I wanted to believe that I had deeply offended someone somewhere and was paying the price. The number one suspect was my Indian roommate in college. On one occasion, when I was annoyed with him burning his incense in the room, I went into the toilet to create a disturbance. I flushed the toilet eight times in a row. That must have offended him so he put me into a nightmare, one that I couldn't wake up from for three years. Faced with such supernatural forces, I knew I had to behave lest I end up with a fate even more gruesome. That was the story of Mr. Li at the cadre school.

While Mr. Li labored at the cadre school, I was stationed at a commune in Yunnan where I met Chen Qingyang, so I didn't think much about Line anymore. But once in a while, I thought about Mr. He. I figured out why he wanted to tell a kid to move right before his death. It was because when he died, he didn't want anyone to see him.

Before the Cultural Revolution, the mining school had a club that would light up with games of poker and chess on every summer night, from eight to eleven. The room had a ceiling fan and a sofa with a floral trim. It was both cool and spacious. Every night, our department went there to play chess. One time, someone told Mr. He that Wang Er's game was terrific. At the time, Mr. He had a head of slick black hair (dyed), polished nails, a deep voice, and was generally winsome. He played a good game of chess but he couldn't beat me. Still, he played with me often and never got embarrassed when he lost.

When Mr. He died, a section of his hair was black and a section of it was white, a very unattractive look. His hands lay at his sides and his neck caved in at an unnatural angle. Basically, he died like a gopher. Mr. He must have predicted that he would look hideous after his death; that was why he didn't want to let anyone see him.

After Mr. He's body was taken away, pieces of his brain remained. The police said to the mining school folks, you guys figure out what to do with the rest. The mining school folks thought about it and said: let the family of the deceased decide what to do, leave a few people here to guard the remains, the rest can clear out. When it was dusk and still no family members appeared, the guards grew angry and grumbled: their own loss, we're out of here, leave this crap for the crows. As the day's last remaining light faded, the wind picked up. It was cold.

When I was in Yunnan, I thought about another thing related to Mr. He. When they were doing the autopsy, Mr. He's big gun was thick and long, and categorically erect. Thinking about it before sex can quell all desire and make you not want to do it anymore.

7

DURING MY TIME IN AMERICA, I often ran into Mr. Li's Indian roommate. He was the dean of my department, as well as my thesis adviser. Strictly speaking, he was my *shifu,** and by extension, Mr. Li was my *shifu-uncle*, and Line would have to be my *shifu-aunt-in-law*. When Mr. Li and I addressed each other as brothers, we had already mixed up our relative seniority; and not to mention the fact that I would say things to him like: Line should have been my wife. Good thing they don't care about seniority in America. I have long forgotten the name of my thesis adviser, not that I ever remembered it to begin with. His name was extremely difficult to pronounce. The first time I went to see him, I stared at the nameplate outside his office for a long time before entering. I said: teacher, I've learned to spell your name, can you teach me how to pronounce it? Every time I saw him, I asked him to teach me how to say his name, but I still don't know how to say it. Good thing

---

*Shifu means "mentor" or "master."

I never acknowledged him as my *shifu*, this way Line wouldn't have to be my *shifu-aunt*.

I never acknowledged this Indian *shifu* because he was far too strange. When he talked to you, he often zoned out and you couldn't ever get his attention back. He talked science during class, but as soon as class ended, he got together with a bunch of Americans to read sutras. He even let people rub his head because the Dalai Lama had once rubbed it. Even with all that nonsense, the school still treated him like a treasure. That was because the man had published a well-known book. In my view, the more he published, the more suspicious he seemed. For Mr. Li to suspect that his blood-swollen turtlehead had something to do with his Indian roommate wasn't at all unreasonable.

Mr. Li said to me, of all the ordeals he faced in the Mainland, the thing that bothered him the most was when he got beaten up by an old farmer at the cadre school. At the time, they had put him on night watch. They specifically told him that old farmers like to steal human manure. If he saw one, it was imperative to snag the thief so as to uncover who was freeloading on other people's squats. Mr. Li was determined to execute his orders, but ended up getting whacked by a bamboo pole so hard that he was almost paralyzed. In retrospect, it all seemed extremely uncanny. How did a *doctor* end up fighting old farmers over some stuff? And somehow that stuff had to be shit, *shit!* He had returned to the Mainland to protect the East, to protect the West, and finally to protect shit. "If this isn't a nightmare, then I must be the reincarnation of a dung beetle!"

8

AFTER I LEFT YUNNAN AND joined a commune on the outskirts of Beijing, Mr. He was still on my mind. Not long after his death, a bunch of us kids convened on top of a coal pile behind the canteen to discuss Mr. He's erection. Some were of the opinion that Mr. He became erect before he jumped. Some were of the opinion that he became erect midair. Others believed that he had become erect as a result of his head hitting the ground. I was of the second opinion.

I imagined that while in midair, Mr. He must have felt like a bomb that had been dropped out of an airplane. The wind must have hissed in his ears as the ground drew nearer. He must have palpitated, the "bang" of his collision would have already resonated in his heart. Since Mr. He wanted to die, he must have foreseen all of it. He must have known the gravity of death. He must have anticipated the thrill of nevermore.

When I was stationed in the outskirts of Beijing, my family returned home from the cadre school one time. Old Mr. Liu, who was locked up in the same room as Mr. He, also returned from the cadre school, and lived next door to us. I asked Old Mr. Liu if Mr. He had had any last words. Old Mr. Liu said, I wasn't in the room before Mr. He died, I was in the bathroom. If I had been there, wouldn't I have stopped him? And obviously, after Mr. He jumped and his brain fell out, he couldn't have left any last words. Therefore, on the matter of what Mr. He was thinking before his death, there were no clues and therefore no way of knowing for sure why he tumesced.

On the night of Mr. He's death, at around two in the morning, I got out of bed and went to the place where Mr. He had died. I knew our campus was crawling with feral cats, they were always moaning through the summer nights; and there were crows on top of the old pine trees that were always squawking in the dusk; so I figured, there must have been animals partaking of Mr. He's brain. The more I thought about it, the harder it was to fall asleep. Not being able to sleep led to masturbation, and masturbation wasn't good for my health. That was why I went outside. I turned a corner and arrived at the spot only to confront a sight that scared the hell out of me. Like tiny stars on the ground, there were dozens of candles lit. By the light of their wavering flames, I could see a few dozen circles drawn in chalk. Inside the circles were pieces of brain matter that wriggled as if trying to escape. Beyond the candlelight squatted a large shadow. The whole scene looked like some sort of necromancy to bring Mr. He back from the dead. Later in my life people would say that Wang Er was a brave man, but that was all later, after my twenties and thirties. At age seventeen, my balls had not yet hardened; in that moment, I was ready to bolt.

The reason I didn't run away was because I heard someone say: little classmate, do you need to walk across? Come. Be careful not to step on anything. Upon closer inspection, the candle flames wavered because there was a breeze; the reason why the man's shadow was so large was because the candles lit him from below. The chalk circles were left there by the police during the day and

Mr. He's brain matter wasn't actually moving. I was finally able to gather the courage to slowly cross. The man across from me was in his forties, he was Mr. He's oldest son. He didn't live on campus so I wasn't familiar with his face, but I knew who he was. He wore a thick coat. By his feet was a briefcase that was unzipped. Inside the briefcase were candles. I asked him: why didn't I see you during the day? He silently reached for his cigarettes. His hands trembled so much that he couldn't light a match. I took the matches from him and lit his smoke. Then, I squatted next to him and said: I used to play chess with Mr. He. A moment later, I added: they already did an autopsy. He broke his silence: little classmate, you have no idea. There was no autopsy. There was never an autopsy. He clenched up as he spoke. Finally, he said: little classmate, you should go.

I walked home slowly. It was a moonless night, but there was light from the stars. For someone who was accustomed to night walks during those years, it was bright enough. I wondered, what was Mr. He's family planning to do? Mr. He was already dead, there was no coming back. When I thought about his family, I felt sad.

In the freezing wind, Mr. He's children kept vigil around his brain matter. No one bothered them. The pieces of brain gradually dried up. By the time they tried to scoop them up, much of it had already been infused into the pavement. In the end, a large portion of Mr. He's brain became a permanent part of the sidewalk. Old Mr. Liu, who told me about Mr. He's dying words, has also passed. When Old Mr. Liu was alive, I didn't have a good impression of him. He had a habit of taking back moves on the chessboard, especially when he knew he would lose, but refused to give in. I don't like to speak ill of the dead but if I say nothing, how will anyone ever know? His mouth stank. No one could stand talking to him face to face.

As for the matter of Mr. He's erection, I have one more thing to add. No matter at what stage of his fall Mr. He had gotten his erection, it all proved the same thing: in Mr. He's body, there was still plenty of life force left. That was all that it could prove.

9

THE YEARS FLOW LIKE WATER, in the blink of an eye, I have reached my doubtless years. Just like everyone else, I have grown accustomed to the world around me. Things that happened happened, things that have yet to happen no longer surprise me. Only Mr. Li's blood-swollen turtlehead and the matter of Mr. He remain on my mind.

That winter, Beijing didn't get one nice day, you just couldn't see the sun. At the time, the mining school had a one-square-kilometer campus, of which two-thirds were covered in pine trees. It was crowded (revolutionary classrooms, revolutionary staffers) with people pouring in from all directions to be at the mining school. After they ate their corn bread and couldn't find a bathroom, they took wild shits in the woods, leaving terrifyingly thick logs everywhere. The walls that were covered with layers upon layers of big-character posters had grown by a finger's width. Occasionally, with a loud crash, a wall would collapse. Xu You's grandmother was in her eighties when she came across a collapsing wall of big-character posters and died of fright. Back then, the campus was full of loudspeakers that blared day and night. As a consequence, many people in my generation have trouble learning English: they have become hearing impaired and can't hear the softer consonants. Back then, there were a lot of waste papers and kids collecting them. The kids rode out in homemade tricycles that made beautiful loops on the road. All sorts of crazies came out of the woodwork, and received admiration. I had just grown out of my idealistic youth. I opened my eyes wide and took in everything before me.

If I wanted to write about all that had happened, I would need a magical pen of history. I am not in possession of such a pen. That's why I can only write about my years as water flow, about the blood-swollen turtlehead and Mr. He jumping from a building. These events didn't happen to me (thank heavens), but they had a big impact on my life.

Before bringing this topic to a close, there is one more thing I want to point out. When Xu You and I experienced the bomb incident and were taken in by the police, I had a manuscript of a short story on me. It was something Chicken Head, a campus prodigy, and I had been working on together. Wang Er was credited, but he had not lifted a pen, the one who had penned it was Chicken Head. He made a big mistake, which was to use real names in a story that repeatedly mentioned several of the mining school's great vigilantes, describing our various feats of righteousness, climbing on walls, smashing windows, and the such. The worst part was he even included the scene where I broke Driver Feng's window. Later, when I ended up in Driver Feng's hands, he left my lower back permanently wounded. The moral of the story is: never use real names when writing a story, especially the names of the good guys. That is why in this book, not a single name is real. Maybe Little Bicycle Bell isn't Little Bicycle Bell but Big Bronze Bell. Maybe Wang Er isn't Wang Er but Scarface Li. Maybe the mining school isn't the mining school but the Sun Yat Sen Medical School. Maybe Line isn't Line but Scarface Bao. And maybe the place where Mr. Li was sent wasn't Anyang but some other place in China. No real names, no real places, the only things that are real are the events that I describe. From the blood-swollen turtlehead to Mr. He jumping from a building, all of it is real, why would I make this stuff up?

10

AT THE END OF '72, Mr. Li was sent to a small coal mine in Anyang, Henan province, to work as an accountant. Henan winters were full of sandstorms. Black water flowed through ditches, bordered by white ice. If you looked inside a ditch, you could find small chunks of black coal mixed in with the gray gravel. The water sprung up from underground and brought the coal up with it. After every mighty gust of wind, clouds of sand and gravel settled against windbreaks. On the surface of the piles of gravel was fine black soot. It was perfectly reasonable because when the wind blew past the coal pile by the railroad tracks, it had picked up the fine coal particles. When he walked from his dorm room to the accounting office in the morning, Mr. Li took note of the orderliness of the universe. Everything seemed too normal for a dream.

Back then, Mr. Li looked upon everything with suspicion.

When Mr. Li got to work at the accounting office, he was always wearing a floppy felt hat on his head. This type of felt hat had a brim that could fold down and cover his entire face, allowing his whole head to stay warm. It was a wonderful feeling. Mr. Li would have liked to, wanted to, and hoped to wear the felt hat from morning to night. Henan winters were freezing, and the mine was on top of a coal mountain. Despite the firewood, the buildings were so leaky and poorly constructed that the rooms were always cold. But when the leader saw him wearing a felt hat indoors, he grew angry: stop scaring me with that devilish thing all right? Then he snatched the hat off Mr. Li's head. That was suspicious.

When Mr. Li went to work, he wore a big blue coat. The coat was huge, but he had gotten it for free. Though it didn't make much sense, it was still a fortunate turn of events. The one who gave him the coat was the chief of the labor section, a man from Guangdong. Mr. Li felt an affinity for the man right away because of the three languages that Mr. Li spoke, Cantonese was second only to English. He tried to speak Cantonese to the guy but the chief said: "comalade," do not speak Cantonese to me la, or else people will think we're insulting them la. That made sense, it was the same way in America. It was rude to speak Chinese in front of the Americans. The chief from Guangdong gave him the coat and said it was a worker's entitlement. Mr. Li asked, what is a worker's entitlement. The Guangdong guy said: waka'sh entitlement meansh the country caresh about you la. He didn't fully understand, but Mr. Li didn't press on the issue. Among the worker's entitlements were other things like a rubber raincoat, a pair of gloves with rubber grips, a dust mask, and so on. Mr. Li asked innocently: I'm not going down the mine, why do I need these? Someone nearby rolled his eyes at him and said: you wanna go down the mine? Easy! Mr. Li shut up instantly. He had already spent two years at the cadre school and had learned a thing or two.

Mr. Li didn't take off his coat when he worked. The advocate stared at him with a dour face until Mr. Li started to get goose bumps. Is it that cold? Why are you hunched over like that? Are you really that cold? Confronted with such questions, Mr. Li chose to remain silent. He walked over to the window and studied the thermometer. After he had availed himself of the information, he returned to his seat. The advocate followed him to the thermometer and said: fifteen degrees Celsius, and here I thought we were in a refrigerator!

Mr. Li knew that refrigerators for storing vegetables were set at fifteen degrees, isn't that cold enough? But he kept silent. Inside of a nightmare, anything you say can and will be used against you. Had he spoken out loud, his world would have instantly transformed into a refrigerator, and he might have turned into an onion. He had learned much from his time at the cadre school. For example, if he pinched his nose in the bathroom, that afternoon, he would be shoveling shit until the smell killed him. When the advocate declared fifteen degrees to be not cold, Mr. Li was certain that if he didn't stop himself and blurted out a complaint, big trouble would necessarily have followed. Mr. Li thought to himself: "This must be my Indian roommate trying to turn me into an onion!"

By 1973, Mr. Li had already internalized the rules of his Indian roommate's games. Whatever he said, happened, just like magic. The basic rule of the game was you had to do whatever people told you to do, and you weren't allowed to refuse; however uncomfortable, you had to do it without complaining. As long as he followed these two rules, even his roommate couldn't do anything to him.

When Mr. Li worked, he wore a pair of a fur-lined boots. He was unaccustomed to the northern climate and got frostbite year after year. Back in America, it had gotten cold as well, but he had never gotten frostbite. Undoubtedly, this was one of his Indian roommate's tricks, but as far as Mr. Li was concerned, this was one of the less impressive acts. For example, the blood-swollen turtle-head was a truly hilarious prank. A headful of bumps wasn't bad either. Sometimes his roommate's imagination was impeccable, like how he was sent to Anyang, in Henan. There was definitely no such a place in China, but the name was perfect: Anyang. What a Chinese sounding name! If I were Indian, I definitely would not have been able to come up with such a name. But the frostbite wasn't a good touch; it wasn't all that realistic, and it was hard to turn into a good story to tell later. The other gags were great, full of humor; but there is no humor in frostbite, only pain.

Mr. Li wasn't entirely unshakable in his belief that the world before him was a nightmare, an illusion that the Indian created. That morning, as he walked to the accounting office, he faced strong headwinds. He could feel the texture of the sand and gravel that pounded his face. It was hard to be convinced that the Indian could have imagined all those details. As the wind coursed, the utility pole, the branches, and the grass all howled in distinctive pitches. It would be unbelievable to suggest that the Indian had created every single one of those details. Humans can only think one idea at a time. It would have been impossible to create so many sounds simultaneously. Therefore, if in fact everything was an illusion created by the Indian, he would have had to harness some sort of a natural force to conjure it. That is to say, everything he saw had an element of reality in it, in addition to an element of fiction. The difficulty was in trying to figure out what was fictional and what was real.

That morning, when Mr. Li arrived at the accounting office, the labor chief wasn't there. He felt a weight lifting. The chief was a nuisance, forever looking for problems. Mr. Li didn't know how to use an abacus, he always did math by heart. His mental calculations were both fast and accurate. But the man shoved the abacus on his desk and forced him to pluck on the wooden beads whenever he did the books. In the chief's absence, he quickly put the abacus away. The sight of the thing gave him goose bumps.

Whenever the abacus was in front of him, Mr. Li couldn't help but wonder, what the hell is this thing good for? To him, it looked like prayer beads that he had to notch whenever he was doing accounting as a sign of reverence. But these prayer beads were too goddamn inhumanly complicated. He swung his legs onto the desk and sat back to reflect on all the details of that morning. He felt that as long as the chief wasn't around, and no one else was around, when he was alone, everything seemed close to its natural state. But as soon as people showed up, everything fell under the control of his Indian roommate. There was only one purpose for all this manipulation, which was to drive him crazy. It wasn't as if he had committed some sort of treachery, all he did was flush the toilet a bunch of times. For his Indian roommate to try to snuff him out for such a trivial thing was just plain evil!

Mr. Li later said that at the time, he thought he was on the verge of insanity. On one hand, he couldn't shake off his habit of using the scientific method to analyze everything he saw, looking for causes and effects, means and ends, arriving at explanations that didn't have anything to do with his Indian roommate. On the other hand, no matter how hard he tried, he always ended up turning his suspicion toward his roommate. At that point, he felt like he was going to lose it: just think about it, we lived together for years, we had decent rapport, but this is how he treats me! The only thing he could do to keep from going over the edge was to tell himself over a long sigh: alas, let's keep an open mind about this. Only then could he shut it all out of his mind.

That day, someone came to the accounting office to tell Mr. Li that there was someone at the bottom of the hill looking for him. Mr. Li locked the door and headed down toward the white houses in the distance that were the mine's administrative unit. He was in good spirits, so he returned to his analytical habit.

He thought about how the houses on the sunny side of the hill had a favorable climate. It was relatively dry and warm during the winter. Not only that, but it was at the foot of the hill so there was no need to hike up after every outing. It would have been fitting to base all of the coal mine's party, state, labor, and youth there. Yet, most of the housing was situated in a dark and humid gorge at the top of the mountain. But that also made sense because the entrance to the mine was inside the gorge. It wouldn't have made sense to make all the workers climb four hundred flights of stairs to go to work every day. Had that been the case, the workers would have been worn out and out of breath by the time they even got to their place of work (the tunnel entrance). Therefore, the fact that the mining facilities were placed in two separate locations was perfectly sensible and not at all suspicious.

The houses at the bottom of the mountain had snow-white walls and gray roof tiles. They looked appealing, which seemed reasonable. After all, it was the face of the whole operation. But upon closer inspection, they weren't all that appealing. The white surface was only a layer of dust. Where there wasn't as much dust, you could see the earthen structure below made of yellow mud (adobe— Wang Er's note). Looking up, the beams under the roof weren't painted and had turned black from weathering. Several of the windows were pieced together with broken shards of glass. The paint on the doors and window frames was so thin that you could still see the striation on the wood underneath. None of that was hard to explain. The economic situation of the mine wasn't exactly superb.

In regard to the mine's economic situation, the president of the mine probably knew more than anyone else. He said: "comrades, remember to be economical. After all we are a regional state enterprise." What exactly a regional state enterprise means is a mystery, but one could hazard a guess. The term often appears on the packaging of cigarettes and matchboxes. Whenever you see those words, it means low quality and modest prices. It was the same way in America; the big famous brands offered high-quality goods at high prices. The small less-famous companies sold things that were cheaper and of a lower quality. And then, there were the generic products that they sell at supermarkets. Those were probably made by regional state enterprises too. Therefore, since the mine was a regional state enterprise, it was economically limited and the shabbiness of the office was to be expected.

Even if he didn't know what a regional state enterprise was, Mr. Li would still have been able to deduce the economic condition of the mine. They were still using chisels and dynamite down in the tunnel. There were only two electric mine carts that went out of order every few days. When they malfunctioned, Mr. Li was no longer an accountant; he became a mine cart repairman. Mr. Li said, I don't know anything about fixing mine carts. But they said: it doesn't matter what you know, it just matters that you're from the mining school. Even if you have never eaten pork, you must have seen a pig run, right? You can sit there and help come up with ideas. If the electric mine cart couldn't be fixed, the miners would have to haul everything out manually. And if the generator broke, then even the doctor from the infirmary had to sit and help. When she got bored, she used her stethoscope to listen to everyone's lungs. The mine also had three automobiles, one of which he must have seen before at the American National Museum of Industrial History. He didn't want to dwell on it. Had he done so, he would undoubtedly have begun to suspect his Indian roommate again.

When Mr. Li arrived at the conference room door, he was mentally stable. It was because his empirical investigations that morning had been a success. Had it gone on like that for much longer, his psyche would have recovered and he would no longer have been his awkward and goofy self. Had that been the case, perhaps Line wouldn't have thought that he was like E.T., and perhaps she would not have liked him. If she hadn't liked him, then she wouldn't have married him and I might still have a chance to have her as my wife. Yet, the years flow like water and the things that happened happened. Things that have already happened do not have the potential of ever not happening.

11

MR. LI WALKED INTO THE CONFERENCE room. It was a big room with a big square table in the middle. There were two people sitting at the table. One was the vice president of the mine. The other was a girl wearing an army coat that was unbuttoned; under the coat was a blue uniform with the rim of a bright red sweater peeping out of the collar. She had fair skin, a peach round face, and watery eyes; with her small mouth and red lips, she was beautiful. This situation wasn't hard to explain. A pretty girl showed up at the mine and the vice president was welcoming her—what was so peculiar about that? *But why was she looking for me?* Then, when I thought about it, I realized I recognized the girl. I had seen her at the mining school and at the cadre school, but I didn't know her name. When the girl looked up and saw Mr. Li, she let out a brisk: uncle! Mr. Li was perplexed: what? I'm her uncle? I don't have any siblings, where would I get a niece from? The vice president said: a reunion of uncle and niece, I will be out of your way. Mr. Li thought: *you think I'm her uncle too?* Line (this girl was Line. The two were uncle and niece in name, but villains in fact!—Wang Er's note) said: goodbye, mister. After he left, Mr. Li asked: am I really your uncle? Like a bolt of lightning, Line pinched him on the shoulder and said: I'll fuck your ma! Are you trying to play seniority with me? I'm Line! Mr. Li thought: *a niece fucking an uncle's mother, wouldn't that be an affront to her great-aunt? Let's keep an open mind about this.*

But the name Line wasn't entirely unfamiliar. At the cadre school, every day when he got home from work, there was a note left by someone by the name of Line under his pillow. It was something Line snuck in to put there when everyone else was out working. The notes revealed the love she felt for Mr. Li. Some of the notes were plainly written:

Blood-swollen Turtlehead, I love you!—Line

Some of the notes were rather formal:

Dear Blood-swollen Turtlehead, hello!
I love you.
And hereby offer
the salute of the Great Proletarian Cultural Revolution!
—Line

Some notes were flirtatious:

My darling big turtlehead, I really miss you. Do you miss me?—Line

Some were minimalist to the point of being incomprehensible:

Blood, turtle: love. Line.

When Mr. Li saw those notes, he was all the more convinced that he was trapped in a dream.

AS FOR LINE'S personal conduct, aside from what I have already described, I would like to add the following: this person dared to say anything and everything. During the Cultural Revolution, in addition to *fuck*, there was another commonly used word that sounded like cunt but with a velar sound at the beginning. After becoming the professor's wife, she gave up using profanities, at least in Chinese. Nowadays, she works at my school's English department. Once, when she was giving a sabbatical abroad prep course, she called one of her students (who was actually a high-ranking official) a "silly cunt." For that, she had gotten a reprimand from the school. They told her to write a confession. She confessed: I was afraid that she would run into trouble abroad so I wanted to prepare her. After said comrade goes abroad, I am certain someone will call her a "silly cunt," because she is a silly cunt! When the school read the confession, they didn't say anything. They probably thought: let's keep an open mind about this.

Line said she had already fallen in love with Mr. Li at the cadre school. But there was no opportunity to get near him. Later, when Mr. Li was transferred to Henan, she tailed him. Of course, it wasn't easy to accomplish; but her motto always was, where there's a will, there's a way. She used her old man's solid connections to become a nurse in Anyang, figured out where Blood-swollen Turtlehead was, and delivered herself. She had an elaborate plan for all of it, including calling Mr. Li uncle. When they were finally alone together, they were in a small ravine on the coal mountain. That was a part of the plan also. She suddenly said to Blood-swollen Turtlehead: I want to be with you! That was an essential element of the plan. After that, she looked for an expression on Mr. Li's face. She found Mr. Li's expression to be completely out of her expectation: he closed his eyes. Suddenly, she was flustered: this Blood-swollen Turtlehead can't possibly be rejecting me, can he?

Mr. Li said he thought a long time about it and decided that it was a trap. This was more than likely the work of his conniving Indian roommate. How did a pretty young girl just show up to tell me that she wants to be with me? After thinking about it for a long time, he decided to look for some answers. He opened his eyes and asked, what do you mean? The question made Line feel self-conscious and a bit embarrassed. After a long awkward silence, she said, what do I mean? I want to be your wife, duh.

When people learned that I could write novels, they came to me with their love stories. In their minds, their love stories were worthy of being written into novels, and even entering the literary canon. To these people, my door was always open. But when I turned their stories into novels, I always used the first-person male perspective. It was partly because it was easier to write what I knew, but it was also so that I could get some vicarious thrill out of it. But when it comes to Mr. Li's love story, I refuse to use the first person because for me, it is a sad story. Line should have been my wife, but she became Mrs. Blood-swollen Turtlehead!

When Line said, "I want to be your wife, duh," her heart nearly skipped a beat. Frankly, the notion had never crossed her mind before that moment. She really just wanted to have some fun with Mr. Li and maybe mess with his head a little. But when Mr. Li said, you should think hard about this, she became agitated and said, I'm going to be your wife if it's the last thing I do! You think I'm scared? Thus, tragedy ensued. Mr. Li added: this isn't something to joke around about; Line said: I want to slap that mouth of yours. Mr. Li thought: *let's keep an open mind about this*.

After that, Mr. Li said, of course, as far as I'm concerned, there are no problems; that was all he said. Line snarled back, as far as I'm concerned, there are no problems either. Suddenly, she screamed: oh crap, it's eleven thirty. I have to catch the bus. It turned out that there was only one bus that went from Anyang to the mine, it departed early in the morning and returned at noon. If she missed it, it would have been two days before the next bus. She quickly told Mr. Li how to find her and reminded him to say that he was her uncle. With that, she ran out to catch her bus. She needed to run fast so she took off her coat and handed it to Mr. Li. Like that, Line ran off. Had it not been for that coat, it all would have amounted to nothing because Mr. Li was convinced that a girl showing up out of nowhere wanting to be his wife must have been the sequence from a dream. He doubted if there was actually a person called Line in this world. Under such a circumstance, he would have thought it much too risky to go to Anyang. If after a three-hour bus ride to Anyang, it all turned out to be a prank played on him by his Indian roommate, he would have been crushed. But the coat provided some sort of reassurance, it gave him the courage to go to Anyang. If he found Line, that would have been great. If not, at least he would get to keep the coat.

When Mr. Li recounted the events of that day, he pointed out that a girl announced she would be his wife, said a few words, then disappeared. When he ran out after her, all he saw was a figure speeding toward the road where a bus was just arriving. After a minute, a sandstorm blocked his line of sight (Mr. Li was extremely myopic, he wore the bottoms of glass bottles on his face—Wang Er's note); a minute later, the sandstorm settled, erasing all traces of person and bus. It was like seeing a ghost in the middle of the day. At the time, he didn't know that Line was a star runner of the four-hundred-meter dash, eight-hundred-meter dash, and fifteen-hundred-meter run. She was in the habit of using this skill of hers and ran everywhere. Her standing on her high school track team wasn't the only proof of this, you could also tell just by the contour of her body. Her body didn't look yellow, white, or black, it looked like the bodies of those runners first to the finishing line that you see on sports TV. Had it been twenty years in the future, no one would have allowed someone like her to go running off doing who knows what in Henan because they would have tossed her into a stadium and made her earn a gold medal and raise the national flag—such things would have been more important than blood-swollen turtleheads.

As for the last point, I was exaggerating when I said that she ran everywhere, but Line was known to use her talent indiscriminately at school, which had led to controversy. She was already a forty-year-old woman, right around the age of your typical midlife crisis, but she wasn't interested in putting on a pair of high heels. In the summer, it was too hot to wear sneakers, so she wore a pair of soft-soled sandals. Her hair was as short as it could go and she wore no accessories (accessories don't affect speed but can easily be lost during running, leading to financial loss—Wang Er's note); while chatting on the lawn, she realized that it was time for class, so she tied the bottom of her pongee blouse into a knot, rolled up her pencil skirt, revealing her black silk panties and a pair of thin, long, muscular legs that didn't at all appear like those of a middle-aged woman, and broke into a sprint. The faces of the Chinese professors went pale. But when the foreign professors with their suits and briefcases saw her, they cheered: Mrs. Li! Fucking! Good! They swung their ties over their shoulders as if they were nooses and ran after her.

In this chapter, we talked about how Line first expressed her feelings to Mr. Li, about how she left her coat in Mr. Li's hands, and about how she ran to catch the bus. From there, we discussed Line's passion for running. In the summer, when she spontaneously ran, her imperious legs were fully unleashed. But none of these ideas get to the heart of the problem. That task would be better served by describing our time at the pool together. Allow me to illustrate. She climbed out of the pool—pushed against the edge of the pool with her hands—and pushed herself up, the critical moment being the push. In that moment, I saw the sleekest elegant line, and after seventeen years, that line hadn't changed. If you were to scrutinize, you would notice that the breasts had gotten slightly larger; but that is a change for the better. Originally, those two breasts of Line's weren't big enough. Even taking into account the fact that she is the lean, agile type, they were still relatively small. Now, she was flawless. I refuse to believe a woman like her can remain loyal to Blood-swollen Turtlehead for a lifetime, or that we have been in love since age seventeen, but we have never made love; it just isn't right. So I said: if your red plum flower were to ever reach over the fence, don't forget about me.

When Line heard this, she paused for a moment and said: if your words are to praise my beauty, then I am very pleased, and would like to treat you to a meal. To be able to receive such a compliment at the age of forty is rather satisfying. But if you were meaning something else, then I should slap your mouth. Supposing that you won't mind, of course. If you do mind, then I won't. It wouldn't be worth it to lose a friendship of twenty-some years over a slap. So which do you mean? Of course I didn't want to get slapped so I said: the first one, of course. But I also wanted to know why. She said she didn't know why, but she had made up her mind long ago that other than Blood-swollen Turtlehead, she would never sleep with another man.

12

THAT'S JUST HOW LINE WAS, always acting crazy and stupid. Even she understood that everything she did was crazy, but she insisted on crazy. For her it was intoxicating. This sort of intoxication has been described by writers such as Old Shaw (George Bernard Shaw—Wang Er's note) in *The Flower Girl* (aka *Pygmalion*—Wang Er's note); the common flower girl Eliza goes to Professor Higgins to be a student. In addition to these two characters, there is also Mrs. Pearce the housekeeper and a Colonel Pickering. Mrs. Pearce understands that a university professor taking in a common flower girl for a student is not only madness but a sort of intoxication. Even though the girl from the gutter is dirty, she could easily be made into a nymph. So she said to the colonel:

"Sir, please don't teach our master drunken madness!"

When Professor Higgins heard this, he said: "What a life for? What is but drunken madness. Some can't even be mad! Drunken madness, Mrs. Pearce, you're really *geng*!"*

THE EDITOR MIGHT at this point note the errors, but it isn't necessarily so. Professor Higgins's specialty was in phonetics and dialects, so in his excitement, he spoke in Tianjinese.† But here, I digress, I was talking about Line and how she lived her whole life under such an intoxicating madness.

THE FOLLOWING EVENTS were told to me mainly by Line. After returning from the mine, two days passed before Blood-swollen Turtlehead made good on his word and returned the coat. That day, Line's roommate was there too. Not only that, but she hung out with them. Outside the windows was a sandstorm rumbling like a boiling pot of millet porridge. It wasn't easy to kick someone out in weather like that. Besides, it had already been established that Blood-swollen Turtlehead was her uncle. There was no reason to ask a roommate to leave just because an uncle was visiting. Line had no choice but to play the sweet niece, peeling apples for uncle Blood-swollen Turtlehead. When she took him out to eat, she introduced him to everyone: my uncle! But people said: I don't see the resemblance. So Line said: I don't look like my mom. They said: he's too young. Line said: he's my little uncle. They said: how come you are so casual with your uncle? Line said: my little uncle grew up at my house; we played together ever since we were little. When they reached a place with no one else around, she stared Mr. Li in his eyes and said: what are you so smug about? Do I look like your niece?

Geng here would mean "clever."
†Tianjinese is a Mandarin dialect.

Mr. Li returned to the mine in the afternoon. As Line walked him out, they finally had a chance to speak in private. Line told him to come see her again on Sunday, after dark, because her roommate worked a night shift that night. After reminding him to be as inconspicuous as possible when he came, she went home to wait for Sunday. Mr. Li couldn't make up his mind. The only way for him to get to Anyang at night was by train, which arrived nine o'clock at night. Was he sure that Line would let him stay the night? Without company documents, he couldn't book a hotel. Spending the night at the train station would have been unbearable. Mr. Li was born in the south. He was terrified of the cold. If he had the choice, he would rather shovel shit on the hottest day of the summer than sleep a night in a room without fire or heating. On this fact his mind was made up, but Mr. Li went nevertheless. When Line recounted the event, she said with pouty lips: our Blood-swollen Turtlehead is good to me.

Line said, before Mr. Li got together with her, he was a virgin boy. When a man says something like that, all you can do is nod, it's not like there is a hymen to speak of. But Line was convinced of this truth. According to Mr. Li himself, before entering into a relationship with Line, he once dated a female classmate one year above him at his university, but they were very proper about it. When I was studying in America, I looked into this story and it turned out to be true. This *shifu-aunt* of mine wasn't my *shifu's* undergraduate classmate. She wasn't a classmate from his master's program either. It wasn't even the 1970s yet; one might think, what was an American girl doing getting a PhD in science unless she was not fit to have a family? She was short and plump, and when they sat shoulder to shoulder, she let out farts that could practically kill a man. Mr. Li said: I did find her ugly, but no matter what, I couldn't hurt a girl's feelings, so I never turned her down.

Even if Mr. Li had been a ladies' man, I wouldn't question his loyalty to Line. I wouldn't want to slander anyone. But if some woman were to seduce him by playing on his pity, he would not have been able to resist. I know this one girl in his graduate seminar who is beautiful beyond belief but also dumb beyond words. When she failed a test, her tears fell like flower petals from a pear tree under the rain. Before letting her retake her test, Mr. Li asked me to tutor her. He gave me all the questions on the test but pretended like it was an accident. After finishing the test for her, I gave the girl all the answers and said: memorize it. If you still can't pass, you should just kill yourself. That was how she managed to pass with sixty points. From this example, we can assume that if a girl were to go up to Mr. Li and say, "If you don't have sex with me, I'll kill myself," he wouldn't have stood a chance.

Mr. Li became a revolutionary precisely because his heart was so soft. It wasn't just a woman's tears but also the suffering of humanity. He liked to quote Che Guevara: how can I simply let the suffering of others pass me by? That was how he got caught on my *shifu-aunt*'s fishhook. But later on, the *shifu-aunt* cried and said, even if you were black, I still wouldn't be with you. Yellow and white together make strange combinations! In fact, yellow and white mixes are only ugly as infants. When they grow up, every last one of them is a gem like those small but smooth watermelons with pitch-black seeds and crimson red flesh. Even with her clear sampling bias and logical misdirection, Mr. Li believed her. All the farts he smelled were for naught. Nowadays, this woman teaches at the university we all went to. She married an extremely racially complicated Latin American and gave birth to mixed-race kids comprising all different shades and sizes.

Let us now talk about the tryst between Line and Mr. Li. In order to maintain the story's continuity, the rest of the chapter will be entirely in the third person, without my extra commentaries.

Mr. Li's second visit to Line was not only on a Sunday but it was December 31. It was a windy day. The wind had turned the sky yellow. The lamps inside the room glowed with a bluish tint. The building where Line lived was a two-story Western-style mansion with a slate roof. The once imposing structure was now a crowded mess. Half a dozen families lived in it, in addition to a woman's dormitory. That was why when they renovated the building, they added a separate entrance that went directly to the first-floor unit. Her room was spacious with huge windows covering an entire wall. As the wind blew, the window panes clacked like Ping-Pong balls. At dusk, the roommate who lived with her left for her night shift.

As I mentioned, Line's room was huge. It was three meters wide and nine meters long. The original owner of the home most likely used it as the billiard room. It was probably the most formidable mansion in all of Anyang, but its original inhabitants were no longer around. Its subsequent owners were also no longer around, but the room was still filled with their things. The chests, wardrobes and mirrors took up two-thirds of the space. That was the reason why only two girls lived in such a large space. In the middle of the room hung a mercury lamp, the same as the kind they use on the streets. They were rarely used inside homes because not only did they waste electricity but were blindingly bright. That wasn't a problem though. It was a dorm room after all, so the electricity they used was all public. Two unmarried young women lived there, so the electrician was willing to install any kind of light they wanted. The girls didn't mind the brightness. Aside from those things, there were two iron-frame, single-person beds.

That evening, Line was full of energy. She hoisted two buckets of water and placed them in a corner of the room. She put away the clean sheet that was on the bed and put down a sheet she prepared especially for the occasion. The reason for it was because the last time Mr. Li visited, he sat on her snow-white sheet and left an inky black butt print in the shape of a lotus leaf. Line didn't mind doing more laundry, but she didn't want to leave any evidence that someone had been in the room. That was why she also changed out the pillowcase and tossed a dirty blanket over the other bed. In addition, she changed into some dirty clothes. When the set dressing was complete, she sat down to wait. The last bit of daylight was fading (the room faced west, so it had a clear view of the sunset), it was around eight o'clock at night. Mr. Li was just coming out of the train, heading her way against the heavy winds. It would normally have been a forty-minute walk, but in that weather, it took over an hour. Line stood up and kept watch at the window. She couldn't see anything so she shut the curtains.

Line returned to her bed and sat down to wait for Mr. Li. As the wind howled, she thought about how difficult it was for Mr. Li to come see her. Next time, she would go to him at the mine. But still, she felt anxious. She took a dirty shirt out of the laundry pile under her bed, walked over to a mirror and looked at herself through its dusty surface. She picked up a rag and wiped the mirror before undressing herself in front of it. Before putting on the dirty shirt, she said to herself in the mirror: letting Blood-swollen Turtlehead play with a body like this, have I gone mad?

That night, when Mr. Li arrived at Line's door, he was blacker than she had expected. This was because on his way to the train station, Mr. Li had passed the coalfields. As he walked, a dust devil made the coal dust gyrate in midair. When he got out of the coal-field, Mr. Li looked as if he had just come up from the mine shaft. After he got off the train, he walked for a long time. The icy wind nearly made his ears fall off. Though every man was by nature horny, that frigid wind had sapped any desire Mr. Li had. All he could think about was: if I don't show up, a girl will be very sad.

Not only was Mr. Li covered in soot, but he was exhausted to the point of collapse. As the end of the year neared and the mine realized that they weren't even one-third of the way to their quota, the administrators met and decided to send everyone down into the mine. They had to dig up some more coal before the New Year. At first it was eight hours per shift, then it became twelve and eventually sixteen. At the end, there was no break. They ate in the mine and dozed off when they could no longer stay awake. Like that, they survived thirty-six hours (the original plan was to work into the New Year, which would have broken their own record) but after that, because of exhaustion and the inability to focus, there was an accident and someone died. The leadership felt defeated and let everyone back up. The thirty-hour shift left Mr. Li with just enough time to take a shower before setting out for Line's place. He took a short nap on the train but it wasn't nearly enough. As he stood in front of Line's door, he was in a daze.

Before Mr. Li arrived, Line sat on her bed and mused: even though Blood-swollen Turtlehead was fun to play with, there was no need to go too far with it. Even though she said she wanted to be Blood-swollen Turtlehead's wife, it would obviously also have been better if she didn't have to be. It was the same feeling that many women have when shopping: they want to save more money but also buy more things. A better example might be those naturally beautiful young women who want to feel the thrill of romance but don't want to think about marriage. Yet Line felt different from both of the above-mentioned types. To Line, Blood-swollen Turtlehead was neither a product on a shelf nor a romantic lover boy but rather something in between.

Mr. Li entered through Line's door and said sleepily: your place sure is warm. After a couple of gaping yawns, he added: hello, Line. Merry Christmas and Happy New Year, may God bless you. He was so out of it; his words didn't pass through his brain. Had he used his brain, he would have realized: we live in the land of the proletarian revolution. Even if there is a God, the old man has no authority here, just as He has no authority over Khomeini.

13

THAT NIGHT, AFTER MR. LI ARRIVED, Line had him wash his face and brush his teeth. Mr. Li kept an open mind and did as he was told. As Line studied his stubbly mouth, she thought: if he tries to kiss me, I can just refuse, no need to make him brush his teeth. But when she heard the wind howling outside, she felt bad for what Mr. Li had gone through to see her. She didn't have the heart to refuse him so she made him brush his teeth after all. There was soot in Mr. Li's teeth. A kiss from him would have dyed her black.

Line judged her own actions based on if she was "keeping it real" or not. During the Cultural Revolution, we all used "keeping it real" as a criterion. It was slightly different from the American standard of "be reasonable." The American's reasonableness is like the standard used by two businessmen, whereas our "keeping it real" is more like honor among thieves. Applied to Line's specific case, her attitude toward Mr. Li needed to be as "keeping it real" as that of a gangster woman to a gangster man.

In terms of what "keeping it real" meant to Line, I offer the following anecdote. In the summer of '68, it was trendy to trade commemorative Mao pins (the term "commemorative pin" was rather strange, he wasn't even dead yet, what was there to commemorate?— Wang Er's note). Around Beijing's Haidian District, there were gatherings everywhere, like flea markets. Line was always going to them. In addition to trading Mao pins, it was also a place to pick up girls. When someone caught sight of Line and wanted to hit on her, she would put on a smug smile and unfurl the folding fan in her hand. On the fan was a word written in calligraphy (written by me— Wang Er's note), *Taken!* That was twenty-two years ago. Line was an elegant maiden with a beautiful smile.

If the suitor continued to pester her, Line would change into her mean face and command: "Wang Er, get him!" Wang Er would jump out of nowhere and kick some troublemaker's ass. If the troublemaker had brought a buddy, Wang Er would also bring a buddy, which was Xu You. Xu was out for blood; his bellicosity was well-known throughout Haidian. After that, we would take the wounded to the hospital. If the injury was serious, we would have to treat the patient to a meal. That would have been "keeping it real."

As Mr. Li brushed his teeth, Line knew she had to "keep it real." But she also realized that "keeping it real" meant having limits. It was a blurry line. If he had gotten gropey, she would definitely refuse. But there also had to be the possibility of consent, so Line mentally prepared herself. If Mr. Li had wanted to encroach on her chastity, that would have been a red line. If he pestered her, she would beat his ass. At the time, Line wanted to play with men, but she also wanted to remain a virgin forever. For her, that would have been the ideal situation.

When Mr. Li finished washing up, they sat down on the beds. At first, Line sat on her own bed and Mr. Li sat on the other bed. But then, she called him over to sit down next to her. She could tell that Mr. Li was tired. The dirty blanket was only big enough to protect the bed from Mr. Li's butt. Had he lain back, it would have been a disaster. Then, she began to study Mr. Li. Her first take-away was this: Mr. Li had big monkey ears. The second was that there was coal dust in Mr. Li's pores. Just as she was about to point out her observations, Mr. Li said: let me lie down for a minute. With that, he leaned to a side and fell asleep before he even hit the mattress. Line later said, "I wanted to kill him right then and there (mariticide!—Wang Er's note)!"

As soon as Mr. Li hit the bed, he began to snore. Line wanted to cry. But eventually, she settled down and thought: fine, go ahead and sleep. Mama's gonna have her fun with you! She took off his shoes and laid him out flat on the bed. She unbuttoned his shirt, took off his belt and reached in with her hand only to feel a bunch of cotton patches (a bachelor's shirt—Wang Er's note). Later, she would describe her first experience caressing her lover in the fol-lowing way: if you tied Blood-swollen Turtlehead to a pole, you'd end up with a mop.

Still, Blood-swollen Turtlehead wasn't entirely a mop. As she reached in farther, she felt Mr. Li's chest. In that moment, she almost screamed. Of course, she became accustomed to it eventu-ally, but the first touch was something else. Mr. Li's chest was sparsely populated with thick, coarse hair that ran down the length of his sternum like the mane on a pig's back. By pig, I mean Chi-nese pigs, the mane on foreign pigs aren't bristly enough to make brushes with. But whether or not Mr. Li's chest hair was bristly enough to make brushes with, Line was having fun. She kept feel-ing her way down until she found an object, like a big sea cucumber. At that point, she paused and pondered for a bit until she finally remembered Mr. Li's moniker. As she chewed on her fingernails, she thought: oh dear, how can this be an organ, it's clearly a murder weapon.

As soon as she touched it, Mr. Li woke. He was in the middle of a dream. He had just gotten out of the mine shaft and was going to take a bath. The public bath was a pot of soot stew. Several butt-naked miners would jump into the muck one at a time. Everything in his dream was true to his real life. He couldn't believe what he was seeing then, but he also had trouble believing what he was seeing now in his dream. How could there be so many male genitals crowded together under one roof? He suspected that he was dreaming; he also suspected that he was gay. Only if both of these conditions were true could he have seen what he saw.

Mr. Li said, when he woke up and found Line touching him, he was startled. Line's face was red, with a big smile. He had just woken up from a dream, so he figured what he was seeing wasn't a dream. He didn't want it to be a dream. It was his years as water flowing, not mine. Time flows like the moon arcing across heaven, shining down upon each of us, but we each live a different life.

After that, Line made Mr. Li solemnly swear that he wouldn't have any unwarranted ideas, that he would stop the moment he was told. Under such conditions, she would let him reach in from under her blouse. This was their second tryst, one week after the first one. Line said, Mr. Li's hands were as rough as if they had fish scales. But through those hands, she was able to feel how thin her waist was, and the roundness of her breasts, the flatness of her abdomen. Furthermore, she also felt pleasure (with a bit of fear). It was a lot more fun than chitchatting in class.

Meanwhile, I was at the farm in Yunnan stealing pineapples. In the middle of the night, I felt my way around and cut down pineapples one at a time. With each pineapple, I first took a sniff to see if it smelled good. If it smelled good, I put it into the sack behind me; if not, I tossed it. The two of us were made from the same mold, incapable of sticking to the straight road. The straight-thinking folks of those years were busy reflecting on the suffering of two-thirds of humanity, even in their dreams. But I had to ask: do I know who these suffering people are? Besides, wasn't I also suffering? That night, I stepped into an ant colony. I had gotten such bad athlete's foot from walking in the rice paddies that the skin between my toes had rotted away. When the colony of ants bit me, it felt like a barrage of arrows piercing my heart.

Of the three of us, Mr. Li was clearly having the best time, but he just had to overthink it. He felt suspicious. When a person gets to be that paranoid, even drugs won't help much. His fingers slid past Line's breasts. Her nipples felt icy cold. In his encyclopedic brain, he wondered: this thing is cold—that can't be right, can it?

In his stupor, Mr. Li's hands moved down her body. Line reacted quickly and broke away. She gave Mr. Li a shove and said: how dare you! Mr. Li said: sorry, sorry, sorry! I didn't mean it. Line replied: I don't care what you mean, she's (her roommate, the girl from Henan) getting off work soon, you should go.

14

WHEN THE CULTURAL REVOLUTION BEGAN, some people were happy while others were unhappy. Old Mr. Liu once told me that he had wanted to kill himself as soon as it began. He could tell by the momentum that he wasn't going to make it through. But when he thought about the Dongpo pork belly they served at the Uh-Mei Pub, he realized death wasn't worth it. He belonged to the unhappy category of people. Line was one of the happy ones because we were in eighth grade at the time and she was failing all her classes. Her dad said: if you don't test into high school, you'll be digging pits at the Nankou Tree Farm. That was how they dealt with people who couldn't make it into high school back then. But her mom said: no one from these academic quarters will be digging pits. She told her husband to go talk to the college's affiliate high school. But the old man replied: I'm a party secretary, how could I do such a thing? In those years, it was as if the suffering of two-thirds of humanity and Party principles were real things. Her old lady was so scared of losing face that she asked me to tutor Line. But the challenge was too great, I didn't stand a chance of success. Wang Er wasn't an idiot and he had a soft spot for young women, so he laid out the following plan:

1. Line was solely trying to get into our high school, not some other school; as long as she took the final exam and passed, she would get in.
2. There was no limit to the number of bathroom breaks one could take during the final exam.
3. Between the boy's and girl's bathrooms, I had already dug a tunnel.

Even with such careful planning, Line was still deathly afraid. One week before the final exam, she told me that she had scared her period back in. One day before the exam, she woke me up with a revolutionary battle hymn. As it turned out, out of revolutionary necessity, all high schools closed and all exams were canceled.

I would never have guessed that Line would later not only go to college but go on to get a master's degree. Whenever a foreign professor came to lecture at our school, she was always the interpreter. At first, the foreigners thought she was just a pretty face, but once they began to talk to her, they realized that she was an expert on everything from set theory, recursion theory, to cybernetics, relativism, and the old three systems theories and the new three systems theories. Not only was she an expert, but she was published (co-authored with Mr. Li). The foreigners would shake their heads and lament: in our country, there are women as well learned as Mrs. Li too, but they don't look much like women.

Our neighbors say: what's so strange about that? She's Mrs. Blood-swollen Turtlehead after all. They talk as if Mr. Li's sperm had some sort of intellectual nutrients that fertilized Line's budding intellect; such talk is clearly nonsense. Her conversation with Little Bicycle Bell three days ago provides ample evidence. This conversation took place in my living room:

Line: Bell, do you guys have any more of the things?

Bell: What thing?

Line: What thing, the thing the husband does the wife with, the rubber *condom* (in English)! Oh my mother, I'm getting aphasia! (A mental ailment afflicting only those with amazing English skills, not just anyone can get it.—Wang Er's note)

Bell: (embarrassed) I have some, but only in extra large.

Line: That's perfect. Our Blood-swollen Turtlehead's is huge! Definitely no smaller than your guy's.

Bell: His isn't 'my guy.' He's a jerk to me!

Line: You need to control him a little, use a smaller size. Do that a few times and he'll behave.

From the above conversation, we can see that they were using condoms, and therefore, not transferring intellectual fluids. The point I want to make is that Line was an early bloomer sexually but a late bloomer intellectually. Line post-marriage to Blood-swollen Turtlehead was a completely different person from the premarital Line.

After having gotten rid of Mr. Li that time when he had come straight from the mine, Line had had her work cut out. First, she had to change the dirty sheet on her bed, then she had to wash the cup that Mr. Li drank from, and hide the towel and toothbrush that he used, because there was soot on them. Then, from some hidden place, she took out a big white towel. She took off all her clothes and stood in front of the mirror. Before the mirror stood a fair and lithe young maiden (in regard to this concept, Line and I have a disagreement. I said she was twenty-one years old at the time, no longer a young maiden; but she said, at the time she one hundred percent looked like a young maiden. She was willing to stake her life on it, so that's what I wrote—Wang Er's note). Said maiden had watery eyes, ivory skin, and long straight legs. Her thin waist would have made even Marilyn Monroe jealous. Below her abdomen was a small patch of pubic hair. Glistening black, it covered only a small area. It made Line proud. She said it was very important, without it, she wouldn't look as good, but had it been too big and bushy, that wouldn't have been pleasing either. When she later went overseas with Mr. Li, they rented a bunch of video cassettes. After some comparison, she saw that even the most famous porn stars didn't stand up to her in this arena. There was only one Krystal who, in a film made when she was nineteen, once possessed such a beautiful lower abdomen (I have not seen the film and cannot vouch for her—Wang Er's note).

Line added, this beautiful body was exquisitely juxtaposed against streaks of black. This beautiful maiden stood with blackened lips and fine black streaks across her breasts and lower abdomen. At a glance it might have looked dirty but upon a closer look, it revealed astonishing beauty; where did such beauty come from? It was the soot that covered Blood-swollen Turtlehead's body. Line dipped the towel in cool water and wiped away the streaks of soot one by one. She then washed her face, brushed her teeth, put on her clothes and walked out to dump the bucket of dirty water. The hallway was pitch-black. Line wasn't as brave as Wang Er. When she heard a rumbling sound, she was quaking in fear.

Line said, the hallway didn't have any lights, but there wasn't anywhere for a person to hide. The sound horrified her. She put down the bucket and crept back inside to get a big flashlight. The thing not only provided light but also protection. She held it as she moved toward the source of the sound. She noticed that under the staircase, there was a tiny nook. It was just large enough for Mr. Li to sleep curled up in a fetal position. His worker's entitlement coat was left out in the hall because there was no more space for it. The scene made Line furious, she wanted to say: Blood-swollen Turtlehead: didn't I tell you to go sleep at the truck stop? She wanted to wake Mr. Li up and give him an ass-kicking, followed by a get the hell out of here, and a never come back. Had she done that, she would have taught him a good lesson, and I may still have had a chance with her today.

But Line didn't do that. She made a different decision, which is why the head of household line on her Household Registration form is now Mr. Li's name; and on Line's own line, it says wife of something something Li. How corny! After she made that decision, she just totally went downhill.

In the years as water flow, Line made the decision to be Blood-swollen Turtlehead's wife and never looked back. I will never understand such a decision. But as long as Mr. Li isn't dead, nothing will change. Time, like the moon, flows in cycles, and everything eventually passes; but still, there are moments, and once they have passed, they have passed forever.

15

WHEN MR. LI HEARD LINE SAY: you can do anything you want to me, he immediately thought of that fat *shifu-aunt* of mine. *Shifu-aunt* often said those words to him but he never knew what they meant. Only after they broke up did *shifu-aunt* explain that it meant: make love to me! When he thought about it, he was grateful that he didn't understand. Had he understood, how could he not agree? Had he agreed, he would have had to make good on it. Whenever he thought about making good, his vision went dark and he wanted to pass out.

Because of the above-mentioned history, that day, Mr. Li understood those words right away. He said with frankness: let's make love. When Line heard this, her face turned red instantly. In a stern voice, she said: you're smarter than I thought! She thought it over, then added: let's do it.

Mr. Li and Line planned to make love in a temple on a hill near the mine. The time was set to be the day the authority turned off the heaters in the spring.

Mr. Li decided to trust in Line and stake what remained of his rational understanding of fate on her. On March 15 of '73, at twelve o'clock noon, he went to the dilapidated temple. For future reference, he took extreme care to write down every detail. The education he had received was British. That was why he was meticulous like the British, why he liked to analyze everything like the British, why he was difficult to get along with like the British, and why, like the British, once a friend, he was a friend for life.

Mr. Li said: the ramshackle temple at the top of the hill had a main chamber that was only a dozen square meters in size. The walls were surrounded by grass that was waist-high. The vegetation growing on top of the roof dangled off the eaves like a waterfall. The temple's doors, cabinets, window frames, and any other movable pieces of wood had already been carried away. All there was in the main chamber was a pile of broken roof tiles and a brick altar. The statue of the deity was long gone. He remembered wondering who the temple was devoted to. Typically, these hilltop temples were devoted to the Jade Emperor because it was the closest spot to heaven, if only by a tiny bit. As a Chinese person, he had spent a good amount of time reading books on traditional folklore. But the inside of that temple offered him no clues as to whether or not it was a temple devoted to the Jade Emperor. There was nothing suggesting that it wasn't a temple devoted to the Jade Emperor either. In that temple, he couldn't be sure of anything. There were no statues, no words, no nothing. For that reason, Mr. Li harbored no suspicion toward the temple.

Mr. Li added: the temple's walls should have been white, but at the time, much of them were black. Beneath the spot where the roof leaked, the wall and the ground were all black. After years of rainwater, much of the paint on the walls had been washed away. Underneath the peeling paint, the walls were black. Some parts of the walls grew mosses while other parts grew mold. The ground was covered in a layer of muck. The muck had fallen in through a hole in the roof. At the edges of the gaping hole, wooden beams jutted out like fangs. The wood was rotten like decayed limbs. Had that not been the case, they would have been salvaged as well. Mixed in with the muck on the ground were rocks. At the edges of the rocks grew tufts of grass. But even the grass was black. There was mugwort growing in the courtyard from last year; it was yellow. The grass that fell in from the hole in the roof was also yellow. Wind blew in from the door and out through the hole in the roof. As the grasses swayed, the light that shined into the room also wobbled. Line still hadn't arrived. Mr. Li climbed onto the altar to look outside. Through what was once a window, past the tunnel on the road, he could see far into the distance, but he couldn't see Line. He exited to the courtyard and looked around from the outside. He saw barren rocky hills and patches of withered grass but he couldn't spot Line. But Line had to be there. Just as Mr. Li decided to go on a search, Line appeared like a miracle. She stepped out from behind the temple with her coat in her hands. Her small face looked pale and her body shivered ever so slightly. Meekly, she muttered: Blood-swollen Turtlehead, you won't kill me will you?

Line later explained: at the time she was truly afraid. She had never known what fear was, and had never felt it since. The fear she tasted, she is no longer able to describe; she can only remember a vague panic. It reminded her of the time in '67 when we went up to the fifth floor of the lab building and climbed out of a window. We walked over a six-inch-wide concrete beam to another window and climbed back in. But climbing through windows was much more enjoyable than this experience.

Mr. Li said: Line put her coat down on the altar and sat herself on top of it. She said: don't say anything, and don't touch me, let me do everything myself. Okay? After she said that, she sat there for a long time without moving.

Line said: Mr. Li really did keep his mouth shut.

Mr. Li said: after that, Line looked up and tried to make a funny face at him but the expression froze halfway on her face, so she looked like she was on the verge of tears. She trembled as she unbuttoned her uniform and pulled her red sweater over her head. The sweater tousled her hair. She ran her fingers through to straighten it. She wore a checkered shirt with loose threads at the shoulder. Then, as if she were eating olives, she undid one button after another. It was as if time had come to a stop. She unclipped her bra and set it down. The thing was made of fine white fabric with a floral trim. Then, in one motion, she took off her pants (including outer pants, wool pants, and long johns) and crawled into the coat. She sat vacant on the altar.

Line said: I felt like a sacrificial lamb.

Line said: Mr. Li revealed his big musket, it was frightening.

Line added: The first time was the scariest. I felt a warmth in my lower abdomen and then made a mess. Only then did I realize that that wasn't the end of the so-called lovemaking. I also had to pull my legs apart like I was giving birth. After those experiences, I never wanted to make love to anyone else again.

16

I N THE YEARS AS WATER FLOW, there was one thing that worried me day and night. But first, I should explain what I mean by years as water flow. Proust wrote a book about everything that happened to him. The story is like a person under hypnosis lying at the bottom of a river looking up at the slithering currents, bubbling lights, the leaves, rotten logs, and glass bottles passing by one at a time. As to the question of how best to translate the title, translators have spent volumes debating. The latest title in the debate is *Chasing the Memories of the Water-like Years*.* It sounds like Proust had already died and wrote the book as a zombie. And it doesn't roll off the tongue.

In my opinion, years as water flow would be a good translation of Proust's title. It's a good name. For now, the name has no owner so I'll take it. If in the future, Proust wants it back, I can always return it. I have respect for deceased forebears.

---

*Wang Xiaobo's translation of Proust's *Remembrance of Things Past*.

Years as water flow is everything a person possesses; it is the only thing that truly belongs to you. Everything else, the momentary joys and sorrows, will all go running back to the years as water flow. No one that I know seems to appreciate their own flowing years. They don't even seem to know that they have this thing, which is why they all act like they've lost their souls.

Now let's talk about Old Mr. Liu. To tell this story, I have to provide some background information, starting with what Old Mr. Liu looked like. At this time, he hadn't passed away yet. He was still living next door to us. His hair was white and his cheeks were ruddy, always full of goofy grins. He held a cane made out of a tree root, and traveled swiftly, but his feet had deformed with age and his ankle joints had gone soft so his gait was more like a fierce hobble. When he wasn't eating over at my place, he was mooching off some other neighbor's dining table and when he ate something tasty, he would brag to us about it. He was a wastebasket of words. He never stopped once he started talking. He would often play chess with my father until midnight. As far as I could see, his game was crap. How else could they have gone through twenty games in a night.

When Old Mr. Liu had to go, he would hobble toward the public bathroom, untying his belt as he ran. Once, a middle-aged woman came out of the woman's side of the bathroom and thought that Old Mr. Liu was charging at her. She screamed and fainted.

Subsequently, I need to describe the location of the story—the mining school. Of course, it's also possible that it isn't the mining school. At the time, the mining school had been relocated to a gorge in Sichuan to continue its activities (Chairman Mao had said university activities should continue), but the faculty said there was coxsackievirus in the gorge, which can cause enlarged heart syndrome. When everyone fled back to Beijing, they found that their dorms were all occupied, so everyone squeezed into a crowded warehouse behind the school. My father and mother came home. I was stationed at a commune on the outskirts of Beijing at the time so I came home too, bringing Bicycle Bell with me. The family gathered under one roof and enjoyed some wholesome pleasures.

But who would have guessed that after pleasure came the pain. The higher-ups sent an army propaganda team over. They left notices everywhere: all returnees must go back to work in Sichuan, or else their wages will be frozen. Only those with third-stage enlarged heart syndrome and the old and useless were exempt. Then they added another rule, those with third-stage enlarged heart syndrome and the elderly will have their wages reduced to cover only basic necessities so that they wouldn't be tempted to lend money to the healthy. The cadre in charge later gave birth to a baby without a butthole. My mother had to perform surgery to give the child a man-made sphincter. This story teaches us that with the advancements in medical technology, we can now accommodate more karma blowback than ever before. A baby born without a butthole can simply have one put in; what's there to be afraid of?

Finally, I need to mention the time frame of the story, which was after the arrival of the army propaganda team and the departure of the mining school faculty. My father and mother both went back. Two days after their departure, Old Mr. Liu passed away. Before his death, there were only the three of us, me, Bicycle Bell, and Old Mr. Liu, living in the warehouse behind the school. It wasn't a bad deal. We lacked freedom when my father and mother were around. They didn't let me and Bell sleep in the same bed.

17

I CAN STILL REMEMBER THE BUILDINGS behind the mining school. They were never meant to be lived in. A row of tall buildings stood over the area so it was perpetually without sunlight. They didn't want sunlight when they built the buildings because they were meant to be warehouses to store chemicals and drugs. There was no running water, you had to walk a long way to a well; there was no electricity, a long cord had to be pulled; there were no bathrooms, to pee or poo you had to walk a long, long way to a public toilet. Once upon a time, several hundred mining school folks had to share this one single public toilet. For that reason, the place was always filthy. It was practically built out of piss and shit. No one cleaned it out because there was no way they could possibly keep up.

The situation inside the warehouse was just as bad. The space was broken up into rooms that all pointed inward. In other words, it was a hallway with a bunch of rooms. The whole building had no air flow. During the summer, people living there didn't have the luxury of modesty. All day long, I had to look at saggy breasts and fat bellies, gnarly legs, and swollen eyelids. Of course, there were some people living in the warehouse with good-looking body parts, but they kept those hidden out of sight.

In the hallway hung all sorts of women's undergarments. It would have been weird to dry them outside so they hung them in the hallway like some sort of an art exhibition. I wouldn't have minded looking at the bras and panties of young women but that wasn't what was there. In the hallway were bedsheets rolled into tubes and a festoon of strung-together flour sacks. If you were wondering what that last thing was, you'd be grossed out to know, but like me, you would want to know anyway. The worst looking of the bunch was a thing that looked like a felt insole but was covered in what may have been shit stains. That's why I regard disposable menstrual pads as a great invention. It has saved countless men's lives. Middle-aged women are like a natural disaster in China. It's not because they are ugly (I've been abroad and middle-aged Chinese women look a lot better than their foreign counterparts—Wang Er's note), but because they deliberately gross people out!

I once heard about a study that someone did, which found that kids who lived in big communal courtyards had lower grades and easily went astray precisely because after seeing those things, they generally lost faith in life. I wasn't led astray because I was already a bad kid, but it did make my will to live a little shaky.

It seemed to me that rather than living in such an awful environment, it would have been better to die a glorious death, like Mr. He jumping off a building, creating a spectacle that caught the gaze of thousands, marching to his death unflinchingly. Before going to sleep every night, I thought of a new way to die, each death rich with poetry. Whenever I thought about those various manners of death, my little monk got hard.

The crowd staring at the gallows, the bloody and cruel execution, the white horses pulling the silver carriage to the funeral, it all aroused me. To become tumescent under torture, to copulate under the executioner's blade, and to scream out my final curse while ejaculating, that was my wish ever since I was a child. Maybe it was because I watched too many movies as a kid (there was no sex in those movies, only ideology, the sex part appeared on its own—Wang Er's note). My father had noticed my obsession with death early on, a tendency he clearly rejected. According to him: I don't care if you want to kill yourself, but don't drag your family down with you. In my view, that was a despicable attitude. If he was really that afraid of being dragged into it, then he should have murdered me himself.

My father and mother had no objections toward Little Bicycle Bell. First, she was from our academic quarters (my father believed in status and reputation). In addition, she was very pretty. And to top it all off, she had a sweet mouth, always calling them mom and dad. My mother would blush and say: it was all our fault that we couldn't make a better son-in-law for your family (she's nitpicking—Wang Er's note). Little Bell said: mom, dad, he's good enough. Is that how a daughter-in-law is supposed to talk to a mother-in-law? But have you seen a mother-in-law who insists on sleeping in the same room as her daughter-in-law? I slept with my father and he snored. I proposed the following solution: you two aren't that old yet, people say at twenty a wolf, at forty a tiger, and at fifty you can outrun the golden leopard. Right now, mom is a tiger and dad is a golden leopard. You two should be working on your committed matrimony and not waste all your time monitoring us. It would be better for everyone to switch; you guys sleep in one room and the two of us sleep in one room. My mother's reaction was laughter and my father wanted to beat me. But no matter what, they refused to take their eyes off us, and didn't allow us to do any premarital infractions. Even when they went back to Sichuan, they told Old Mr. Liu to keep his eyes on us.

18

'D KNOWN OLD MR. LIU FOR a long time. When he was locked
in a room with Mr. He, I had seen him. At the time, Line and
I were dating. We were always crawling around looking for
places where no one could see us. We crawled around inside the lab
building and found a place between the ceiling and the roof where
we could look down to see Old Mr. Liu and Mr. He below sitting
face to face. Mr. He sat with a grim look on his face, but Old Mr. Liu
wore a goofy grin with his face tilted to a side. Drool seeped out of
a corner of his mouth but he was oblivious. At times, he would
raise his hand and in a crisp falsetto say: reporting! I have to go to
the toilet! The guards wanted to beat his ass so he took off his
pants and showed off his snow-white butt cheeks. He climbed onto
a table and raised his ass high in the air. That was just who Old
Mr. Liu was. It was hard for anyone to take him seriously. I suspect my father cozied up to him just to borrow money.

By the time my father left, it was wintertime. The others had
all gone back to Sichuan already. It wasn't only because they ran

out of money but also because the rear battalion kept sending comrades over every day to mobilize. But no one dared to come to my house to mobilize because they were all afraid of me. I had a personal vendetta against those guys, so as long I was alive, they were cautious. The fact that my father made it to the end was all thanks to me. But still, we had our moments of deprivation. We not only ate everything we had, but we had to sell watches, coats, and eventually even newspapers. Anyone with money to lend had moved away. The ones who couldn't move away had no money. The warehouse was finally empty and we could finally settle in, but by then, my folks we no longer there to enjoy it.

Even though my father never thought much of me, he still offered some amount of biological affection; at his age, he could see that there weren't going to be any more opportunities available to him (later when he realized he still had opportunities, he reverted to condescension and even envy—Wang Er's note). He could also see that there was a 1.9-meters-tall son and a beautiful daughter-in-law—a pair of lovebirds—right in front of him, and it made him reluctant to leave. That was understandable, but I began to worry: you guys ate all the food and used up all of Old Mr. Liu's money. Once you leave, how are we going to live? Of course, I didn't voice my concern.

Before leaving, my father told me to call Old Mr. Liu grandpa. Fuck that shit; that wasn't the order of things. Father bowed with his hands folded in front of him as he said: Elder Liu, I place my son in your care, please teach him the way. It's okay if the idiot can't learn, but don't let him lead Little Bicycle Bell astray; she's a good girl. Old Mr. Liu accepted wholeheartedly. My father then turned to Little Bell and said: Bell, take good care of Grandpa Liu. Bell also agreed wholeheartedly (my father borrowed a lot of money from Old Mr. Liu, leaving us as ransom was a part of his ploy). Finally, he said to me: boy, watch yourself, don't end up in there (jail—Wang Er's note) again. After that, they left. The mining school used a big truck to take them to the train station and they refused to take anyone else to see them off. The moment my folks left, I said to Old Mr. Liu: old man, are you really going to be in my business? Old Mr. Liu said: oh nah nah, we were just saying what they wanted to hear. Wang Er, let's play a game of chess, Mr. He says you play a good game!

When Old Mr. Liu asked me to play chess with him, I knew it was going to be a chore. Just think about it: it had been months since Bell and I had a chance to be intimate. At long last my father is gone, my mother is gone, and if you leave and let me shut the door, we will finally have the world to ourselves. Even though she probably wouldn't have agreed to taking off her clothes in the middle of the day, she would have at least let me near her. Unfortunately, Old Mr. Liu wasn't that perceptive, and I didn't have thick enough skin to lay it out for him. Goddammit!

I hated Old Mr. Liu, not only because he was ruining my good times but also because he was a coward in the face of death. When he asked me to take his blood pressure, he would stare at the mercury meter going up and ask: how high?

Not bad, 180.

Frightening. Bell, hand me my medicine. Systolic pressure at 180! What's the diastolic pressure?

Not bad, 160.

High diastolic pressure! Oh no, I need to go to sleep. Measure again when I wake.

WHEN HE WAS diagnosed with atherosclerosis, it was like receiving a death certificate. They say eating sour things softens blood vessels so he went on a pregnant woman's diet. He ate so much sour food that he ruined his gut. Had he not done that, his mouth wouldn't have smelled like a vat of shit. Is death really so terrifying? In literature, ancient and modern, Chinese and foreign, there are plenty of references to the subject of death.

"General Lü Bu! Death comes for us all, why fear?"
—Zhang Liao in *Romance of the Three Kingdoms*

"What is death? It is nothing but to be with Napoleons* and with Caesars?"
—*The History of the Life of the Late Mr. Jonathan Wild the Great,* by Henry Fielding

"Seven have I hewn in pieces, nine have I pierced with my lance, many have I trampled upon with my horse's hoofs; and I no longer remember how many my bullets have slain."
—*Taras Bulba,* by Nikolai Gogol

(In the above reference, Gogol is describing a battle between the Cossack and the Polish. The Cossack all have heroic dying words so the Polish must also have their own dying words: I have been hewn in seven pieces, pierced by nine lances, and I no longer remember how many bullets killed me, or else there wouldn't be enough Poles to go around!— Wang Er's note)

"Afraid of death? Without death there is no revolution! Afraid of death? Then how can you call yourself a member of the Communist Party!"
—Protagonist of Model Films

"Si La Si La Deyo!"
—Antagonist of Model Films

---

*Wang has changed the original "Plato" in the Fielding to "Napoleons."

I have two entire notebooks full of quotations like these that I copied out. But most people's dying words tend to be shaped by their moment in history. Within the formalism of the "Cultural Revolution" era, only the very last dying words counted; shouting long live so and so while you were still alive didn't count. When I was in the hospital in Yunnan, the next bed over was a guy with lung cancer. His wife reassured him by saying: baby's daddy, if you feel unwell, just yell at me or the kids okay? The guy started spasming and spent the whole night yelling: long live Chairman Mao! No one could get any sleep. Eventually, the head of the hospital came and said to him: you are already dead, those last dying words counted! Only then did he find release. Compared to above-mentioned attitudes toward death, Old Mr. Liu was nothing short of a spineless coward!

Old Mr. Liu and I started to set the chessboard. Clearly, he was no match for me, so I went with the Delayed Opposite Direction Cannon opening. Apparently, Old Mr. Liu knew about the strategy. He muttered, ah, so that's what you're trying to do! I said quietly: give it a try, it's not too late to talk after you win. When he heard this, he became nervous. The DODC strategy calls for brute force; you can't be subtle about it. He hesitated and immediately lost pieces and after twenty rounds, he was dead. He praised, amazing! During the rematch, I pulled another DODC. In that one afternoon, I played fifteen games using DODC, and Old Mr. Liu's brain was annihilated!

Old Mr. Liu took endless beatings from the cannon play. People who have studied such things know that it's a vulgar strategy. At night, he wanted to play me again, what a drag. I wanted to go to sleep, but it would have been impolite to say it out loud. So of course, I kept at it with the DODC. When he saw that I was doing the cannon play again, he said: Wang Er, do you know any other openings? I said: like what? He said: for example, Screen Horses. I said: sure, I know them all, but why don't you win against my DODC first. He said: it's not good to always use the same opening. I said: that's strange, why do you care what I play? Old Mr. Liu had no choice but to play on. He lost before we got to fifteen rounds. The old man let out a long sigh: it looks like I should call you *shifu*. I said: who am I to teach a venerable elder like you? Old Mr. Liu walked off in anger.

It has been twenty years, and I have reached my doubtless years. With regard to Old Mr. Liu's chess skills, I have arrived at the following conclusion: his game wasn't all that bad. When he played with my father, they could go head-to-head for twenty matches. Of course, my father's game kind of stank. But when we were playing, I could have said to him: you are losing because you are too afraid of risk. He may have lasted a bit longer. I understood this at the time, but I was in such a hurry to make love to Little Bicycle Bell that I just wanted the old man to go away. Had I known that he would die the very next day, I would have put off the lovemaking and given him more of a chance on the chessboard.

Old Mr. Liu was always holding his cane and dozing off in his chair while drooling on the front of his shirt.

19

OF ALL THE PEOPLE I'VE ever known, Old Mr. Liu had the worst craving for meat. Back then, we all ate together and the two of us were hungry too. A problem like this should not have been difficult to solve (like buy some meat and cook it), but we didn't have money. Old Mr. Liu only got a forty-yuan stipend, which he had to use on things other than food as well. So the problem wasn't easily solved. As I mentioned, before my parents left, we ate everything up and even sold scrap paper. All we could afford to eat was cabbage and a bit of Cantonese sausage. Little Bicycle Bell figured since Wang Er was 1.9 meters tall and had to sacrifice energy for his sex life, eating the same amount as her wouldn't have been enough. So she tried to eat as little as possible. But on the first night, Old Mr. Liu arrived at the dinner table like a hungry demon. With flying chopsticks, he packed away all the pieces of sausages. Even though I wasn't raised with traditional decorum, fighting with an old man over food was still not something I could bring myself to do. So I ended up making love to Bell on a half-empty stomach. After that, I thought even less of Old Mr. Liu.

Now I understand that Old Mr. Liu had reached the point in his life where he couldn't feel full without eating meat, not to mention the fact that he had spent the first half of his life eating steak. His system didn't digest stuff like cabbage boiled in water; even rice had no impact on him; eating those kinds of foods was like lying to his stomach. In the final hours of his life, he was constantly in a state of hunger. Old Mr. Liu was a lifelong bachelor, and I never heard any scandals or innuendos relating to him. At his age, he wasn't doing scholarships anymore either. So his life revolved entirely around food. But at the time, it was hard for me to empathize. I thought the gluttonous old fool should just die already.

Now, I also know that after eating that meal of boiled cabbages, Old Mr. Liu woke up in the middle of the night starving. He rummaged through all the cabinets and drawers until he found a piece of pickled radish. He sat there grinding his teeth on it until sunrise. As soon as day broke, he dashed to the farmer's market: our food money was all in his hands, he bought the produce and we cooked, that was our division of labor.

That night, after Old Mr. Liu left, I knocked on our shared wall to tell Bell to come over, but she wouldn't. So I said: I'm angry, I'll ignore you, I don't want to be with you anymore. When I got to the last sentence, she came over. We only cuddled for a bit before she wanted to leave. I told her to not go. She said: your mother reminded me again and again to not sleep with you. I agreed to it. I knew that when Little Bicycle Bell made a promise, that meant she staked her life on it, but I still wouldn't give up. After some persuasion, she agreed to stay and to sleep with me. It almost made me blush: if even Bell was willing to break a promise for me, my power of attraction must have been formidable! I felt delighted. My little monk became as hard as iron but quickly, my excitement faded. Little Bell insisted on putting a condom on me. She said: this is your mother's order! Apparently, when my mother got Bell to promise she wouldn't sleep with me, she still wasn't satisfied. She said: you think I don't know about young men and young women? Promise me this, and you have to keep this promise. Remember, you have to use a condom, none of the other methods work! Wang Er is clumsy so you have to make sure it happens. You have to promise me! So in the end, the promise Bell made was to make sure I wore a condom and not to not sleep with me. Had she agreed to not sleep with me, I would have only gotten a hand job that night.

I resented my parents for the whole thing. They had to control everything, even condoms! I hated my father the most because it had to have been his idea. I hated Bell too, because she didn't listen to me; she listened to my mother. That was why I didn't marry her.

Now, I finally understand why my father and mother spent so much time worrying about my sex life. At the time I was twenty-three and Bell wasn't yet of age. If for some reason, she ended up pregnant and needed an abortion, we would have needed to get a reference letter. The only agency that could have provided such a letter was our commune. Put yourself in my place for a moment. Supposing something like that happened, what would have happened to me? My father and mother's overbearing parenting was hardly enough. If they really wanted to go all the way, they should have castrated me. Now, I finally understand that Bell loved me more than anyone else. I want to marry her, but she has changed her mind.

There's more to the story that night. Before we did it, I made up a story about how I was getting my head chopped off. Outside the window was a gallows built for me. The executioner was outside the door sharpening his blade. A red line had been drawn on my neck and the hair on the back of my head had been shaved. They called Bell over and gave her a crate. They told her to pad the crate with straw—"don't let the face get all scratched up, it's your fiancé's after all!"—to catch my head when it fell. But somehow, she managed to convince the jailer to let us spend our last half hour together.

It made Bell cry: then hurry up and put on the condom. Every time she heard me die a new manner of death, she cried. When I was on my second condom (death by hanging this time—Wang Er's note), Old Mr. Liu began clamoring next door and continued until I was on my fourth condom (when my heart was ripped out of my chest—Wang Er's note). During the sixth condom, which was already the next morning, he went outside. That night, it was six times in total but Old Mr. Liu's disturbances kind of ruined all the fun.

When he came to knock on our door the next morning, we weren't out of bed yet. At the time, I was massaging Bell's breasts with intense focus. And Bell's breasts were the best pair of breasts I had ever seen: they were perfectly hemispherical, with soft white skin, and small, pretty nipples. Had there been a world boobs competition, she would have definitely qualified. Bell was never much interested in the other aspects of sexual intimacy, she was only interested in breast massage. Making love to her breasts could give her orgasms, it was the only method by which she could enjoy sex. But of course, it wasn't always easy to accomplish, one could only hope for the best. That day, her desire was unstoppable (two months of abstinence will change a nun or a Bell), with her head on her arms, eyes closed and cheeks a flush, she was about to come. Right then, Old Mr. Liu started banging on the door, *bang bang bang*, so when I went to opened the door, I muttered: this old dickhead needs to die already.

When I opened the door, my first reaction was: this old man must have drunk from the River of Immaculate Conception and become pregnant. His belly was round on top and pointy below, the white hair circling his bald head was all sticking up, and on his face was a Mona Lisa smile. Then, like a midwife, he pulled a fat duck out of his belly. When I saw that, I couldn't help but gasp: did you steal that? He was appalled and replied: steal? How can you steal? Stealing will get you arrested, this was bought. I asked how much he paid. He said it was cheap, only five yuan. I said you fool, if you spend money carelessly, we'll have to eat shit for the second half of the month. He listened and felt embarrassed. That was when Bell ran over and said: Wang Er, how can you talk to Grandpa Liu like that, apologize now. Frankly, I didn't give a crap about the five yuan, I just thought the Old Liu was a loser. Can you guess why he hid the duck in his bosom? It was because he was afraid the rear battalion guarding the gate might call him a pig. His reason for being back in the city was because he was sick. He feared that people might accuse him of not being sick, eating a fatty duck a day like that. In any case, it was all because he had gotten hit a few times during the "Cultural Revolution" and had become spineless.

If we wanted to talk about getting one's ass kicked, Old Mr. Liu had absolutely nothing on me, even taking into consideration my youth and his old age. All the beatings he ever took in his life happened in that lab building, you could count the number of times with your fingers. My ass-kickings, on the other hand, were too many to count. During the authoritarian phase at the school, Driver Feng had called me into a basement. The ceiling lights were on and I was surrounded by a group of men. He had said: take a good a look, we won't touch you. The Worker's Propaganda Team has arrived on campus, so we don't beat anyone up anymore. Then the lights went out. When the lights went back on, I picked myself up from the floor, dripping blood. Driver Feng smiled and said: we didn't touch you, right? Can you point to someone who hurt you? Of course I couldn't. I said: fuck your ma! Then the lights went out again. When you are beaten in the dark, you can't even keep count. The ones who beat me were the rear battalion guys, the same ones who beat up Old Mr. Liu. But I wasn't afraid of them. Even the one called Feng had to call me grandpa, who else was there to fear?

Now that I'm in my doubtless years, I understand that the beatings I took can't be compared to the beatings Old Mr. Liu took. This was because I was one of them; so much of my punishment was a result of my own actions. When Old Mr. Liu got beaten, there wasn't that element of him asking for it. I was still young, so I still had many opportunities for payback; but Old Mr. Liu had already reached his final chapter, he couldn't seek revenge so every blow he took was his to keep. Naturally, Old Mr. Liu was terrified.

Old Mr. Liu tried to pump the tires on his bike but he couldn't line up the nozzle. Unable to pump the air, he gave up out of frustration and pushed his bike over.

20

N THE MORNING, OLD MR. LIU said to me: I couldn't sleep last
night thinking of two things; one was to eat a duck, and two was
to learn chess from Wang Er and figure out just why DODC is
so hard to beat. I said to him: this particular version of DODC is a
new variation. In the year 1966* of the Common Era, the greatest
Chinese chess players under heaven including Yang Guanlin from
Guangdong, He Shunan from Shanghai, Liu Dahua from Hubei,
Wang Jialiang from Heilongjiang, and more—about fifteen in
total—gathered in the city of Hangzhou. Everyone said: Hu Ronghua
from Shanghai is too good; he won several championships in a row,
the nerves! Let's conspire against him. Everyone agreed Opposite Direction Cannon was a vulgar opening so they decided to
tinker around the strategy to give Hu a big surprise and hence,
defeat! They pondered for seven weeks or forty-nine days before

---

*1966 was the year a ban on chess was imposed in China, under the Cultural
Revolution.

coming up with fifteen moves that were as unconventional as they were vicious! As Old Mr. Liu listened, his eyebrows danced in fascination and he smacked his lips. Bell laughed and said, don't listen to Wang Er's tall tales. Old Mr. Liu said: Bell, you don't understand chess, don't interrupt! This story is real! Keep talking, what happens then? I said: then the gang decided to each memorize one of the new-fangled moves, and the move could only be used against Hu Ronghua, never against one another—Bell, go clean up the duck, you won't understand—but in the end, none of them used a single move. Hu Ronghua was still the champion! Old Liu, you know chess; can you guess what happened?

Old Mr. Liu thought for a long time before stuttering: earlier did you say, He Shunan?

I said: that's right! An elder after all! That son of a bitch was from the same county as Hu Ronghua, always playing the spy (had Old Mr. Liu not given me the prompt, I wouldn't have known where the story was going—Wang Er's note)! The day before the championship, all the chess players who gathered in Hangzhou received a letter which read: chariot eight cross five. It was signed: you know who! Old Liu, can you guess what happened there? He slapped the table and shouted: what a Hu Ronghua! Truly amazing! He Shunan knew one of the moves, but he couldn't have remembered the other fourteen. Old Hu knew he was in trouble so he wrote down the first variation of DODC and sent it to everyone. When they received the note and knew that Hu knew they were going to use the DODC, they no longer had the confidence to go through with it. He used the old trick of a dead Zhuge Liang scaring away a living army! I'm certain that you know all fifteen moves; no wonder I can't beat you. This DODC certainly has a feted origin, just teach it to me already. I said, sure I can teach you, one yuan per move. He said, that's a deal!

It's true when they say old people are like children. Old Mr. Liu set up the chessboard, cut out a few pieces of paper, and prepared a pencil to take notes. With his eyes wide open, he stared at me from top to bottom. I felt an itch to bop him on the head. After only one move, Old Mr. Liu announced in a high-pitched voice: chariot eight cross—five! He lifted up his arm to write. He made me laugh so hard that I knocked over the chessboard.

Later when I told him there was no new-fangled variation and that I had made everything up to just to mess with him, he became upset. But in the blink of an eye, he was happy again because he remembered the duck. Old people are innocent like that; they always do what you expect them to do. Old Mr. Liu stared at the poor duck's corpse and thought up many ways of partitioning it. One portion he wanted to deep fry, one portion he wanted to poach, one he wanted to make a soup with, and the last portion he wanted to grill. If the dead duck still had a soul, it would have wanted to ask: Old Mr. Liu, why? If after my death, someone chopped me up into four pieces, cremated a quarter me of, buried a quarter of me, fed a quarter of me to vultures and mummified the last quarter of me, I too would ask: why? Unfortunately in our kitchen, there was only some condensed soy sauce, so we could only make soy sauce duck. Old Mr. Liu said, the soy sauce duck won't taste good until the meat falls off the bones, which won't be before dark. He had used up the last of his food budget to buy the duck, which meant he had to go hungry for lunch. Old Mr. Liu said, good food requires patience, but he was constantly opening the lid to check. Apparently, even looking at the food gave him some amount of satisfaction. His gluttonous expression was hard to watch. The room was filled with the aroma of a boiling duck. Old Mr. Liu couldn't sit still, he paced back and forth like a maniac. There was still a whole day before nighttime. With his high blood pressure, he wouldn't have made it. That was why Bell called me over, gave me some money and told me to take him out to lunch. She added, she wasn't hungry. So I said to Old Mr. Liu: old man, take a ride with me. I got on a man's bike, he got on a lady's bike, and we rode out the school gate. At that point, I said to Old Mr. Liu: I still have some money on me; let's go to the new restaurant street to eat some lamb chowder with croutons. But with a sudden *clang*, Old Mr. Liu fell on the ground along with his bike.

I stopped and turned to look only to see him crawl back onto his feet while drooling: lamb . . . chowder with croutons!!

I treated Old Mr. Liu to the chowder because I had yelled at him in the morning and felt guilty. But later, he died. He never got to eat the duck. That evening, the duck was the only thing on our table. I threw up after the first bite. Bell couldn't swallow it either so we threw it out. The duck was sticky and slimy, it left a morbid feeling in your mouth. Even now, I don't much fancy eating ducks.

When I ate the lamb chowder with Old Mr. Liu, we got to talking about Mr. He. The old man's eyes bulged as he said: eat, eat, don't talk about those things, it's too creepy. I said: we're just talking, old man, what are you so afraid of? He said: don't talk about dead people. I said: that's funny, at your age, you're still scared of death? The old man said innocently: I'm not scared. I said: can you avoid death by fearing it? Old man, look what you're eating; it's all lamb intestines, full of cholesterol. It'll clot your blood vessels and bring you closer to death. The old man looked funny with his trembling hands.

After that, Old Mr. Liu gathered his courage (he said, I'll drink some vinegar at home, that'll take care of it—Wang Er's note), and began to tell me about what happened before Mr. He's death, but it wasn't very interesting. Before Mr. He jumped off the building, he said, tell my family to not grieve too much. He didn't say anything like, in twenty years I'll come back a new man, or even something like, let my sons avenge my death. At the time I thought, people like Old Mr. Liu are so boring that even their stories become boring.

After lunch, I told Old Mr. Liu to go home while I wandered around until dark. I was lethargic as I wandered around like an aimless dunce. When a person reaches that point, he begins to think grandiose thoughts. At the time I thought: if only we were at war or something.

People bored with life and hoping for war is nothing out of the ordinary. My generation grew up under constant expectation of war. Take me for example: even though I feared neither pain nor death, all I could do in those peaceful years was dig holes. It wasn't as if China had ever been short of hole diggers.

In peaceful times, life was just a competition for digging holes and planting grains. Even though I had the physique of a stallion, I was no better than anyone else. First of all, I didn't grow up doing farm work so I wasn't used to it. Second of all, I had lower back pain and you can't farm without a good back. So I was always hoping for war. On a battlefield, my heroism would have surpassed that of all others. Had I become a prisoner of war, I could have secreted away a shard of glass with which I could cut open my stomach and choke my enemies with my intestines. I would have made an effective soldier. But without a war, I was as useless as Old Mr. Liu.

Now I understand that wrapping your guts around someone's neck is a really bad idea. Just because I wasn't happy with my life, I wanted to start a fight with somebody, anybody. If everyone thought that way, we would never get any peace. Now I also understand that for Old Mr. Liu to fear death was the most natural thing in the world. He had nothing left in this world other than his short and final days.

When Old Mr. Liu peed in the bathroom, his urine often ended up on his pants.

21

AFTER OLD MR. LIU PASSED AWAY, I thought that maybe when I got old, I'd end up like him too.

When Old Mr. Liu was still alive, I often said behind his back: spineless people tend to live longer. The difference between Mr. He and Old Mr. Liu was like heaven and earth. Mr. He plunged righteously off the top of a building whereas Old Mr. Liu was beaten once or twice and broke his gall. But when he died, I was nonetheless worried. When I got back home, Bell said to me: go see how Old Mr. Liu is doing, he's snoring on his bed and won't answer. When I entered his room, I saw that he was drooling all over himself. When I lifted his eyelids, I saw that his eyeballs weren't moving. Immediately, I turned and bopped Bell on the head: are you dead? Hurry and get a cart, we're taking the old man to the hospital!

According to Bell, when Old Mr. Liu came home, he rode at a flying speed and his forehead oozed sweat. The moment he got in, he checked on the duck; the meat was already falling off the bones. He rubbed his hands and wiped his drool. But then he said he didn't feel well and needed to take a nap; ask Wang Er to check his blood pressure when he gets back. But when Wang Er got back, he didn't check anyone's blood pressure but bopped Bell on the head instead: look at what state the old man's in, why would you wait for me?

Bell was never the oil-saving kind of lamp. As I pedaled Old Mr. Liu to the hospital in a tricycle cart, she sat in the back and bickered: uh-huh, so you can hit me now! I'll get you back no matter what. I said: Old Mr. Liu had a stroke. If he recovers, he'll end up with a crooked mouth and a paralyzed eye, check if his mouth is crooked. I only said those things to distract her. When we got to the hospital, we rolled Old Mr. Liu to the emergency room. After only a short while, a gurney with a white sheet covering it rolled out. A doctor said to me: the old mister has already passed. I said: stop kidding around. When we brought him in here, he was still snoring: you've got the wrong guy.

The doctor said: I'm sorry for your loss, but we only had one patient in there. My eyes bulged as I said: no way! We just sent him in, you didn't even take a look! He said: when your grandpa came in here, he had already stopped breathing. Can you stop pulling on my collar! Someone! Help!

A bunch of white gowns gathered around us, but I still wouldn't let the emergency room doctor go. A guy in a uniform showed up and yelled: stop stirring up trouble! What department are you with? I want to talk to your superior. I said: you sure as hell can fucking try! I'm a goddamn intellectual youth! When they heard that, they backed off. Everyone knew that our kind had nothing to lose, so no one dared to fuck with us.

The story of Old Mr. Liu ended like this: in the end, the head of the hospital sat down with Bell and me in his office. He said: everyone dies eventually, it is an unavoidable fact of life. Some illnesses are so serious that we cannot save the patient. If you have doubts about our medical practice, perhaps you would like to have the body examined? We have to be responsible not only to the patients, but to the doctors as well. By then my head had cleared. I said: I'm not related to the dead guy; you guys can wait for the mining school's rear battalion to come and sort this out. With that, I went home with Bell. On our way, I said to Bell: he died out of craving for that duck.

That night, as Bell and I slept together, we recounted all sorts of frivolous little stories about Old Mr. Liu. For example, when he got to the dark cluttered hallway, he would hit everything with his cane because he couldn't see. His cane looked like it had been chewed on by a dog. When Old Mr. Liu had his cravings, he baked a sausage on the charcoal burner only to have us walk in on him. He was so afraid that we would yell at him that his face turned red. He stared at us as if to say: if you dare to speak a word, I will kill myself! I'll die! How did he all of a sudden, actually die? How uncanny. We should empty a bottle in his memory.

We told each other many of Old Mr. Liu's stories. They were all funny except for one. Once, my father said to me: Old Mr. Liu wasn't always a fool; everyone at the mining school knew that he was a genius. But he played a fool for so long that eventually he became the real thing. So once when I asked him: old man, why don't you care about dignity? He replied instantly: don't have the luxury!

Later on, I got out of bed and walked to the window. The night outside was dark; a sea of stars glimmered. Everything was just as it was last night, with the exception of Old Mr. Liu. Suddenly, I realized that even though Old Mr. Liu was really annoying and his mouth stank, I didn't actually wish for him to die. I wished he could continue to live in this world.

Years as water flow, the sun and moon shuttle like a loom. Many things have come to pass. Looking back at the end of '67 from New Year's Day of '73, many things had already happened, but there were some things that hadn't yet. Whether I have been talking about the things that had happened, or the things that had not happened yet, my explanation has not been very clear. The reason for this is that in my above narration, the most important thread has been missing—this thread being the changes that happened within me. Some of the changes had already taken place and some had not yet taken place. As I mentioned earlier, when Old Mr. Liu told me about Mr. He's dying words, I was not very impressed. But that night, when Bell and I were in the middle of lovemaking, I stopped and walked to the window. I thought about those words again and it felt tragic. When I saw the stars outside, I thought about the candles flickering around his brain and it felt tragic. Old Mr. Liu's death was also tragic. The fact that there was nothing I could do in the face of death was also tragic. When I began to talk to Bell about this, she cried; I also wanted to cry. To look death in the face and do absolutely nothing about it wasn't really in my character.

When I said, in the years as water flow, there were things that worried me day and night, I was worried precisely about these things: when Mr. He died, he was erect. When Old Mr. Liu died, he just wanted to eat a duck. When I was in America, my father passed away at his desk. He was in the middle of writing a letter to me, discussing the topic of relativism. Although they died in various ways, what all of them had in common was the strength to live on. I sincerely wish for them to have had the opportunity to live for longer, to continue to live. As for me, I no longer wished to wrap my intestines around anyone's neck.

22

YEARS AS WATER FLOW, IN the blink of an eye, I have reached my doubtless years. I feel bottled up inside because nothing ever went my way. In fact, it feels more and more like everyone is just putting on a show.

Line is always putting on a show. Every morning before she leaves for work, she has to shout in the stairwell:

"Turtlehead, don't burn the house down! Remember to take your pills!"

When she returned from work, she screamed: "Big Turtlehead! Hurry on down, look at how much stuff I brought!"

MR. LI ALSO PUT on a show. He pushed the door wide open and rushed downstairs; they may as well have been performing for an audience. Had I not been their friend, I would have pushed my door open and put them in an awkward spot—Professor Li, Mrs. Li—the two of you combined add up to over ninety years and you're still playing house; is that corny or what?

Line and I go way back. During eighth grade, in the summer, Line and I often went swimming at the Deep Jade Pool. She gasped: Wang Er, what happened to you? Why is there a rolling pin hiding in your trunk; does it hurt?

I said: you don't understand because you don't read. I have a good book called *The Decameron*, I'll lend it to you when we get back. I bookmarked the important parts. You only have to read "Putting the Devil Back into Hell" and "The Mare's Tail."

She said, I don't know what you're talking about, but let's go somewhere where no one can see us and you can show it to me. So we went to a secluded place and I showed it to her. When Line saw it, she panicked: Wang Er, you must be sick! Your peepee's all swollen, you should go to the hospital!

Of course, I didn't go to the hospital. That night, I lent the book to her. When Line returned it, she said with a blush: Wang Er, you're not planning to give me the devil now are you?

What? You don't want it?

It's not that. I'm just saying, if you wanted to give that to me, maybe wait till I'm a bit bigger. If you had to give it to me now, I might die!

After I showed her my little monk, Line's grades took a plunge. She failed Chinese, English, math, physics, and chemistry. And because the teacher caught her telling other girls about the mare's tail, her behavioral assessment was also terrible. Had it not been for me letting her cheat off me, she would have been done for. Line had been the smartest girl in school. Our elementary school teachers all thought she would grow up to be Marie Curie. Never would they have imagined that this Marie Curie almost didn't make it into high school.

Line said of herself, in eighth and ninth grade, she was so very haunted by a nightmare that she couldn't even pass music class. At the time, she felt like she had to marry Wang Er or else she had no future, but that big gun of his . . . when she woke from her nightmare, her windpipe itched.

Once, when I talked about the good old times with Line and brought up this story, she got upset. She said: Wang Er, you're not so little anymore, why are you still talking about that old story! No offense but compared to my husband's big gun, yours is more like a sorghum stalk.

I was quickly reminded of why you can't be friends with women. I didn't even need to mention how many times I let her copy my homework or cheat off my test back when we were kids. I only needed to think about that time when I was at the commune outside of Beijing, and received a telegraph saying: "Need money, Line." I sold my Omega watch for two hundred yuan and sent it to her.

I know how to fix watches so I know the value of watches. Even though that Omega watch was old, it contained all original parts. Later when I was living in America, my neighbor was an old man who fixed watches. He had a collection. When I mentioned the watch to him, he said: if you have it, hand it over, five hundred, a thousand, all negotiable. If you don't have it, then don't get my hopes up for nothing. I have high blood pressure; I don't need the excitement. Not only was that watch a premium collector's item and a paragon of mechanical craftsmanship, but it was also a memento given to me by my father. My mother knew someone from the United Nations Relief and Rehabilitation Administration, so our household was never short on food. My father got that watch by trading away a bag of foreign noodles. In ordinary times, there was no way he could have afforded the watch. But it took only one sentence from Line for me to sell it, which I did not regret in the twenty-odd years since. It wasn't until she called me a sorghum stalk that I felt regret!

I said to Line, I'm never going to make another friend again, to avoid further pain. Line said: is it that bad? Fine, fine, I take back sorghum stalk. You're being a dork. My husband is your friend and I'm Bell's friend. Why are you after me? Bell's pretty great isn't she?

Mr. Li was my friend and I didn't want to dump Bell, I knew these things to be true. But I just wanted to hold her for a bit, why couldn't I just hold her for a bit. Like I said, she was putting on a show.

Little Bicycle Bell was also putting on a show. Every time we made love, she put a medium size condom on me. My little monk and I both suffocated because of it—like in the movies with those bank robbers who wear stockings over their heads. So the fact that I followed up on those homeopathy fliers that said, "(for treatment of) rises but not firm, firms but not for long!" shouldn't at all be surprising. Suppose you stuffed a 1.9-meter-tall astronaut into a 1.6-meter suit, he too would have shriveled up. Hence, I complained to Bell: "Bell, this condom is too small."

"Nothing we can do. The entire hospital only has that size."

This pharmaceutical company was also putting on a show. People of our age can all recite these two lines of poetry: "in that world of peace and equality, the whole world will feel your heat and your cold." But no one ever said anything about the whole world being equal in endowment. I knew for a fact that when the family planning department handed out contraceptives, they had condoms of every size. Bell said: "Wang Er, let's just make do with what we have. Do you understand what it means to be a divorced single woman?"

If she really went there and tried, she could have gotten some. But Bell said: her company was handing out promotions. If they knew that she was sleeping with a size 37-mm man, it would affect her prospects for the open assistant editorship at work. To put a man in a medium size just for assistant editorship, isn't that putting on a show?

If I really wanted to, I could have gotten some, but my work unit was also considering promotions, and I was also a divorced single man. If I had gone to ask for a 37-mm condom, it would have affected my prospects for assistant professorship. So then, I had to put on a show.

Even my mother was putting on a show. I asked her to get me some extra larges and she said: but Wang Er, I'm a widow, which means I'm also single!

I said: Mom, you're almost seventy years old, no one will suspect you of anything. Besides, you already have your professorship, what are you afraid of. If you are too embarrassed to say it's for your son, you can just tell them you want to make balloons at home.

"Shush! To tell you the truth, I could get some but I don't want to. You still owe me a grandson!"

This is my life now, forty years old and still putting on a show. Just like my little monk, I got put in a medium size, unable to straighten my neck. When I was a kid, I had three whorls in my hair (those with three whorls fight to death—Wang Er's note), now I only have one, the other two fell out. The courage I once had, like the two whorls, has also fallen. Anyway, life is short and like everybody else, I'm making do.

Right now, I'm teaching mathematical analysis to an undergraduate class. Integrations that once took less than a second now take me five minutes to think through. In class, I'm close to inanimate. The first half of my sentence doesn't line up with the second half. Even I know that the students are laughing behind my back. One smug graduate student said to my face: I heard you were a math machine—I don't see it.

I replied: machine? Do machines go bald?

An even more smug graduate student said: teacher, I think you often repeat yourself.

I replied: is that right? Well, when a record runs for long enough, it'll skip too.

A female graduate student said to me: teacher, I heard you were an accomplished speaker, you certainly live up to your reputation.

That I rather enjoyed hearing, but behind my back, she continued: this one's gonna be a blabber when he's old, probably annoying as hell.

But what my mother said to me was: the forties are the hardest years to get through. It's a time when your mind is still clear but you can tell you are getting old. Later, when everything gets to be a blur, you won't notice it anymore.

Arthur Schopenhauer said: before forty, people live slowly; after forty, people live quickly.

But what our Confucius said was: at forty, you're doubtless; at fifty, you know heaven's will; at sixty, you learn to listen; at seventy, your desires no longer transgress. Things sound like they just get better and better; how wonderful! But what happens after your desires no longer transgress? That's why I'm afraid he had gotten himself all excited over nothing.

Aside from the forty-year-old things I and the people around me tend to talk about, I also find myself often unable to remember things. I just finished reading a book. Full of praises, I lent it to someone else to read. But only a few days later, I noticed that I couldn't recall a single word of the book. In the past, I was famous for being able to read ten lines at a time with a photographic memory. But for me, the change wasn't necessarily a bad thing: in the past I never had enough books to read; now I'll never run out of the joy of reading. But because of these patterns, my doubtless years have turned into a state of constant anxiety. I have lost interest in all things and all I can think about all day is having an affair with Line. To be more specific, I just wanted to fuck her, but of course, not too much. My current state of health is like this: once at a time is more than sufficient, twice is pushing it. So really, I just wanted to do her a couple of times.

When Line and I talked about it, we were sitting in a student-run café at the mining school. Our discussion grew heated and we even yelled a few times. The first time was at the mention of sorghum stalk, another time it was about Mr. Li and Bell. I said, so what if they found out? Bell loves me and Mr. Li loves you, they'll forgive us eventually. Whenever I think about you I get hard. So one thing is for sure: if I don't do it now, I'll regret it when I can't get hard anymore. With Heinrich Heine's elegy as proof:

> *Inside my head,*
> *burns a violet.*
> *That sweetheart! Never did I bed!!*
> *Damn, how I regret!!*

Of all the poetry I have ever read, this was the most tragic. Line: my student is here, standing right there behind the bar counter. If you want to make a fuss, let's go outside.

Line and I left the café to take a stroll outside. The sky was covered in constellations. I was instantly reminded of a time twenty-three years ago, on another summer evening, when Line and I climbed to the top of the lab building to gaze at the constellations. We declared in the most grandiose way: if a hundred Wang Ers and a hundred Lines teamed up, they could shake the world!

Even now, I don't think we were over the top. If you have two hundred identical weird things in the same place, it's already a miracle of thermodynamics. It would be weird if it didn't shake the world. For example, two hundred famous celebrities join in a performance, that would definitely shake the world. If a hundred people with only left eyes and a hundred people with only right eyes appeared together, that would also shake the world. If a hundred seventeen-year-old Wang Ers and a hundred seventeen-year-old Lines teamed up, that would make two hundred male and female martyrs. How could that not shake the world?!

That night on top of the lab building, in addition to those grandiose statements, I also did another thing that gave me a deeper understanding of women's undergarments. I reached in through her collar and undid the clip on the back of her bra. With the thing wedged between her shirt and her skin, my hand slipped easily onto her breasts. I learned that a woman's breasts were cooler than the rest of her body. They felt like two little apples. Other than that, we just said some more crazy stuff like: we were born in a time of martyrs; how fortuitous for two martyrs like us! We must come together to accomplish great things!

That night, I said: to accomplish great things in this world, you must be willing to be a martyr. Take Giordano Bruno for example. His insistence on the Copernican model, in spite of the Inquisition's persecution, was proof of his willingness to die. He was burned to death. For a man to be burned at the stake is nothing out of the ordinary, but he was also subjected to endless torture, which is hard not to respect. The Inquisition even said, as long as you admit you were tempted by the Devil, you can be spared the torture. Decapitation, hanging, poison, take your pick. You can even hire a whore before you die; the Church will cover the expense. But he chose the glorious road of thorns, so he was tied to the rack. Two ropes, one around his hands and one around his feet, creaked as the levers turned, stretching his body. His once 1.6-meters frame got stretched to 3.8 meters by the time they pulled him off the rack. The executioner forked his body onto a pyre and curled him up (like a snake—Wang Er's note), before burning him alive. Giordano Bruno was a champ! There was also Joan of Arc, who when captured, was also given the choice of saying she conspired with the Devil in exchange for a hanging and burning. But she wouldn't say it, which meant she chose to be burned alive. Young women have tender skin that burns especially fiercely. According to historical records, that day, Joan of Arc wore a skimpy dress and a woven sash around her waist as she was led to the stake. The iron chain she wore stopped her advance. She noticed a bed of oily pine needles covering the pyre. This was a particularly heinous trick. When Joan of Arc saw it, she furrowed her brows and said to the executioner: may God have mercy on you. This Joan of Arc was one hell of a broad! When the fire was lit, the pine needles exploded with embers that burned away her hair, her brows, and her dress. Not only that, but they covered her body with boiling blisters! It wasn't enough to turn a pretty young lady into a toad but she had to endure a slow roast. They put mirrors in front of her so that she could see herself boil. The blisters cracked as they baked, spraying pus. While Joan of Arc stood in the middle of the fire with her hands together and prayed to Mother Mary until she was turning into a Peking duck, not one curse word passed over her lips. By the time she was fully burned, she lipped the name of Mary no more. In my opinion, Joan of Arc was more heroic than Giordano Bruno because Wang Er could have been a Bruno but never a Joan. When it got really hot, I would definitely have cursed: fuck your ma. Had the saint done that, it would have ruined everything.

I said to Line: Granddaddy Heaven will thank us personally and arrange an execution for us. When that time comes, you and I have to stand firm; we have to be a good champ and a good warrior woman!

But Line said: she wishes for a five-minute bathroom break before the execution because seeing bloody things made her want to pee.

Twenty-three years later, Line said to me: now is the opportunity: we have to join forces and accomplish something great. Before us is precisely the cruelest of all executions. I will go bald, lose my sex drive, turn presbyopic, get stomach pains, swollen prostate leading to difficulty peeing, leg pains; the lower back wound that has plagued me all my life will turn into paraplegia, and hunchback, weight loss, dizziness, and death. As for her, breasts will sag, periods will cease, and with the shrinking of her vaginal canal, she will be tormented by an empty desire. Her face will grow wrinkly, her hair will fall out. She will turn into an ugly hag and eventually die of multiple organ failure. This is what Granddaddy Heaven has planned for us, death by aging. You only get this one chance in life; pick yourself up, prove that you're a champ!

Line's suggestion was: before old age came for us, we needed to accomplish something important like Bruno advocating the Copernican model or Joan of Arc protecting Orléans. We mustn't back down from the oncoming hardship; stand firm until our last lucid moment: just like how Bruno stood firm on the Copernican model even as he was being stretched into a noodle and how Joan of Arc prayed the name of Mother Mary even as she was being roasted. We need to do this not for some other reason but to prove that we are champs!

The thing Line suggested was very much worth doing. At least I can't think of anything that is more worth doing. She also said, she chose me to do this thing with not because I have any special ability or qualification but because we were companions when we were young and we once swore we wanted to prove we were heroes (heroines)!

Line said, even though Wang Er seemed like a champ when he was young, when he got to his forties all he could think about were nearsighted pleasures, not at all heroic. Besides, he had never been through any real ordeal so he couldn't prove himself a champ. But Wang Er said: he was struggled against, he was beaten; he stole swill with his mentor Liu Er (stealing swill requires more courage than stealing a car—Wang Er's note)—don't those qualify as ordeals? If Wang Er isn't a champ, then what has Line done to prove that she's a champ (warrior woman)?

Line said: I fell in love with Blood-swollen Turtlehead. That alone was enough to prove that she was a champ. If you needed details, it would be as follows: she was once somewhere in Henan, Anyang, inside a ramshackle temple. Cold and frightened, she lay naked on a brick altar, trying her best to part her legs, and gave her virginity to Mr. Li without any conditions. She also decided to devote her entire life to loving Blood-swollen Turtlehead, even though Mr. Li was just as unlovely as any other man. This alone was enough to show that she had passed her test.

Line's nonsense was sheer sophistry, unworthy of discussion. But her line of reasoning was enough to explain why she had followed Mr. Li to Henan. She said, in her own way, she also walked the road of thorns up to the present day (referring to

Hans Christian Andersen's "The Thorny Road of Honor"). Now she was offering us an opportunity to unite in our pursuit of honor. This honor meant I should write down all the years as water flow to be passed down generation after generation, no matter how tragic or how many people it offends.

I thought I had been doing it all along but Line said that only good things happen in the stories I write, while all the bad things were avoided; that's not the complete picture of years as water flow, it's not the way of the true pen. To truly write the years as water flow, you must write down everything, including the unbelievable things and the things you don't dare to write about, or else it's just kitsch.

For example, not writing about the following would be considered kitsch: there is a new construction site outside the mining school's front gate. Some of the buildings there are half-finished; some are still only foundations. The workers found a few square meters of black soil. All the surrounding soil was yellow but that patch was black. The young workers couldn't figure out what it was. Someone said it was coal, another said it was bitumen, yet another said it was buried grain that had turned to dust. In order to determine what it was, one of them picked up a chunk and tasted it, but in the end, he came to no conclusion. From this story, we learn: if it ain't coal, and it ain't food, then it's somebody's shit.

In our years as water flow, we've seen many things like these: when I was eight, during the Great Leap Forward, our plan was to grow fifty thousand kilos of grain every mou,* so we needed a lot of fertilizer. Fresh manure isn't fertilizer; it's poison; it'll burn the crops alive, so we dug a whole bunch of deep pits, as deep as wells, and poured fresh manure into them. Because of the bacteria in the soil, the manure began to ferment and even bubble. When I was a kid, I used to stand next to the pits and throw matches into them so that I could see the eerie blue flame floating on the pit.

---

*A mou is a Chinese unit of land measurement equal to roughly 806.65 square yards or 0.165 acre.

When I was a kid, I thought the blue flame was incredibly mysterious. In the silent night, I wanted to lie prostrate and pray to it, forgetting completely that it was emitted by feces.

The sad thing is, the story of the manure pit didn't really lead anywhere because after the fermentation was complete, people found it impossible to get the stuff out: too thick to scoop and too watery to dig, it was hard to know where to start, not at all as simple as it was on the way down. The pits were unfathomably deep. If someone had slipped and fallen in one, there would have been very little chance of returning. As a result, the pits, along with the manure, were abandoned.

After some time, the pits became overgrown with weeds and indistinguishable from their surroundings. They became dangerous traps. I had a buddy who stepped in one and paid the ultimate price. That's one story from our years as water flow.

Line said, that's not even the weirdest part, when I was at the cadre school, I heard about another story. At around that time, some local cadres thought that digging holes to ferment shit took too long. They wanted the manure to cook faster, so they told every family before dinner to use their own wok to boil some shit (referencing Peking University Sociology Department's Dr. Shen Guanbao's PhD thesis—Wang Er's note). As it boiled, you had to stir it around with a ladle, just as if you were poaching slices of meat. You also had to add wood ash into the wok as if you were seasoning it. After boiling for some time, the whole kitchen smelled like the stuff. Some people became delusional from the fumes and thought the thing was edible so they scooped it into their bowls and ate it.

The previous story was told by Line. I can tell the beginning is true (with Dr. Shen's PhD thesis as proof—Wang Er's note), but the last two sentences were total crap and its brand of romanticism has got to go. But the story of boiling shit should not be omitted because it is one of the years as water flow's main threads. It shows that there was a time when everyone had to be a *shabi* (what Line refers to as silly cunt—Wang Er's note), and there was no other choice. At the time, we were still young, too young to have been able to make our own choices.

But as we got older, we came to have two choices: be a silly cunt or be a martyr. Our choice was not to be silly cunts but to be martyrs.

As for stories of the martyrs, there were too many to record. Many of my compatriots died. They died for less than a fart. For example, in Yunnan, some friends of mine wanted to liberate the world's two-thirds suffering masses, so they crossed over the border to fight guerrilla warfare and they were shot. A death like that is simply unconscionable. Think about it:

1. The world's two-thirds suffering masses, do you know them?
2. The world's two-thirds suffering masses, do you know what they are suffering from?
3. Just as Chairman Mao said, in this world, there is no love without a reason and no hate without a reason. To die for them without knowing anything about them, don't you find that a bit corny?

Among the dead are my friends. They wanted to become martyrs but they became silly cunts. A story like that is far too tragic; I don't have it in me to write about it. If I asked for a true pen of history to write the years as water flow, I would have already committed the sin of phoniness.

I know even more tragic tales—from what I can see, life's greatest tragedy lies in being duped. Will there ever be an end to those tragedies?

Line said: you think with your plain, underachieving, withering brain, there was going to be any other way for you to leave humanity with some wisdom? If you wrote about how the mining school's patch of black soil came about as a history, people will know right away that it's shit, no way would they take a bite; so doesn't that, at least, make it a real piece of contribution? Don't you think you should thank God for giving you some literary talent, to allow you to write something a little bit real, and not just complete silly cunt talk?

Suppose I did want to write about the years as water flow like that, my worry wouldn't be for a lack of things to write, but that I would never get to them all. To do it, I would need an all-knowing pen of history, or several pens of histories. Where would I find such a pen? Where would I find that many people? Even if I were able to gather enough compatriots, I would need to throw myself wholeheartedly into it and write nonstop until I died. Only then would I be able to stand up straight before God's cruel death-by-aging and prove that I'm a champ. But before I decide to do that, I still need more time.

ABOUT THE AUTHOR

Wang Xiaobo was born in Beijing in 1952 and died of a heart attack on April 11, 1997. Xiaobo taught at Beijing University and Renmin University of China and became a freelance writer in 1992. His novels *Golden Age* and *The Future World* won the United Daily News [Taiwan] Award for Novel twice. He is also the author of the essay collections *A Maverick Pig* and *The Silent Majority* and the novels *Golden Age, Silver Age,* and *Running Away at Night.*

ABOUT THE TRANSLATOR

Yan Yan graduated from Columbia University in 2008 with degrees in English and religious studies. After working at the Alibaba Group in Hangzhou, China, his hometown, he backpacked around the world and eventually settled down in Brooklyn, then the Hudson Valley. As a freelance translator, he translated works by Hans Christian Andersen Award-winner Cao Wenxuan, including the Dingding and Dangdang series, *XiMi*, and *Mountain Goats Don't Eat Heaven's Grass*, as well as updated editions of *Grass House* and *Bronze Sunflower*, for China Children's Press & Publication Group.

More recently, he has been translating works with the Chinese literary icon Wang Xiaobo, which include a novella collection titled *Golden Age* and an essay collection titled *The Pleasure of Thinking*.